SCOT

A Liss MacCrimmon

MICKEY SPILLANE

ZANE

ELLERY QUEEN

I, THE JURY

AGATHA CHRISTIE

RAYMOND CHANDLER

NERO WOLFE

THE BIG SLEEP

MARY ROBERTS RINEHART

KAITLYN DUNNETT

KENSINGTON
U.S. $7.99
CAN $8.99

**Don't miss these other
Liss MacCrimmon Scottish Mysteries!**

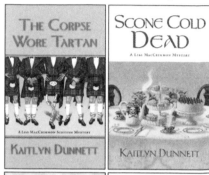

Books by Kaitlyn Dunnett

KILT DEAD

SCONE COLD DEAD

A WEE CHRISTMAS HOMICIDE

THE CORPSE WORE TARTAN

SCOTCHED

BAGPIPES, BRIDES AND HOMICIDES

Published by Kensington Publishing Corporation

SCOTCHED

KAITLYN DUNNETT

KENSINGTON BOOKS
www.kensingtonbooks.com

KENSINGTON BOOKS are published by

Kensington Publishing Corp.
119 West 40th Street
New York, NY 10018

ISBN-13: 978-0-7582-3882-5
ISBN-10: 0-7582-3882-7

First Hardcover Printing: November 2011
First Mass Market Printing: July 2012

10 9 8 7 6 5 4 3 2 1

Printed in the United States of America

For
mystery readers
especially those who have had the good fortune
to attend
Bouchercon, Bloody Words, Cluefest, The Great
Manhattan (Kansas) Mystery Conclave, Killer
Nashville, Magna Cum Murder, Malice Domestic,
Mayhem in the Midlands, Murder in the Grove,
or the New England Crime Bake

And special thanks go to
Peggy Baker (Blair Somerled), Angie
Hogencamp,
Betty Jean Neal, Patricia Ruocco (Glenora), and
Sandra Sechrest for their invaluable help with
character naming
and to Sally and Dina
(they know why)

Chapter One

From Liss MacCrimmon's Scottish Emporium to Angie Hogencamp's new and used bookstore, Angie's Books, it was only a short walk across the town square of Moosetookalook, Maine. Liss could have been there in two minutes flat. Instead, she dawdled, enjoying the delights of a glorious morning in mid-May.

This particular spring in the mountains of central Maine was warm and sweet-scented. The apple blossoms were in bloom, all pink and white and pretty. One tree stood next to the merry-go-round and two others flanked the bandstand. Volunteers had spruced up the flowerbeds that lined the paths through the square, putting in their own particular favorites. Liss strolled past an eclectic assortment. She recognized pansies, bright yellow daffodils, blue forget-me-nots, and the purple of grape hyacinth but was less certain she was correct in identifying creeping phlox, candy tuft, and star of Bethlehem. There were tulips, too, but they were a bit bedraggled, having almost reached the end of their season. The crocuses had already gone by.

There would be varieties of iris in bloom soon, Liss thought, and the ever-present lupines would show up in a few weeks, followed in July by one of her personal favorites, orange day lilies. Smiling to herself, Liss began to sing under her breath as she left the square and crossed Main Street. "It's May! It's May! The darling month of May."

Frowning, she broke off, glad no one else was within hearing distance. Not only couldn't she carry a tune in a bucket, but she had a habit of plugging in the wrong words—"darling" went with "buds of May" and came from some old poem, not a Broadway musical. The song she'd been trying to sing talked about the *merry* month of May. Didn't it?

Shaking her head, Liss took the porch steps at Angie's Books two at a time. She should *not* try to sing. Her voice was bad enough all by itself, but the effort was always a disaster when combined with her terrible memory for lyrics. She'd always had a tendency to get the words mixed up. And if she hadn't realized it before, this failing had been brought home to her just a few months earlier. She'd committed a major blooper, and in public, too.

In late December, Moosetookalook had celebrated "The Twelve Shopping Days of Christmas." Liss had been put in charge of the pageant. To go with the lyrics of the yuletide carol, she'd duly rounded up nine lords a-leaping and ten ladies dancing, as well as appropriate representations of the gifts named in the other ten verses of the song. That no one appeared to have been bothered by her mistake did not make Liss feel any better. She was certain dozens of people had noticed and just been too polite to say anything to her. She'd been horrified when the music director from the local high school had casually mentioned—in February!—that "The Twelve Days of Christmas" actually featured *nine* ladies and *ten* lords, not the other way around. It had been some consolation to realize that he assumed she'd rewritten the lyrics in order to accommodate a casting problem, but the whole incident embarrassed her whenever she thought about it.

Angie's Books, like all the other storefronts around the square, was a converted residence with a shop on the first floor and living quarters above. The front porch was big enough for a couple of chairs and a small table. They'd been pushed back to make room for a huge, freestanding signboard.

"Great advertising," Liss said as she opened the screen door and stepped into the shop.

"One of Ms. Quinlan's people brought it by," Angie Hogencamp said.

"I don't think I've ever met anyone who had 'people' before," Liss said with a laugh.

The featured author for Angie's Saturday afternoon reading and book signing was actress-turned-mystery-writer Yvonne Quinlan. The sign featured a life-sized photo that showed a willowy beauty with dark brown eyes and a short cap of blue-black hair highlighted with purple streaks.

Angie had big brown eyes, too, and dark, wavy hair, but the resemblance stopped there. The book-store owner was a little overweight and a lot flustered. Her face, devoid of makeup, had turned pink with exertion. Cartons of books surrounded her, three of them clearly labeled with the title of Yvonne's latest novel.

"I may have ordered too many copies," Angie said.

"Think positive." Liss made her voice bracing as she approached the sales counter.

Liss, too, was a brunette. She was taller than Angie. At five foot nine, she loomed over most of the women in town. Like Yvonne, she was on the slender side, but her eyes were light, not dark. Liss herself called them blue, but she'd been told more than once that their color changed with the clothing she wore and was, on occasion, closer to green in hue. Today, Liss was certain, they were a very ordinary shade. Her outfit consisted of well-worn jeans and a baby blue sweatshirt that said MOOSE-TOOKALOOK, MAINE on the front—right beneath the picture of a cross-eyed cartoon moose.

"There are around a hundred mystery fans coming to the conference." She rested her elbows on the sales counter. Additional cartons of books were stacked on the floor behind it. "They all love crime novels. They will buy the latest titles from you because they want to get them signed by their favorite authors." Almost a dozen mystery writers would be attending the conference and taking part in panel discussions.

Angie swatted at a lock of hair that kept falling into her face. "I hope you're right. At the moment, I'll settle for getting these boxes out to the hotel. It's going to take forever to set them up on the tables in the dealers' room. They'll have to be alphabetical by author's last name so people can find what they're looking for. Do you think I should put hardcover books in one place and paperbacks in another or lump them all together?"

"Better put all the books by one author next to each other. As for schlepping books, that's why I'm here. I can take some of the cartons over to The Spruces now and swing back for more if you need me to. Take a deep breath, Angie. We have plenty of time. It's not even noon yet, and the festivities won't get started until six this evening. And we don't open the dealers' room to customers until nine tomorrow morning."

Angie plopped herself down on the stool behind the counter. "A whole three-day weekend! What was I thinking? I never do this kind of thing."

"It's a new venture for all of us. Consider it a challenge."

"The challenge was conning my sister-in-law into agreeing to babysit and keep this place open for me while I'm at the conference." Angie grimaced. "I really hate owing her a favor."

Liss sympathized. She'd thought about asking someone to work at Moosetookalook Scottish Emporium in her place but opted to close down instead. These days most of her business came through online orders anyway.

"It'll be fun, Angie. How can it not be? Readers. Writers. Books."

"And what is this conference called again?" There was a hint of sarcasm in Angie's voice.

"The First Annual Maine-ly Cozy Con," Liss admitted, wincing a little at the name. Still, it fit the occasion. The attendees would all be fans of the traditional mystery—crime stories with limited violence and no graphic sex that tended to feature amateur detectives inspired by such classic sleuths as Agatha Christie's Miss Marple and Ellis Peters's Brother Cadfael.

"Do the people coming to this conference know there was a homicide at the hotel only a few months ago?" Angie asked.

Liss gave a snort of laughter. "Are you kidding? Apparently that's what sold the organizers on The Spruces. How many gatherings of fans of fictional murders can say they met at the scene of a real one?"

The worried furrow in Angie's brow deepened. "Beth wants to help out. You don't think she's too young, do you? She's only ten, and I have no idea what the people who attend these conferences are like."

"I've never been to one, either," Liss said with a grin, "but I don't think the fans are violent. They may like to read about murder and mayhem, but they aren't likely to commit either."

Angie looked sheepish. "Of course they aren't. Silly of me to worry, I guess. Well, okay then. I'm keeping three cartons of the new Yvonne Quinlan hardcover here for the book signing on Saturday, but everything else that's boxed up goes out to the hotel. Some woman named Nola Ventress sent me a list of all the attending authors, and I ordered the three most recent titles by each one of them. Plus I'm bringing some books by other mystery authors, just in case people are interested in them. If you'll drive around to the side of the building, we can load up from there."

A few minutes later, Liss and Angie began piling

cartons of books into the back of the pickup truck Liss had borrowed from her fiancé, Dan Ruskin. It was already half-full with stock from Moosetook-alook Scottish Emporium. On the second trip out from the bookstore, Angie stopped to stare at the distinctive, dark-colored vehicle just turning in at another of the businesses on the town square. Like the bookstore, it also had a side entrance.

Curious, Liss glanced that way and grimaced. "I'm glad I don't have a view of this from the Emporium," she remarked. Nor could she see it from her house, which was situated on the lot next to her store.

"I could live without it," Angie muttered. "Fair warning. Doug's son is a klutz."

Frank Preston, age fifteen, emerged from the passenger seat while one of the men his father regularly called to make pickups slid out from behind the wheel. Almost invisible wires ran from Frank's earphones to his pocket. He was very obviously listening to music. He jerked and hopped to the beat of the song on his MP3 player as he made his way around to the back of the vehicle and started to unload the cargo. It, too, was unmistakable.

Liss felt neither shock nor surprise when Frank hauled a body bag out of the back. His father, Doug, was the local undertaker. It was hardly unusual for the hearse to arrive with a new "client" for Preston's Mortuary. But Frank's cavalier treatment of the remains bothered Liss. Without waiting for Doug's assistant to help, Frank tried to sling the body over his shoulder in a fireman's carry. He lacked both the physical strength and the coordination to manage the maneuver. The corpse slipped out of his grasp. One end hit the pavement with a dull thump that made Liss wince. The thought that it might not have been the feet that struck the ground made her a little queasy. Frank wasn't just clumsy. He had no respect for the dead.

The assistant mumbled something Liss couldn't hear. She hoped it was a rebuke, but she was too far away to catch the words. She doubted Frank heard them, either, over the music blaring in his ears. He grabbed one end of the bag while the assistant took the other and together they carried the deceased the rest of the way into Preston's Mortuary.

"That boy could care less about tending to the family business," Angie muttered.

"He's always been a handful," Liss agreed. The previous winter, young Frank had gotten into trouble for joyriding on a snowmobile. "Who died?" she asked, certain Angie would have heard.

Moosetookalook was a very small town. The population barely topped a thousand, even after several recent additions. The local grapevine was quick to spread news of births, deaths, elopements, and other assorted rites of passage. Anything even remotely scandalous also spread like wildfire.

"Lenny Peet," Angie answered. "Well, he had a good long life, didn't he? Ninety-five, I heard."

Liss hadn't known Lenny well, but she'd seen him just about every day. He'd walked his dog in the town square in the early morning and again in late afternoon, no matter what the weather or the season. You could set your clock by him. Incensed that Frank Preston should have treated Lenny's remains so carelessly, Liss promised herself that she'd speak to Doug about his son's attitude the next time she saw him. Then she had another thought.

"Who's taking care of Lenny's dog?" she asked.

"It's at the animal shelter down to Fallstown," Angie answered.

Liss added another note to her mental list—do something about the dog. When Lenny's ancient hound, Tatupu, had passed away over a year before, he'd promptly acquired a cute little fox terrier named Skippy. Liss was sure she could find someone in the village who needed a new "best friend."

Filing away both chores to think about later, Liss returned to loading the back of the truck with cartons of books. The weekend ahead would be a busy one, but she fully expected to enjoy every minute of it. How could she not? She was a huge fan of traditional mysteries herself. She planned to slip away from the dealers' room now and again to attend some of the sessions. And she'd definitely be putting in an appearance at that evening's opening reception.

Sherri Campbell, née Willett, had her booted feet propped up on the desk in the inner room of the Moosetookalook Police Department. Leaning back in the creaky wooden swivel chair that went with it, she held one hand out in front of her so she could admire the shiny gold band on the ring finger of her left hand. She was three months mar-

ried, but just looking at that wedding band still
gave her a thrill.

A loud knock had her all but jumping out of her
skin. Her feet hit the floor with a thump and she
sat up straight.

A very tall, very stout woman in a gray pantsuit
stood in the doorway. She had a big head to
match her big body—a long oval squared off at
the jawline. The shape was accentuated by the way
she wore her hair. Her iron gray locks were cut
very short. The effect put Sherri in mind of an old-
fashioned swimming cap of the sort her grandmother wore in family photos taken in the 1950s.

"Can I help you with something?" Sherri's voice
came out a bit higher pitched than she'd intended. They didn't get a lot of walk-in customers
at the police department. The abrupt arrival of
this one had caught her off guard. Most people
phoned in with their questions and complaints,
and, as a rule, there weren't very many of those.
Most of the time, Moosetookalook was a quiet, law-
abiding place.

"Are you Officer Willett?" the woman demanded.

"It's Officer Campbell now," Sherri corrected
her. "I recently married."

"Congratulations." The stranger stepped into
the office, at once making it seem considerably
smaller. Without waiting for an invitation, she settled her bulk into the bright red plastic chair on
the other side of Sherri's desk. It groaned omi-
nously under her weight. "Since you're not busy,
I'd like to ask you a few questions."

"I'm here to serve the public."

Sherri put more warmth into the words than

she was feeling. She told herself that it was ridiculous to feel intimidated. At five foot two, almost everyone towered over her. She should be used to it by now. But this woman was nearly three times Sherri's size and made her feel like a house cat facing down an elephant. She upgraded herself to lioness and reminded herself that she was the one with claws.

"You say you have questions?" Sherri asked.

The woman had burrowed into a briefcase-sized black leather purse and come up with a plain white business card. She handed it over and waited while Sherri read the lettering. It didn't tell her much. In the center were the words THE NEDLINGER REPORT and a Web site address. In the lower left-hand corner was a name—J. Nedlinger—with a P.O. box, e-mail address, phone and fax numbers.

"So, Ms. Nedlinger . . . what kind of questions are we talking about?"

J. Nedlinger's carefully shaped eyebrows shot up. "You've never heard of me?"

"Sorry, but no."

"Oh, well. They say fame is fleeting."

Sherri didn't like the way the other woman was looking at her. That intense stare seemed to her to contain a strong undercurrent of mockery. It was as if this Nedlinger woman knew something Sherri didn't and relished hugging that secret knowledge to herself. Sherri tried to tell herself she was being fanciful, as she had with that lioness and elephant image, but the impression remained.

"I'm a journalist," J. Nedlinger said. "I collect information, in this case statistics. I'd like to know about the crimes your little town has suffered over the course of the last two years. Is that going to be a problem?"

Sherri tried to put her finger on why the woman made her uneasy. Ms. Nedlinger was quite stout, but there was nothing soft about her. She was physically fit. There were muscles beneath the sleeves of the plain gray suit, and she wore sturdy walking shoes. She was not someone Sherri would fancy meeting in an alley on a dark night. But, curiously, it was the image of a bulldozer that replaced that of an elephant. No predatory beast—just one of those pushy people determined to get her own way.

Sherri had no reason to deny the woman's request. When it came right down to it, she didn't suppose she had any choice but to comply. What Ms. Nedlinger had asked for was public information, data that Sherri had, literally, at her fingertips. She tapped a few commands into the keyboard in front of her and heard the printer whirr into action.

One of the routine jobs Chief of Police Jeff Thibodeau had assigned to Sherri when he'd first hired her had been compiling the monthly statistics and feeding them into a computer program specifically designed to keep track of such things and report them to the state of Maine. The task didn't take much of her time. Moosetookalook had been known to go for weeks at a time without a single complaint that ended up creating paperwork. Arrests were not an everyday occurrence.

Two sheets of paper spilled out of the printer. Sherri glanced at them, then handed them over.

"Here you go. This runs from May two years ago up to this week."

The stout woman seized the pages with an eagerness that had Sherri tensing up all over again. She knew there was one statistic that was out of proportion with the rest for a village as tiny as Moosetookalook. Sure enough, Ms. Nedlinger zeroed right in on it.

"Three murders in two years? Isn't that a bit excessive?"

Hidden by the desk, Sherri's hands clenched into fists. When she felt her fingernails bite into her palms, she forced herself to relax. She made an effort to keep her voice level. "These things happen even in small towns, Ms. Nedlinger. Now, is there anything else I can do for you?"

"Were you personally involved in any of the murder investigations, Officer Campbell?"

Sherri glanced at the card in front of her on the blotter. J. Nedlinger's P.O. box was in Boston, Massachusetts. Sherri wondered why an out-of-stater would care what crimes were committed in rural Maine.

"Criminal investigations, Ms. Nedlinger, for the more serious crimes, especially homicide, are handled by the state police. And for almost anything more complicated than a traffic violation, Moosetookalook usually asks for assistance from the county sheriff's department."

"That was a somewhat evasive answer." Ms. Nedlinger's pale blue eyes gleamed with amusement.

Abruptly, Sherri stood. "I'm afraid that's the only answer I have to give you, ma'am. May I sug-

gest that you contact the Maine State Police? They
have an officer specifically assigned to public relations."

"I'll do that." She tucked the printout into her
purse and gave Sherri a tight-lipped smile as she
also rose from her chair. "Nice talking to you, Officer Campbell."

After she'd gone, Sherri snatched up the business card she'd left behind. What an unpleasant
woman! She was tempted to tear the pasteboard
rectangle into tiny pieces and toss it in the trash.
Instead, she turned back to her keyboard and
typed in the URL for *The Nedlinger Report.*

A blog came up on the monitor.

Sherri skimmed a piece criticizing how a police
investigation into cyber-harassment was being con-
ducted, then read an item lambasting the parents
of a recent victim for not supervising their daughter's presence on the Internet.

"Well you just hate everybody, don't you," Sherri
muttered to herself as she scrolled down the page.

She stopped when she came to something a little different. Instead of an op-ed piece on some aspect of real-life crime, this blog entry was a review
of a recently published mystery novel. J. Nedlinger
had nothing positive to say about the book. In fact,
she was downright nasty in her comments and,
worse, gave away the ending.

Sherri was about to click away from *The Nedlinger Report* when the movement of a line of type
at the bottom of the screen caught her eye. Next
to the words "today's readership," going up even
as she watched, was a number. Sherri stared at it,

then glanced at the clock on the wall. It was barely noon and, if this was legitimate, the most recent blog entry on *The Nedlinger Report* had already attracted over forty thousand hits.

The possibility that the rude woman who'd invaded her office had that many fans made Sherri even more wary of her interest in crime in Moosetookalook. Whatever she was investigating now, it could not be good for the village.

Sherri wondered if she should alert the town selectmen to a potential public relations problem. Better to wait, she decided. She'd just as soon avoid unnecessary contact with the three elected officials who had charge of the police department's budget. One was her newly acquired mother-in-law, another the local mortician, and the third a slippery character who sold real estate. None of them numbered among her favorite people. It didn't take much effort to talk herself out of taking action. What could any one of the town officials do about J. Nedlinger's interest in local crime anyhow? Besides, if the blogger were left to her own devices, she might well decide their sleepy little burg wasn't worth the time to trash.

Sherri set the phone to forward any calls to her cell, locked the office, and headed for Main Street, pausing only long enough to exchange friendly waves with the town clerk. In addition to the police department and the town office, the municipal building also housed the public library, which took up the entire second floor, and the fire department.

Just as Sherri stepped out onto the sidewalk, on

her way to meet her new husband, Pete, at Patsy's Coffee House for lunch, she spotted Liss Mac-Crimmon driving past in Dan Ruskin's truck. Liss braked and rolled the window down. She was blocking the narrow street, but it hardly mattered. There was no other traffic.

"I'm heading out to the hotel," Liss said when they'd exchanged greetings. "I've got a load of Angie's books in the back."

"Right. Conference." It was on Sherri's radar, as was the Saturday-afternoon book signing. Both were only distant blips, since she did not expect any problems with traffic or crowd control. "Have fun."

"I plan to." With a cheerful wave, Liss drove on.

Sherri resumed her trek to the coffee shop. She didn't have far to walk. The small restaurant was right next door to the municipal building. Less than a minute after she'd seen Liss on her way, Sherri pushed open the door and walked in. Pete was waiting in a corner booth, the same one he always chose if it wasn't already occupied. She slid across the bench seat toward him and lifted her face for a quick kiss.

"Hello, handsome," she murmured after he complied.

Black-haired and brown-eyed, at five-ten Pete Campbell had the tall and dark down pat. As for handsome, he wasn't a classic Adonis type, but he suited Sherri just fine. He was built like a line-backer, square and solid, and he looked a treat in his brown deputy sheriff's uniform. He was work-ing the two-to-ten shift this week, patrolling Carrabassett County's rural roads to keep the community safe.

"Hiya, gorgeous," Pete replied with a grin. "How's your day going?" At her grimace, his smile faded. "You want to talk about it?"

"Not till after lunch. I don't want to ruin my appetite."

Pete had already ordered ham and cheese subs for them, along with chips and the diet root beer Sherri had lately become addicted to. When the last chip was gone, she felt calm enough to repeat her conversation with J. Nedlinger and share the discoveries she'd made on the Internet.

"Sounds to me like she might be doing a story on small-town police forces," Pete said, "and since she seems to go in for the negative, I'll bet she's planning to argue that they're useless in this day and age."

"Oh, that's a cheerful thought!"

Sherri turned her gaze from the dregs of her soda to the view through the plate glass window of the coffee shop. From that vantage point, she could see two sides of the town square. Directly opposite Patsy's place was Stu's Ski Shop and, next door to it, Moosetookalook Scottish Emporium. Then came Liss's house. Sherri's gaze rounded the corner, lingering only briefly at the post office. The Clip and Curl took up the back half of that building. Upstairs there was an apartment. Their apartment. The place where Sherri now lived with her brand-new husband and her precious son, Adam, a boisterous seven-year-old. And, best of all, they lived there without her mother.

Cheered by that thought, Sherri was almost smiling when she continued her visual survey. Next to the post office stood what had once been The Toy Box and, before that, Alden's Appliances. Now it was a jewelry store that featured items made with Maine tourmaline. Beside it, on the corner, sat Preston's Mortuary.

Sherri couldn't see the side of the square she and Pete were on, but she knew what it looked like well enough. The bookstore came first, then the municipal building at the center—the only building of red brick in a sea of white clapboards. Patsy's Coffee House occupied the corner lot. The remaining side of the square likewise had three structures. First was the house of John Farley, an accountant. Then came Dan Ruskin's place, which wasn't a business yet but would be once he converted his first floor into a showroom for the custom woodworking he did in his spare time. And finally, around the corner from the ski shop, was a building that had once been a consignment shop. It had recently been sold to a young couple Liss knew from her days as a professional dancer. They were going to open a dance studio there.

All in all, Sherri thought, Moosetookalook was a nice quiet little village with a charming, picture-perfect town square. Except for the fact that two of those twelve buildings, within the last two years, had been the scenes of violent crimes. When you added what had happened at the hotel the previous January and the murder of the manager of Liss MacCrimmon's old dance troupe down to Fallstown. . . .

Sherri sighed and reached for Pete's hand. She took instant comfort from his firm grip on her fingers. "Let's hope J. Nedlinger *is* going to argue for the elimination of small police forces," she said, "because if that's not her plan, then the topic of her next blog is likely to be the high incidence of murder in Moosetookalook."

Chapter Two

By five that afternoon, the lobby at The Spruces, Moosetookalook's finest hotel, was swarming with people. In fact, The Spruces was the town's only hotel, but it was a spectacular one. Built more than a century earlier, in the heyday of destination resorts, it boasted 140 luxurious rooms. The management offered every amenity. They had to, to make up for the fact that the hotel was located in the middle of nowhere.

A woman Liss had never seen before clamped one hand around her forearm and gestured with the other toward a small group waiting for the elevator. "Isn't that Dorothy Cannell? Oh, I love her books! *The Thin Woman* is a classic." Her whisper held barely suppressed excitement and there was an awestruck expression on her homely face.

Liss obligingly studied the cluster of guests. She'd already collected and studied the program book for the First Annual Maine-ly Cozy Con. From their photos, she recognized not one but both of the women waiting for transportation up to their rooms. The one nodding in response to something the man next to her had just said *was* Dorothy Cannell, who lived somewhere on the coast of Maine. The other woman was Yvonne Quinlan, the conference's guest of honor. The gentleman with Dorothy sported a splendid beard. The other man wore a loud blazer and had scraped his long blond hair back into a stringy ponytail.

"I think you're right," Liss said to the woman who'd accosted her. The clinging fingers let go so abruptly that she had to take a quick step back to keep her balance.

The woman—obviously the more rabid sort of fan—didn't notice. With a determined stride, she made a beeline for the elevator, all the while burrowing with one hand into the canvas tote bag she carried. The elevator doors closed a fraction of a second before she reached them. With a little cry of disappointment, she turned away, shoulders slumping as she stuffed a hardcover book wrapped in a brightly colored dust jacket back into her tote.

"What was that all about?" Dan Ruskin asked, appearing without warning at Liss's elbow.

Liss gave an involuntary start of surprise. "Sheesh! Don't sneak up on me like that."

"Sorry. Blame the thick, plush carpets at The Spruces. Guaranteed to muffle sound." He grinned, justifiably proud of the job his family had done restoring the turn-of-the-nineteenth-century hotel. For the most part, Ruskin Construction built new homes and added garages and the like to existing structures. The renovation had been a labor of love.

As Liss's fiancé slid an affectionate arm around her waist, she smiled up at him. She never got tired of looking at him. She wasn't so shallow as to have chosen her future husband only for his handsome exterior, but it was certainly a bonus that the things she loved about him—his sense of humor, his loyalty to friends and family, even his instinct to protect those he loved, annoying as that could be on occasion—came wrapped in a superb package. He was six foot two with sandy brown hair and molasses-colored eyes and he had the sort of build that came from years of working in the construction field—muscular without being bulgy. Like the handcrafted furniture he built in his spare time, he was darned close to being a work of art.

Liss admitted to herself that she might be a tad biased. After all, she was in love with the guy. She turned in his arms, rested her hands on his broad shoulders, and went up on tiptoes to give him a quick kiss. When she opened her eyes, her gaze fell on her engagement ring. The stone was an exquisite tourmaline, her own choice over the more traditional diamond. She'd coveted this particular ring from the moment she'd first seen it in a display case in the hotel's upscale gift shop.

At times it was difficult for Liss to believe that they'd been engaged for almost four months. Soon . . . *very* soon . . . they'd be married. Reluctantly, she stepped out of Dan's embrace, before she was tempted to ravish him right there in the hotel lobby! Not for the first time, she thought wistfully of suggesting they elope, as their friends Pete and Sherri had on Valentine's Day.

The date Liss and Dan had chosen for the wedding was in late July—close enough to cause Liss to panic every time she thought about how much she still had left to do. She'd never realized how many details were involved in planning even a simple wedding. And yet, in other respects, another two and a half months seemed way too long to wait. She'd wanted Dan to move in with her, but he'd refused. He was old-fashioned that way. They continued to live in two separate houses on the town square.

"Did you ask me a question?" she murmured, distracted by an enticing, rose-colored vision of what their married life would be like.

"That woman who missed the elevator," Dan prompted her. "She looked as if she just lost her last friend. Problem?"

"Oh, her." Liss forced her wandering thoughts back to the present. "That was just a disappointed fan. She missed a chance to get an autograph from her favorite author, but I'm sure she'll have another opportunity. There are signings after every panel and a group signing on Sunday."

"Fan? You mean some kind of groupie?"

Liss chuckled. "Oh, please! Writers don't have groupies. They have readers."

"But the main attraction at this conference is someone who's an actress as well as an author, right?"

Liss gave him a playful poke in the arm. "And how do you know that? You hardly ever watch television."

"I see the tabloids in the supermarket checkout line, just like everybody else. Yvonne Quinlan. Star of *Vamped.*" Dan made quotation marks in the air and recited a grocery-store headline: "Why does she only come out at night? Could she be a *real* vampire?"

"Well, I guess that theory's shot to hell," Liss said with a laugh. "She was standing in full sunlight just now, over by the elevator."

A party of three middle-aged women scurried across the lobby, heading for the lounge at the ground-floor level of the west wing. That they'd already registered for the Cozy Con was evident from the heavy book bags each of them carried. The totes contained freebies. Liss had been relieved to discover that her own goodie bag had not contained any of the books Angie hoped to sell in the dealers' room. She knew how easily Angie could lose money on this deal. If the attendees were more interested in meeting their favorite authors and going to panels than in buying the books those authors wrote and having them signed, Angie would be in trouble. She couldn't afford to offer the same discounts online bookstores did. She had to sell her stock at close to full price.

"Why the deep sigh?" Dan asked.

Liss felt heat rise into her face. She hadn't realized she'd made any sound. She tried to laugh it off. "I'm a worrywart, that's all. Hadn't you noticed?"

"Worried about what?" he asked.

"Nothing. Everything. Let's just say I'm keeping my fingers crossed that this weekend is a financial success for everyone involved."

"I have an idea," Dan said. "How about you just relax and enjoy the conference? I know you've been looking forward to it."

"Sounds like a plan," she agreed.

"Liss!" someone called. She turned to find the conference's organizer, Nola Ventress, bearing down on them.

An energetic little woman of sixty or so, Nola had silver-blond hair she wore short and curly, and vivid green eyes. She was casually dressed in designer jeans and a purple T-shirt with the conference logo on the front, but she carried a businesslike clipboard.

Next to Nola, Liss felt overdressed. After her last pickup at Angie's and an afternoon spent setting up in the dealers' room, she'd made a quick trip home to shower and change her clothes. The tailored slacks and silk blouse she now wore were business casual, but she had a hunch that most of the attendees would opt for a far more casual look. The ones she'd spotted so far certainly had!

"Have you seen Blair Somerled?" Nola asked. "His panel time's been changed and I want to make sure he knows about it."

"Sorry, Nola. Perhaps he's not here yet."

Somerled was from Kansas, Liss recalled. She wasn't quite sure why he'd decided to attend a small conference in Maine, but she was looking forward to meeting him. His books featured an amiable and sometimes absent-minded retired physician, an American G.P. who lived and sleuthed in present-day Scotland and was attempting, with humorous results, to learn to play the bagpipe. Liss had particularly enjoyed *Homicide with Haggis*, but *Skulls and Drones* and *Eleventh Piper Dying* had been excellent, too.

"Do you know Dan Ruskin?" Liss asked Nola, since Dan showed no sign of leaving.

Nola looked him up and down. "Joe's boy. I can see the resemblance."

"You know my father?" Joe Ruskin, head of Ruskin Construction and father to Sam, Dan, and Mary, was also the driving force behind renovating and reopening The Spruces.

Nola gave a short bark of laughter. "I grew up in this godforsaken burg. Didn't you know? That's how Margaret Boyd persuaded me to hold the Cozy Con here. That and the fact that there's a certain cachet about holding a conference of murder mystery fans in a venue where a real murder took place."

She was off again before either Liss or Dan could comment, but they exchanged a rueful look. "That's not how we want the hotel to be remembered," Dan muttered.

"Aunt Margaret knows that, but it's better to attract business than to drive it away, right?" Liss glanced at her watch. "The opening ceremonies are starting soon. I've got to go."

Dan brushed a light kiss across her forehead. "Have fun. I'll see you later."

He started to turn away, but she caught him by the front of his shirt and tugged. Obligingly, he lowered his head for one more kiss—a proper one, this time.

Grinning like a fool, Dan watched Liss sail up the sweeping staircase that led from the lobby to the mezzanine where the meeting rooms were located. No one would ever know from the graceful way she walked that she'd had knee surgery less than two years earlier. He still couldn't believe his luck. She'd been gone from Moosetookalook for a decade before a twist of fate brought her back. Now she was going to stay on permanently . . . with him.

Liss turned at the top of the stairs and sent a smile his way. The sides of her dark brown hair swung forward over her ears, just brushing her jawline. There was nothing spectacularly beautiful about her face, but Dan liked the way everything went together. And he loved her for her quick, clever mind and her absolute dedication to the things she cared about.

Only when Liss disappeared into the crowd beginning to gather on the mezzanine did Dan realize that he was being watched. His father smirked at him in a good-natured fashion from his post behind the check-in desk.

"Pitiful," Joe Ruskin kidded him when Dan sauntered over. "Mooning over the girl like a lovesick calf."

"If I'm a calf, shouldn't that be mooing?"

Joe chuckled. "If that's the best comeback you can manage, you'd better stick to working with your hands. You're never going to master the art of clever repartee."

"Why would I want to?"

"Listen, son," his father said, leaning forward with his elbows on the counter, "I've got a puzzler for you. Sherri called a little while ago to ask if we had a J. Nedlinger registered. We don't, and I told her so, but then I got to thinking that the name sounded familiar."

It meant nothing to Dan, but he heard the worry in his father's voice. If Sherri had been asking in her official capacity as a Moosetookalook police officer, then no good would come of finding a connection between the hotel and this Nedlinger person.

"A credit card issued to J. Nedlinger paid for a room, just not under that name."

"What name did he use? Smith or Jones? And how good-looking was the woman with him?"

Joe snorted a laugh. "The name in the register is Jane Smoot. She checked in yesterday. A big woman, especially when she's wearing a jogging suit. I saw her first thing this morning when she was heading out for a run on the cliff path."

"Smoot?"

Joe nodded. "I think maybe she's using an alias. I'm wondering if I should call Sherri back and let her know. We don't want some criminal type staying here at the hotel."

Dan shrugged. "Sure. Call her. It's probably nothing. Maybe the Nedlingers have a family emergency and are trying to get in touch with J."

"But why use another name? Normal people don't do things like that—try to hide who they are."

"Maiden name?" Dan suggested. "Or maybe it's a pseudonym. This conference has a lot of writers attending, right? And sometimes they don't publish under their own names."

Joe's tension evaporated. The shallowest of the worry lines in his face smoothed out. "Yeah, that's probably the explanation. But I think I'll let Sherri know anyway, just to be on the safe side." He reached for the phone.

"You'd better try her at home, or on her cell." Dan picked up a pen and scribbled down both numbers on a scratch pad on the check-in desk. "This late in the day there's no point in calling the P.D. You'll just end up being forwarded to the dispatcher at the sheriff's department."

Joe hesitated. "I hate to bother her if she's off duty. She's probably right in the middle of cooking supper for Pete and Adam."

"Pete's on the two-to-ten shift, and Sherri won't mind an after-hours update."

Although he'd been on his way down to the hotel lounge, Dan stuck around while Joe tried Sherri's numbers. Dan and Liss had become close friends with Pete and Sherri since Liss's return to Moosetookalook. Sherri's compulsion to tie up loose ends was almost as strong as Liss's inability to let any puzzle go unsolved.

In spite of the fact that Dan had already worked a full day for Ruskin Construction, adding an office above the garage to a client's house, he'd agreed to put in three more hours tending bar. Everyone in the family—his sister Mary, his brother Sam, even Sam's wife, June—pitched in to help their father as needed. It had long been Joe's dream to restore The Spruces to its former status as a grand resort hotel, or at least to a modern version of those glory days. Although the jury was still out on whether he'd ultimately succeed, his three kids were determined to do all they could to support him.

"Funny," Joe said. "No answer at the apartment.

Not even the machine. Nothing on the cell, either."

"Try Pete's cell," Dan suggested, and rattled off the seven digits. He'd always had a good memory for numbers. That was a definite asset in the building trade, where accurate measurements were important.

This time Joe got an answer. "Any idea where Sherri's got to?" he asked. Then, abruptly, his voice changed. "Sorry to hear that, Pete. You at the hospital now?"

"What happened?" Dan demanded, but his father gestured for him to be patient.

"Hang in there, son," Joe said after listening a bit longer. "I'm sure he'll be fine." But his brow was furrowed with concern when he hung up. "It's Sherri's son, Adam. Pete says they think he broke his arm. They've taken him down to Fallstown General for x-rays. He's probably going to end up in a cast."

"Poor kid. He's only seven years old. How'd it happen?"

"Typical youngster. He fell out of a tree."

Dan winced in sympathy.

"Pete said Sherri just took the boy into the emergency room. He met them outside and he was parking the cruiser when I caught him. Another couple of minutes and he'd have shut off his cell phone. They don't let you keep them turned on inside the hospital."

"They'll be there a while," Dan predicted.

"I didn't tell Pete why I was looking for Sherri," Joe said. "I don't guess this Nedlinger business is all that important. Nothing that can't wait till to-morrow, that's for sure."

"If it was something crucial, I'm sure Sherri would have said so when she called you earlier."

The arrival of a tall, lanky individual wearing glasses with Coke-bottle lenses and a harried expression on his face ended the discussion. While his father checked in the newcomer—under the improbable name of Blair Somerled— Dan continued on his way to the lounge. He dismissed the minor mystery of J. Nedlinger from his mind and concentrated on psyching himself up for his stint as bartender. He didn't resent the dent working at the hotel put in his personal time, but he sure would be glad when he no longer had to pitch in there.

Things would improve once he and Liss were married, he told himself. They planned to live in her house and turn his into the business that was *his* dream—a showroom for the furniture and other items he crafted from wood. As always, that thought brightened his day. He was whistling a cheerful little tune by the time he reached the lounge.

Liss was also in excellent spirits. The largest of the meeting rooms was packed, but she spotted a chair in the middle of a row halfway to the podium. Stepping carefully over feet and goodie bags, she reached her goal and collapsed onto the cushioned seat. What a relief it was just to sit!

She'd been on the go, and on her feet, since early that morning. To carve out the time to attend the First Annual Maine-ly Cozy Con, she'd had to spend extra hours making sure that Moose-tookalook Scottish Emporium was caught up on mail and online orders. Setting up the dealers' room had been time-consuming, too, but now everything was ready. In addition to Angie and herself, there was one other vendor. There was also a display area for the items to be offered in the Friday evening charity auction and another long table, currently empty, where attending authors could leave their promotional material. All that was left to do was unlock the big double doors at nine the next morning.

A smattering of applause sounded when Nola Ventress took the stage. She launched into a brief history of how the First Annual Maine-ly Cozy Con came to be. Since Nola was not a stirring speaker, Liss's mind wandered. She enjoyed people-watching, and this was a fascinating group.

Women vastly outnumbered men in the audience, but one of the latter caught Liss's eye.

She recognized him by his checked blazer and the fact that he wore his long blond hair in a queue. He'd been one of the two gentlemen standing by the elevator with Yvonne Quinlan and Dorothy Cannell. Now he had his back propped against a side wall. His attention was fixed on Yvonne, who currently shared the stage with Nola and two other women. He started visibly when an impressively large woman dressed all in gray sidled up to him. She leaned in close, invading his personal space. He tried to retreat, but he had nowhere to go. Just to be sure he didn't escape, she got a good grip on his lapel, giving Liss a new appreciation of the term "buttonholed."

When Nola introduced Yvonne Quinlan, Liss turned her attention back to the podium. Nola named all seven titles in Yvonne's series of mystery novels and quoted a review in *Publishers Weekly* that praised the author's skill at characterization and her light touch with humor.

The actress-turned-author smiled graciously, acknowledging the enthusiastic applause from the crowd. "Thank you all for such a warm welcome," she said in a pleasant, slightly throaty voice. "I'm looking forward to the weekend."

Liss expected Yvonne to hog the spotlight, but instead of acting like a prima donna, she promptly returned the microphone to Nola so that Nola could introduce the Fan Guest of Honor, Betty Jean Neal.

"You all know Betty Jean," Nola said, "and if you don't, you should. This woman owns more mystery novels than most libraries."

Betty Jean, beaming, bounced up to the microphone. Like the trapped man in the checked blazer, she had blond locks pulled back into a ponytail, but her hair was thick to the point of being bushy. A few strands had escaped to frame a rosy-cheeked face.

"That's right, Nola," she said, and giggled when the microphone squealed. She held it a little farther from her face to elaborate on the number of books she had collected. "Floor-to-ceiling bookshelves in just about every room," she boasted.

"Tell them about the bathroom," someone in the audience yelled, obviously a friend.

"Oh. Well. You don't really want to hear this, do you?" Betty Jean asked the crowd.

Reassured that they did, she launched into a description of her recently remodeled guest bath. The floor was black and the walls white, except for a suggestive spatter of red paint on one wall. The white bath rugs had red footprints on them. The black towels were decorated with the outline of a body. And the toilet paper had been printed to look like crime-scene tape.

"Of course, no one is allowed to use that roll," Betty Jean added, chuckling along with the laughing crowd.

"*And* she lives in a decommissioned lighthouse," said a woman sitting directly in back of Liss.

"No kidding?" A second female voice sounded skeptical.

"Oh, yeah. Betty Jean's the principal of the local elementary school, and the living quarters, which belong to the town, go with the job."

"I never heard of such a thing."

"It's a throwback, that's for sure. And Betty Jean knows it. She's had that job for thirty years and she's not letting it go anytime soon. Well, would you?"

Liss didn't hear what the second woman replied. Betty Jean had stepped aside and Nola was now introducing the conference toastmaster, a mystery writer named Sandy Lynn Sechrest. A tall, slender woman in her thirties, she spoke in a soft Southern accent Liss found charming.

"I've been thinking about the title of toastmaster," she drawled, "and it just doesn't fit. And I don't want to be anybody's toastmistress, either. So

I've decided to call myself the Cozy Con's Toast Chick. You know—like the Dixie Chicks? What do y'all think?"

Boisterous applause and more laughter assured her that the crowd approved. As Sandy Lynn went on to make a few announcements about schedule changes, Liss made a mental note to pick up a copy of her latest mystery, *The Cat Herder Murder.* Apparently Ms. Sechrest's detective was a woman who wrote pet-care guides. Liss liked the premise and thought she might just garner some helpful hints about dealing with stubborn felines while she was trying to solve a fictional crime.

Two cats shared Liss's house in the village. They were not going to be happy with her this weekend. Lumpkin and Glenora wanted regular meals. Since the Emporium was right next door to the house, Liss usually darted back and forth, putting down fresh food and water and doling out attention on a schedule that suited all three of them. For the duration of the conference, however, the cats were going to have to make do with seeing her only in the early morning and late at night, after the First Annual Maine-ly Cozy Con activities were over with for the day. She planned to attend the classic movie festival after that evening's reception, the charity auction on Friday evening, and the banquet on Saturday night.

Enthusiastic applause, the loudest yet, greeted Nola Ventress's announcement that refreshments awaited them in the adjoining room. All around Liss, people surged to their feet and started to move in that direction. She didn't hesitate to join them. The hotel always put on a good spread. The head chef, Angeline Cloutier, produced splendid buffets. Angeline had already agreed to cater Liss and Dan's wedding.

The woman Liss had last seen accosting the man in the checked blazer intercepted her before she could join either of the long lines snaking around two buffet tables loaded with food. "Excuse me," she asked, "but aren't you Amaryllis MacCrimmon?"

Liss frowned. "I prefer Liss." And she was wearing a conference name tag that said so.

"Of course you do. I wonder if I could speak with you for a few minutes."

"Sure," Liss agreed, but she kept walking. She was close enough now to smell delicious aromas, and she could see that one of the buffet selections was a macaroni and cheese bar.

The woman kept pace. She was as tall as Liss and easily twice her weight, but she was solid rather than flabby. Formidable, Liss decided. And there was something predatory about her smile.

"Why don't we get in line?" Liss suggested. "We can talk and collect supper at the same time." Since she'd managed only a peanut butter and jelly sandwich and a glass of milk for lunch, she expected her stomach would start to growl at any moment.

"Are you sure you want our conversation to be overheard?"

Liss hesitated, taken aback by the question. Her gaze wandered to the other woman's shelflike bosom, to the spot where a name badge should have been pinned to the dove gray fabric and was not. "And you are?"

"Jane Nedlinger." The woman's light blue eyes gleamed, but not with good humor.

There were three lines to choose from, two for food and one at the cash bar. For a moment, Liss was tempted to join the latter. If Jane Nedlinger was this intense in her dealings with everyone, it was no wonder that the man in the checked blazer had looked so desperate to escape her clutches.

"I don't believe I'm hiding any deep, dark secrets." Liss managed a flippant tone of voice and selected the food line that looked marginally shorter.

The two women in front of them were engaged in a lively discussion that momentarily caught Liss's attention. She recognized one of them as the conference toastmaster, Sandy Lynn Sechrest. The other had just proudly announced that she'd had her first mystery published in March. Then she proceeded to rattle off the names of every location where she'd done a book signing. They ranged from the Barnes & Noble in Augusta, Maine's state capital, to the sidewalk in front of a local Rite Aid pharmacy managed by her sister-in-law.

"I'm doing that one again during the Apple-Pumpkin Festival this fall," she added. "Signings are absolutely essential, don't you think? I make a point of talking to the manager of every bookstore I come across. Can you believe it? Some of them are reluctant to schedule an event."

"Perhaps they don't think they'll make enough profit," Sandy Lynn suggested in a mild voice.

"Nonsense. Author signings are good for everyone. And essential," she repeated. "Just like bookmarks. And an online presence. I spent my entire advance on publicity."

"I do hope it will pay off for you," Sandy Lynn drawled. "I've given up on bookstore signings myself. They just aren't cost-effective for me, living in a remote, rural area as I do."

The less experienced author looked profoundly shocked. "But you *must* do them," she insisted. "They're *essential.* How else can you hope to boost book sales?"

"I've always found it helps to write a good book," Sandy Lynn said, and turned her attention to scooping salad onto her plate.

The line picked up speed. Liss collected utensils and glanced back at Jane Nedlinger. Like Liss, she had been shamelessly eavesdropping on the veteran author and the newbie.

"So, what can I do for you, Ms. Nedlinger?" Liss asked.

"I write a daily blog in which I discuss real murder cases. I also review mystery novels."

They moved a few steps forward, closer to the spot where Angeline Cloutier, resplendent in a high white chef's cap and a pristine white apron, was slicing roast beef. Covered metal trays displayed a variety of tempting choices—all the makings of a satisfying supper.

Jane loaded her plate, taking some of everything. Liss made more careful selections. She passed on the scalloped potatoes but couldn't resist the macaroni and cheese bar. Small soup bowls had been set out so that people could line them with goodies from an assortment of toppings. Or would that be bottomings? Liss chose the finely cubed ham and held up her bowl so that one of the wait-staff could ladle a steaming portion of homemade macaroni and cheese into it.

"I have questions," Jane continued as she plucked two rolls out of a basket, "about all about the murders you've been involved in during the last two years."

Her words were rife with innuendo. Caught off guard by the unspoken accusation, Liss automatically went on the defensive. "I've hardly been *involved*—"

"Haven't you?" Jane Nedlinger didn't bother to hide her sneer. "I've read all the newspaper articles. I've even seen the police reports. You, Amaryllis Rosalie MacCrimmon, are a lightning rod for sudden violent death." Her eyes glinted with unconcealed malice. "Do you like that turn of phrase? I'm considering using it as the headline for my blog."

Chapter Three

"I pretty much lost my appetite after that," Liss said when she finished recounting her conversation with Jane Nedlinger to Dan.

"So you just walked out?" He was on the other side of the bar in the lounge, polishing a glass with a towel.

The place was all but deserted. Most of the hotel's guests were attendees at the First Annual Maine-ly Cozy Con. They were buying their drinks at the portable bar set up at the reception. Dan's only patrons were a young couple sitting in one of the booths, a nervous-looking man in his early thirties at a table, and an elderly gentleman occupying the stool at the end of the bar farthest away from where Liss perched, nursing a ginger ale.

She scooped up a handful of complimentary party mix from the nearest bowl. "I couldn't see the point in sticking around."

"And she said her name was Nedlinger?"

"Yes. Jane Nedlinger. But she didn't have a name

tag. I'm not sure if she's attending the conference or not. Why? Do you know her?"

"Sherri called earlier to ask if we had a J. Nedlinger registered here, which we didn't. She didn't say why."

"Ms. Nedlinger must have stopped by at the P.D. She said she'd seen police reports. Would Sherri have shown them to her?"

"I'm not even sure Sherri is the one who'd have them. The state police did the investigating."

The name Gordon Tandy hung in the air between them, unspoken. He was the state police detective assigned to Carrabassett County and, until recently, he'd been Dan's rival for Liss's affections.

Liss doubted that Gordon had talked to Jane Nedlinger himself. The state police had a public relations officer to deal with the public. Or would Jane be considered the press? Liss didn't suppose it mattered. The woman had gotten information from somewhere. Now she wanted more, and she didn't strike Liss as the type to give up easily.

"Drat," Liss muttered. "I was looking forward to this weekend. I don't want to have to worry about some scandalmonger dogging my steps."

"You may be making too much of this."

"You mean I'm overreacting." She made a face at him. "Maybe."

They were interrupted by the entrance of a trio of screaming kids in wet swimsuits. "Daddy! Daddy!" yelled a little girl of perhaps six as she ran up to the nervous man at the table. "Mommy says you have to watch us."

The two boys, one who looked to Liss to be eight or nine and the other a little older, started a game of tag around the furniture. A chair toppled over. The little girl's shrill voice rose even higher when the older boy poked her in the ribs in passing.

"Daddy! He's picking on me!"

Dan left the bar and went over to speak quietly to the father. Then he turned to the two boys and told them that if they didn't settle down they'd have to leave. He was perfectly polite and therefore made no impression at all on any of the children. No sooner had he returned to his post than all three of them were racing in and out of the lounge, shouting at the top of their lungs. Liss felt a little sorry for the father, who had probably been trying to hide from his family long enough to have a quiet beer. Her sympathy quickly evaporated when he proved unwilling, or unable, to control his brood. The second time Dan came out from behind the bar to speak to him, he stood up, threw some money down to pay his tab, and stormed out. The children had already disappeared.

"Kids shouldn't be allowed in bars," Dan grumbled.

"Not those kids, at any rate."

As he refilled her glass, she could almost see him collecting his thoughts. Dan's face fascinated her. Unless he was making a conscious effort, all his feelings were right there for anyone to read. She liked that about him. He was as honest, as they said around here, as the day was long.

"The Nedlinger woman said she wanted to interview you, right?" Dan asked.

"She said she had questions."

"And you immediately put up shields." Liss not

only saw the smile on his face, she heard it in his voice.

"I told her that her claim wasn't true, that I'm not some kind of magnet for murder. And she just laughed and said that magnet for murder was an even better turn of phrase than lightning rod for violent death. Sheesh! Some days you just can't win!"

"The point is, she's offered you the chance to talk to her and answer her questions. If you agree, she might end up giving her story a more positive slant."

Liss glared at him. "Or not. Oh, that may be what she *implied*, but I didn't believe her. There was just something . . . *smarmy* about her. I wouldn't trust her to take out the trash." She managed a weak smile and held up one hand with her thumb and forefinger held a quarter of an inch apart. "I came *this* close to telling her to publish and be damned."

When Dan's eyebrows shot up, she chuckled.

"Okay. Dumb impulse. I wish I could remember who said that originally. Somebody famous. If I knew who it was, maybe it wouldn't sound so hackneyed."

Then again, maybe it would. Was Dan right? Was she overreacting?

"At least think about talking to her," he advised, ever the voice of reason.

"I suppose I could. She did give me a grace period. She said that if I changed my mind, I should let her know before the end of the conference."

"Then why don't you go back upstairs and enjoy the rest of the reception? Then maybe talk to

Sherri—oh, damn! I forgot to tell you about Adam Willett."

His sudden change in tone alerted her to expect bad news. "What happened?"

Word of Adam's broken arm banished Jane Nedlinger from Liss's thoughts. She tried phoning Sherri, but none of the numbers she tried were answered. Finally, she just left a message on the voice mail for Pete's cell phone, a sympathetic word and the assurance that if Sherri needed her for anything, she shouldn't hesitate to call.

"I feel so helpless," she lamented after she hung up.

"He'll be okay. Kids heal fast."

"Broken arm, though—that's a bummer." She had plenty of experience with injuries, and with physical therapy, too. Adam would be in pain. And Sherri would suffer right along with him.

"Enough doom and gloom," Dan said. "There are movies showing later, right? Which one are you going to attend? Maybe I'll join you. We can make this into a date night."

She could use cheering up, Liss decided, and she didn't have to fake her enthusiasm for the conference's offerings. "They're all good," she told him. "You pick. The choices are *Rear Window, Dial M for Murder, Murder on the Orient Express,* and *The Maltese Falcon.* The classic versions, of course." She was pretty sure they'd all been remade in less successful, more violent modern adaptations.

Since it was barely seven, Liss was not inclined to hide out in the lounge until the film fest started at nine. Besides, she knew she wouldn't be able to avoid Jane Nedlinger for long, no matter what she did. That being the case, she decided that she might as well go back to the reception.

On her way there, she passed the harried father who'd been in the lounge. A woman, obviously his wife, had him backed up against one of the pillars in the lobby. Her face was a picture of outrage as she demanded, in a voice as shrill as her daughter's, "What do you mean, you lost the kids?"

Liss kept walking.

Back at the reception, she decided it was a good thing she had not yet regained her appetite. In the short time she'd been gone, the contents of the buffet tables had dwindled down to a few scraps of cheese and a single mini-éclair. Liss snagged it and looked around for Jane Nedlinger.

The woman's height and Wagnerian proportions stood out even in a crowd that contained a number of plus-sized, middle-aged women. Jane was still holding a plate heaped high with goodies. Or perhaps it had been refilled. But she wasn't eating. She was talking at Yvonne Quinlan. Her body language was aggressive and her current prey had a deer-in-the-headlights look on her face.

Just how many people did Jane Nedlinger plan to harass that evening?

Liss tried telling herself that what was between the blogger and the actress was none of her business. And that she should be grateful someone else had captured Jane's attention. But when she spotted Nola Ventress chatting with Margaret Boyd, she headed their way, thinking that perhaps Nola knew something about Jane Nedlinger. Something they could use to rein her in. If Jane wasn't registered at the conference, maybe they could even kick her out.

"Here's my lovely niece now," Margaret said as Liss approached.

Almost two years earlier, when Liss had first moved back to Moosetookalook, Margaret Mac-Crimmon Boyd had been a plump and comfortable widow in her late fifties who dyed her hair bright red and had little to occupy her time besides a good-for-nothing son and the family business, Moosetookalook Scottish Emporium. Since then, she had lost weight, let her hair fade to a natural grayish brown, and begun a new career as events coordinator at The Spruces. Margaret still talked a mile a minute and had a cheerful outlook on life, but now her days were much more well-rounded. She even had a boyfriend, if such a term could be applied to a man who was pushing sixty.

"You must stop in and see the Emporium, Nola," Margaret continued. "Liss has worked wonders with it since she took over."

"I'll do that, if I can find the time." Nola started to move away.

Liss spoke quickly. "Nola, do you know anything about a woman named Jane Nedlinger?"

Nola went perfectly still except for her eyes. She blinked several times, as if to process the question. "Why do you want to know?" she asked.

"Because she's here and she's asking intrusive questions. At least she did of me, and I've watched her accost two other people this evening. Neither looked happy about being cornered."

"I've heard she can be . . . abrasive in person."

"That's putting it mildly."

Nola frowned. "I've never met her, but I'm a regular reader of her blog. I do hope everyone's being polite to her, even if she is offensive. Good publicity for our conference is especially important this first year, so there can be a *second* Annual Maine-ly Cozy Con."

"So you invited her here?" Liss asked.

"I sent her a press release and some other . . . material. I was hoping to generate publicity."

"From a blog?"

Liss had designed the Emporium's Web page and now made most of her profits selling online, but she had no experience with social networking or blogging. She'd never had any urge to share her personal observations with the world. As for reading other people's opinions, who had the time? When she did squeeze out a spare half hour for herself, she usually spent it curled up with a good book. Or with Dan.

"You'd be surprised how wide an audience *The Nedlinger Report* reaches," Nola said. "It has more readers than some newspapers."

"So she's here to report on the conference? She'll give you good press?"

Nola sighed. "Good? Probably not. She tends to find fault with things. But she has a huge following."

Liss frowned. None of this was encouraging. And if Nola had known in advance that Jane emphasized the negative, she had been naïve to think alerting her to the existence of the Cozy Con was a bright idea.

"Well," Nola said, visibly stiffening her spine, "I

suppose I'd better have a word with her. Which one is she?"

"She was speaking with your guest of honor a few minutes ago." Liss turned to scan the room. It was easy to locate Jane Nedlinger, but she was no longer with Yvonne Quinlan. Now she was talking to Dan.

Liss wondered why he wasn't in the lounge. He'd been scheduled to work behind the bar until nine. Then again, his father owned the hotel. She knew he could get someone to fill in for him when he really wanted to. He'd probably called for a replacement as soon as she returned to the reception and come up here looking for her, thinking that she still needed cheering up.

He was right about that.

"Jane Nedlinger is the big woman in gray," she told Nola.

"Oh, my," Nola said, her eyes widening. Then she headed in the opposite direction. "Yvonne looks a bit frazzled," she called over her shoulder. "I'd better have a word with her first."

Shaking her head, Liss watched Nola scurry off in the direction of her guest of honor. Wise to run, she thought, trying to picture the petite Nola confronting Jane Nedlinger. It would be like a squirrel facing down an enormous black bear.

Should she follow Nola or rescue Dan? Liss glanced back at her fiancé, torn. She ought not leave the man she loved in the claws of a predator. But Dan was the one who had thought she was making too much of Jane Nedlinger's interest in Moosetookalook's past murders. Maybe a few minutes at the blogger's mercy would convince him that she'd been right to be concerned. Besides, she'd been hoping for a chance to meet Yvonne Quinlan.

Turning her back on Dan, Liss set off after Nola and Margaret.

Dan held his ground with an effort. He had a feeling that if he tried to back away from the formidable woman in front of him, she'd pace him like a lioness stalking her prey.

"Moosetookalook appears to be the murder capital of Maine," Jane Nedlinger repeated. "Wouldn't you say that's correct?" She edged a little farther into his personal space. She seemed to use up more than her fair share of oxygen, too.

"Seems a stretch to me." Dan slid into the laconic drawl he sometimes adopted for the benefit of tourists. In the popular opinion of the rest of the country, all Mainers were laid back and folksy, fished for lobster in their spare time, and said "ayuh" a lot, never mind that most of the state was nowhere near the rockbound coast.

"Oh, come now, Mr. Ruskin! May I call you Dan?" She didn't wait for permission, just assumed it would be forthcoming. "Now, Dan, there's no sense in hiding the truth. Not from a seasoned newshound like me. I was an investigative reporter once, you know. I worked for one of the big Boston papers. There's no deflecting me when I'm chasing a hot story."

And the juicier, the better, Dan assumed. She was all but smacking her lips over this one.

"Sorry, ma'am," he said aloud, "but I don't have anything to say to you. You'd best talk to the police if you're interested in the details of a criminal investigation."

"Investigations. Plural. And the way I hear it, you and your little girlfriend had more to do with solving those cases than the cops did."

Little girlfriend? Oh, Liss was going to love that one! Since Dan couldn't think of a single reply that wouldn't come back to haunt him, he wisely remained silent.

Jane Nedlinger kept talking. She seemed to take a malicious pleasure in enumerating Moosetookalook's flaws, making Dan realize that he'd been dead wrong in the advice he'd given Liss. When he'd lobbied her to consider giving Jane Nedlinger an interview, he'd assumed that the threat Liss had sensed was all posturing and play-acting on Jane's part. In person, however, the blogger was just as alarming as Liss had claimed. The potential danger she posed could not easily be dismissed.

"Moosetookalook is a quiet little town, Ms. Nedlinger," he said, interrupting her.

"Jane."

"We're peaceable folk here, Jane. Minding our own business. Trying to make a living. There's no call to make a fuss just because we had a few unfortunate . . . incidents . . . over the last couple of years."

"Is that how you see it? Incidents? I call them vile murders." Her expression abruptly turned cold and hard. "I hear you're head of the chamber of commerce or whatever you call it here, but I won't be put off by the party line. You're sitting on a hotbed of crime and violence in this dinky little sinkhole you call home. In fact, I think this story is bigger than I first thought. I may just have to devote an entire week to the Moosetookalook murders and Liss MacCrimmon's part in them."

"Now hold on just a minute!"

She talked right over his protest. "You can tell Ms. MacCrimmon that I won't need to ask her any questions after all. I can get all I need for my exposé without her input."

Leaving Dan still sputtering, Jane sailed away. Within seconds, she'd pounced on a new victim, a woman who, by the color of her name tag, was a speaker at the conference. He'd stopped by the registration table earlier, long enough to observe that fans got white name tags while panelists wore light green. Nola Ventress and her helpers sported bright yellow.

The chatter in the room was loud, one conversation bleeding into the next. As Liss passed various couples and small groups, trailing after her aunt and Nola Ventress, she caught a word here and a sentence there. Everyone sounded upbeat. Some were talking about the next day's panels and workshops. Others were saying nice things about the hotel. One remarked that she enjoyed the romantic suspense novels written by Maine writer Susan Vaughan more than the quasi paranormals penned by Yvonne Quinlan.

"Apples and oranges," replied the woman she was speaking to.

The remaining tidbits Liss overheard were all about murder, but to her immense relief, the only crimes anyone seemed interested in discussing were those that took place between the covers of a book.

Nola looked surprised, and not particularly pleased, to discover that both Margaret and Liss were right behind her when she reached Yvonne's side. Rather perfunctorily, she introduced them to the actress-turned-writer and to the man in the checked blazer. His name was Bill Stotz and he was Yvonne's manager.

Bill lavished praise on Nola for her organizational skills, then seemed to lose interest when Liss announced that she was one of the vendors from the dealers' room. He fished a stick of chewing gum out of his pocket, unwrapped it, and popped it into his mouth. He let the wrapper fall to the floor without bothering to look around for a trash receptacle.

"Are you a bookseller?" Yvonne asked.

"I sell gift items with a Scottish theme," Liss replied.

"I must make it a point to stop by and see what you have to offer," Yvonne said with a charming smile. "I always find such delightful gifts in dealers' rooms at small conferences like this one."

If Yvonne was suffering any residual effects from her encounter with Jane Nedlinger, Liss couldn't spot them. Then again, Yvonne *was* a professional actress.

"Was that Nedlinger person bothering you?" Nola's blunt question surprised Liss and thudded into the conversation as awkwardly someone tripping over a piece of furniture.

Bill Stotz scowled. Even Yvonne's easy smile faltered, but only for a millisecond.

"Of course not," she said. "That dreadful woman is just after a story, as always. And she wanted to make sure I knew how much she hated my latest book."

"She panned it?" Nola could not have looked more stricken if it had been her own creation that Jane had reviled.

"I take it you didn't see the review." Yvonne sounded remarkably cheerful. "She loathed everything about it."

"I've been too busy with the conference to read her blog for the last couple of days," Nola admitted. She seemed extraordinarily shaken by Yvonne's announcement. "Oh, my. I never thought . . . I hoped . . ."

When her incoherent words trailed off, Yvonne filled in the blanks. "You sent her a review copy, didn't you, Nola?"

A study in misery, Nola nodded.

"Don't give it another thought," Yvonne advised her. "None of us should allow that awful creature to spoil our day."

"Doesn't bad press bother you?" Liss asked, genuinely curious.

"Well, of course it does," Yvonne said. "No one *enjoys* a scathing review. But you have to consider the source. I learned a long time ago not to let petty people get under my skin. Not for more than about a minute and a half, anyway." She gave a light, infectious laugh.

Liss found herself smiling back at the actress-turned-mystery-author. "Good advice. Too bad it's so hard to follow."

"It takes years of practice," Yvonne admitted. "Are you a writer, too?"

"Oh, no. Just a reader."

"There's no *just* about being a reader. We writers wouldn't have much in the way of careers if no one read what we wrote."

"Well, I do enjoy your books, Ms. Quinlan."

"Yvonne, please."

"Yvonne, then. I'm curious, though. You have a successful career in television, but you made your fictional detective a bit-part actress."

At first glance the character, Toni Starling, might have seemed an unlikely amateur sleuth. She lived in Vancouver, where many U.S. action series and movies were filmed, and worked pretty steadily as "woman number two," "first waitress," and the like. Many of the crimes she solved had to do with the film industry. What made the series unique, however, was that Toni had assistance on her cases from a mysterious associate who might . . . or might not . . . be a vampire. That gimmick had attracted hordes of readers to the books because Yvonne herself had played one of the undead for nearly a decade—a character named Caroline Sweet in the hit television show *Vamped*.

"Toni isn't me," Yvonne said with another soft laugh, the kind that invited the listener to share in the joke. "Besides, if you think about it, unsuccessful actors have to be more observant than successful ones—constantly on the alert for opportunities to show off their skills. That's a good quality in a sleuth, too, don't you think?"

"True. And Simon? Is he really a vampire?"

This time Yvonne's laughter was so full-bodied it attracted attention from all corners of the room. "I leave that up to the reader to decide."

For a moment, Liss considered the question seriously. She'd read all the books, some of them twice. "We never see Simon bite anyone. And there aren't any bodies drained of blood lying around. On the other hand, he never goes out in the daylight."

"That you know of." Yvonne's smile was secretive and her dark brown eyes glinted with mischief. "Vampires don't *have* to kill these days, do they? And sometimes they kill in other ways. It's very easy for them to break someone's neck, for example. Just a quick twist and the deed is done." She mimed the action.

Liss found herself both fascinated and repelled by this conversation. She couldn't resist asking another question. "Is that possible? I mean, is it really so easy to break someone's neck?" She'd seen it done countless times on both the big and little screens, but reality and Hollywood—or Vancouver—weren't always in the same universe. Screenplays certainly got a great many other things wrong, a point Yvonne made over and over again in her mystery novels.

"It is if you know how," Yvonne assured her. "I did a brief stint as a stuntwoman before I got my first gig as an actress. They taught me what to do.

Or rather, what *not* to do. Fatal accidents on the set are never good for business."

Two young women had joined the group surrounding Yvonne and had been hanging on every word the actress spoke. Hesitantly, one ventured a comment.

"A real vampire would drain the victim's blood," she said. She had long, straight hair and wore the conference uniform of jeans and a T-shirt. The shirt featured a skeleton sitting on a bench at a bus stop. The caption read: "Waiting for a Good Agent."

"That's right," her companion agreed. "Breaking someone's neck and leaving the body to rot is just wasteful." Her face was slightly rounder than the first woman's and her hair was shorter. Her black T-shirt had no artwork on it, only words. It read: "And then Buffy staked Edward. The End."

"But for a vampire to do that," her friend said in an authoritative voice, "is a sign of contempt. Remember that episode of *Buffy* where Angel—"

"Please," Yvonne interrupted, her smile slipping. "At least choose an example from *my* show." *Vamped* had lasted longer than *Buffy the Vampire Slayer*, Liss recalled, but it had debuted back when Joss Whedon's cult classic was still on the air. Liss supposed it was only natural that there had been some rivalry between the two shows.

"Will you sign my book?" the first fan asked. Then her face fell. "Oh. I left it in my room. I'll have to go get it."

Bill Stotz paused in the act of stuffing a second stick of gum into his mouth to object to autographing outside the established signing hours.

Maybe it was the third stick of gum, Liss thought, studying him. Bill was starting to look like a chipmunk storing up nuts for the winter in his cheeks, and she could smell the spearmint on his breath from two feet away.

"It's okay, Bill." Yvonne made a little shooing motion with one hand. "I'll tell you what," she said to her fan. "Why don't you go fetch your copy of my book right now? I'm not going anywhere. When you get back, we'll find a quiet spot where the three of us can sit and chat."

"I think that Simon is hot," the second woman said as they were leaving. "Way hotter than Vampire Bill."

Liss blinked and glanced at Bill Stotz before she remembered that Vampire Bill was a character in yet another paranormal mystery series, the one written by Charlaine Harris. She had to disagree on the hotness factor, she thought.

Since she'd obviously not been included in the invitation to chat, she looked around for Nola, intending to steer her back to Jane Nedlinger, but Nola had wandered off. Liss didn't immediately see either her or Jane.

Human, gum-chewing Bill slipped away as soon as Yvonne spotted an empty table where she and her two starry-eyed admirers could settle in. Liss and Margaret continued to chat with the actress/writer until the fans returned with Yvonne's latest novel in hand and the three of them headed for an empty table.

Margaret stooped to pick up Bill's discarded

gum wrappers before they moved on. "She's a real powerhouse, isn't she?"

"And gracious. Talented, too," Liss agreed. "She must be to have written so many novels while working full-time as an actress."

"She probably had a lot of free time on the set," Margaret mused, tossing the litter into the trash can near one of the buffet tables. Angeline's crew was already hard at work clearing away the empty platters and plates and used utensils. "I can easily imagine her scribbling madly into a notebook while she waited to shoot the next scene."

More likely she wrote on a laptop, Liss thought, but she said nothing to dispel her aunt's illusions.

When Margaret veered off to make sure there were no last-minute problems with the rooms where the classic movie night features were to be shown, Liss looked around for Dan. He was Nedlinger-free but on the far side of the room.

She took her time getting to him. It was still early, and the attendees at the First Annual Mainely Cozy Con were an outgoing bunch. She was twice drawn into conversations with complete strangers and once found herself being surveyed for her opinion on how early the first body should turn up in a cozy mystery. Liss found these brief encounters stimulating. She might not have known any of these folks before they arrived at The Spruces, but they all read the same books she did. That was enough to create an instant bond.

Dan's face was set in a fearsome scowl by the time Liss finally reached his side.

"What's wrong?" she asked, although she suspected she already knew.

"You were right about that woman," Dan admitted. "That Jane Nedlinger. She's out to cause trouble, and we have to do something to stop her."

Chapter Four

Liss and Dan stepped into a window alcove, out of the flow of traffic. The recess gave the illusion of privacy even in a crowded room. "What did she say to you?" Liss asked.

"She wanted to know if I thought Moosetookalook was the murder capital of Maine." Dan kept his voice low but it throbbed with irritation.

"And, of course, you corrected her. That honor belongs to Cabot Cove."

Dan looked blank.

"Cabot Cove, Maine? Home of Jessica Fletcher? *Murder, She Wrote*?"

"Oh. The old television show? I never watched it. I heard they got a lot of stuff about Maine dead wrong."

"Well, yes, but . . . oh, never mind! What else did she say to you?"

"She told me that this story may be bigger than she first thought. She's thinking of devoting an entire week to Moosetookalook and all the murders you've been involved in."

"They didn't *all* take place in Moosetookalook."

"That's not the point."

"And there haven't been that many." Annoyance sharpened Liss's voice. "A week implies seven. There have only been—"

"Liss! You're not seeing the big picture here. If she posts these blogs, they will generate very bad publicity for this town in general and this hotel in particular, not to mention for you personally. And she seems determined about it. She doesn't even want to do an interview with you anymore."

For just a moment, Liss felt annoyed. When it had been only her reputation on the line, it had been: "Don't worry, Liss. Go ahead and talk to her." But now that it was the *hotel*—She broke off in mid-thought, appalled by her reaction. Of course they should be concerned about The Spruces, and about Moosetookalook. What Jane Nedlinger wrote could harm everyone who lived here.

All the local residents would be affected by the situation. That meant there was no good reason not to solicit help in deciding how to blunt the impact of *The Nedlinger Report*. She glanced at her watch.

"It's barely eight. If we activate the phone tree, we could convene a meeting of the MSBA at my house in an hour."

The membership of the Moosetookalook Small Business Association included all the merchants on the town square and most of the other business-people in the village, too.

Dan hesitated, then nodded. "I'll alert Dad. You phone Patsy." He headed for the lobby.

Liss made her call from the window alcove,

where the cell phone reception was better. She was about to leave the meeting room when she caught sight of Nola. One look at the other woman's face told her that Nola was not a happy camper. Liss changed course to intercept her.

"What's wrong?" she asked.

"Do you really need to ask? That woman is impossible." Nola's face was flushed and her small hands had curled into tight fists.

"Jane Nedlinger?" Liss asked.

"Who else?"

"Come with me." Liss took Nola's arm and tugged her toward the nearest exit. "We're going to put our heads together and figure out how to deal with her threats."

Liss shivered when they stepped outside. Although the sun had only just set, the temperature was already plunging. She glanced up at the overcast sky. It looked, and smelled, as if they would have some rain tonight.

"You, too?" Nola asked. "I've always hated the great outdoors, especially after dark."

Liss wanted to protest that she was just chilled, but Nola was still talking.

"My parents used to insist on going camping every summer. I loathed every minute we spent in the woods. I don't like having too many trees around even now." She gave a theatrical shudder. "My friends kid me about my phobia, but I won't even visit the local Christmas tree farm at the holidays. I have a nice plastic spruce that suits me just fine."

"How do you feel about apple orchards?" Liss asked.

Nola laughed.

During the short drive into Moosetookalook, Nola supplied details of various posts Jane had written, and Liss began to understand why she was so upset. If Jane chose to pan the First Annual Maine-ly Cozy Con, its attending authors, and Nola herself, it would be very difficult to organize a second annual gathering. According to what Aunt Margaret had told Liss when Nola first booked the conference into the hotel, this conclave of mystery fans had been Nola's brainchild. She had almost single-handedly organized and produced the event, spending almost a year on the planning. She'd used her own savings to bankroll the project, which meant that she had a lot riding on its success.

Liss and Nola entered Liss's house through the kitchen. Nola dragged her feet all the way from the car. "I'm not sure this is such a good idea," she protested.

"Do you have a better one?" Liss asked. She flicked on the light and waved the other women inside.

Lumpkin, Liss's big yellow Maine Coon cat, chose that moment to leap from the refrigerator to the nearest kitchen countertop. Nola gave a shriek and threw her arms over her head. Then, cautiously, she peeked out through her fingers.

"Oh," she said, sounding sheepish. "A cat."

"Hang on a minute," Liss said. "Let me feed him and his little buddy and then I'll lock them in the basement. They'll only be underfoot at the meeting anyway."

Lumpkin and the half-grown black cat Liss had

named Glenora appreciated the food but protested loudly at being banished.

Members of the MSBA started to arrive a few minutes later, and at nine o'clock sharp, Dan banged his gavel—a wooden spoon—on the coffee table in Liss's living room. "Meeting will come to order!"

Liss doubted he could be heard above the babble of voices. She quickly suppressed the cowardly thought that it might be better if he wasn't. They'd called this emergency meeting of the Moosetookalook Small Business Association for a good reason. This was no time for second thoughts. If they *had* overreacted, they'd just have to take their lumps.

A glance at Nola's face told Liss that Nola, too, sensed the potential for disaster. It occurred to her that Nola hadn't told her exactly what Jane Nedlinger had said to her. Whatever it was, it had made the poor woman miserable.

"You okay?" Liss whispered.

"No," Nola said. "I shouldn't have come here. You don't need my input." She darted nervous glances this way and that, as if she expected something else besides an oversized cat to jump out at her.

"You're the best person to explain who Jane Nedlinger is and how influential what she writes will be." Liss used her most soothing tone of voice. "And your presence will emphasize that an annual Maine-ly Cozy Con will bring business to this town. Trust me when I say that money talks."

Nola managed a faint smile, but she did not look entirely convinced.

Her nervousness was contagious. The greater Nola's anxiety, the more Liss worried about what Jane might write.

Dan banged the spoon again, with the same results.

Liss stood. "Everybody? Quiet, please!"

She projected her voice so that it reached every corner of the room, a trick she'd learned while on tour. True, she'd been a dancer, not an actress, but she'd had a few lines to say and she'd learned how to make herself heard from the second balcony.

"We've got a meeting to start here, folks!" she added. "Whenever you're ready."

"Yeah, yeah." Stu Burroughs slanted an irritated look in her direction. It turned decidedly unfriendly and suspicious when his gaze moved on to Nola. She made a soft sound of distress and refused to meet his eyes.

Seeing that he'd successfully cowed their guest, Stu gave a "whatever" shrug and plunked himself down on Liss's sofa, bouncing a little when he connected with the cushion.

Stu was short and chunky and fond of bright colors. His shirt was a deep maroon and royal blue suspenders held up his well-worn jeans. It was only recently that he'd stopped dyeing his hair black. Liss privately thought that had been a wise decision on his part. The flat, lifeless color had not suited his deeply lined face. The salt-and-pepper locks he now sported looked far more natural. Liss had no idea how old Stu was, but he'd owned and operated Stu's Ski Shop for as long as she could remember.

Betsy Twining, proprietor of the Clip and Curl,

settled in next to Stu. The owner of Patsy's Coffee
House, Patsy herself, squeezed in beside her. Betsy
was slender. Patsy was almost cadaverously thin, in
spite of the delicious homemade pastries she
turned out on a daily basis. Patsy was a genius in
the kitchen. She was also profoundly unhappy
about being up this late. She kept glancing at her
watch, a clear indication that she was anxious to
get home and go to bed. Liss knew that Patsy
would have to be up at three the next morning to
start baking and didn't want her to wake up
cranky, not when Patsy was the one who had been
hired to supply pastries for tomorrow's author
breakfast.

They'd been able to round up quite a few members of the MSBA on short notice. The others
found seats, filling all the extra chairs Liss had
brought in from the kitchen. The room was packed.
Aunt Margaret was there, and Angie Hogencamp,
and Joe Ruskin. Liss recognized the retired couple
who had just taken over the old Toy Box building
to turn it into a jewelry store. She fingered her
tourmaline engagement ring. It was one of their
creations. Even before they'd opened their business on the town square, they'd had items for sale
in the hotel gift shop at The Spruces.

A bouncy young woman with ginger-colored
hair and a wide smile rushed in, out of breath. She
was another newcomer, the owner of a hobby shop
located where, until a few months earlier, there
had been an insurance office.

Dan once again tried to call the meeting to
order.

"We aren't all here yet," Stu objected. He smirked

at Liss and Nola. "We need to wait for our friendly local undertaker."

Nola gave a start, causing the Canadian rocker in which she sat to squeak loudly. The sound grated on Liss's nerves. She clenched her teeth. The sooner they got this meeting started, the better.

"Doug's running a little late," Patsy piped up. "He said we should go ahead without him."

"Good enough." Dan banged the spoon one last time. "We're officially in session. Liss?"

Every eye turned in her direction. In her peripheral vision, she saw Nola shrink back, as if she were trying to make herself invisible.

"Evening, all," Liss began. "I apologize in advance if I've gone off half-cocked. If that turns out to be the case, you can all feel free to laugh me out of the room. But when Dan and I talked this over at the hotel, it seemed logical to call in reinforcements. All of us have a vested interest in protecting the good name of our hometown."

She recounted her brief conversation with Jane Nedlinger, then gave them a few of the details she'd learned about *The Nedlinger Report* from talking to Nola.

"This blog is very popular, and the woman who writes it is renowned for her scathing remarks. She'd far rather trash a book in a review than praise it. As for her accounts of true crimes, she gravitates toward salacious details, and if there aren't enough of those, she's been known to drop hints about others—just shy of saying enough to provoke a lawsuit."

"But surely only people interested in crimes and

criminals read something like that," Betsy said,
making a little sound of disgust. "We wouldn't want
that sort of person coming to Moosetookalook
anyway."

"You'd be surprised the people who like to wal-
low in scandal," Angie cut in. "I've got standing orders for stuff so lurid it would curl your hair."

"How is being featured in this blog any worse
than Moosetookalook showing up in a story in one
of the supermarket tabloids?" Stu Burroughs
asked. "Seems to me that it's all free publicity. And
you know what they say about any publicity being
good publicity."

"I hate that old saw," Liss muttered. "It's just
plain wrong. Studies show that people tend to pass
on negative comments far more often than they
repeat positive ones." She was pretty sure she'd
said the same thing the last time someone had
played the "any publicity" card.

"That's just human nature," Aunt Margaret
agreed. She sent a worried look Nola's way, then
glared at Stu.

"In any case," Dan said, "it seemed best that we
warn all of you about this woman and her blog. It's
likely that we're soon going to have a serious public relations problem on our hands." He recapped
what Jane Nedlinger had said to him, reinforcing
what Liss had already told the group.

"And yet," Angie said, "Liss told me earlier today
that this conference came to The Spruces *because*
there had been a murder at the hotel."

"That's true," Liss admitted. She turned to her
guest. "This is Nola Ventress. She's the organizer
of the conference currently being held at The

Spruces. Jane Nedlinger's presence here is a threat to her, too."

Nola nervously cleared her throat. She was still avoiding eye contact, not just with Stu but with everyone. Her voice was barely audible, a far cry from the self-confident woman Liss had seen earlier on the podium. Two or three people had to lean forward in order to catch what Nola said. One of the jewelry store owners surreptitiously turned up the volume on her hearing aid.

"Jane Nedlinger can put such a negative spin on what she writes that no one will ever want to come here again," Nola said. "She's petty and vindictive and she positively *enjoys* ruining people's careers." She twisted her fingers in the bottom of her T-shirt, then looked up at last. "I've been sitting here thinking about it. I don't think she ever has a good word to say about anything."

She was such a study in misery that Liss could only assume she was blaming herself for bringing both the conference and Moosetookalook to Jane Nedlinger's attention.

"Then why do people read her blog?" Joe Ruskin sounded confused.

He was an older version of his son, with a distinguished hint of gray at the temples. Liss hated to see him looking so worried. He'd had to weather far too many ups and downs since the hotel opened. She realized, with a painful lurch of her heart, that he seemed to have aged ten years in the last ten months.

Bitterness made Nola's voice stronger. "For the same reason some people watch reality shows.

They like to feel superior. And Jane's clever with words. I'll give her that much. Some people find her kind of venom entertaining. I did myself until she turned it on me."

"The biggest problem is that blogs reach everywhere," Liss said. "This won't be just a local story."

"Still sounds like a tempest in a teapot to me," Betsy Twining cut in. "It's only been, what? Three hours since you first met this woman? Don't you think you could have slept on the problem before going to Code Red?" Like Patsy, Betsy had to be up at the crack of dawn.

"She threatened to link Liss and, by extension, all of Moosetookalook to a series of four murders over the last two years," Dan pointed out. "That's a threat that's hard to take lightly."

"Are you *sure* she has all that much influence?" Patsy fought a yawn, lost, and apologized for being so sleepy. "Past my bedtime," she mumbled.

"I've never even heard of her," Angie chimed in.

There was an immediate chorus of "me neithers."

"Maybe *we* haven't, but folks from away, the ones we want to attract here as tourists, apparently *do* read her blog."

"If you're right about that," Stu said, looking morose, "then we're already dead."

"Who's dead?" a new voice asked. "Does someone need my services?"

Stu gave a derisive snort. "Like Preston's Mortuary is hurting for business!"

"Join the party, Doug," Liss invited as the newcomer stepped into her living room. In addition to

being the local mortician, he was also one of the
village selectman. Even though he was often
prickly to deal with, Liss was glad he'd been able to
attend the meeting.

The term "gentleman" might have been in-
vented just for Doug. Liss didn't think she'd ever
seen him wearing anything less formal than a suit
and tie. He had an upright carriage and a refined
manner that came very close to straying over the
line into supercilious. How he'd produced a son
like young Frank, best described as careless and
slovenly, was a mystery no one in Moosetookalook
had been able to solve.

Doug was yet another of the longtime village
residents who had seemed so ancient to Liss when
she was growing up. She'd been surprised to realize, when she returned to the village as an adult,
that he was the same age as Aunt Margaret. They'd
gone to high school together. The fact that he'd
married a woman more than twenty years his junior, back when Liss herself had been in junior
high, had once struck her as creepy. Now she supposed, when she thought about it at all, that Doug
would have considerable appeal to women who
liked the suave, reserved type.

Doug glanced around the room, looking for an
empty chair. He froze when he caught sight of
Nola. "Well, as I live and breathe. Nola Ventress."

"Hello, Doug." Nola was back to whispering.

Liss frowned. Was it her imagination, or had
there been a distinct rise in tension in the air?
Nola was actually trembling. While Dan recapped
the situation for Doug's benefit, Liss studied the

faces of those gathered in her living room. Two of them seemed more alert. Stu had an anticipatory gleam in his eyes. Aunt Margaret looked more worried than ever.

"What does this woman look like?" Doug asked.

Liss described Jane, emphasizing her size and her all-gray ensemble. She'd have stood out in downtown Moosetookalook, and Liss wasn't surprised when Betsy spoke up.

"I think I saw her late this morning," the beautician said. "She was going into the library just as I was coming out."

Doing her research, Liss thought. And soaking up gossip. Dolores Mayfield, the town librarian, would have been happy to dish the dirt, even with a stranger.

"Sounds to me as if you and Nola have an irrational fear of this Nedlinger woman's power, Liss," Doug said. He'd dragged the combination stool and stepladder that Dan had custom-built for Liss out of the kitchen to perch on. "I'm sure there's no cause for alarm."

"I disagree," Stu said. "She's a real threat. One we need to deal with. Let's face it, Moosetookalook doesn't need any more bad publicity."

Liss wished she could take more satisfaction from Stu's change of heart, but she suspected he'd come down on the opposite side from Doug just to spite the other man. They'd never gotten along all that well.

"And exactly how do you propose that we do that?" Doug sounded bored.

"We'll think of something." Stu swiveled on the

sofa so that he could look at each of the other MSBA members in turn, but no one had any solution to suggest.

Patsy produced a jaw-popping yawn. "Maybe we should sleep on it."

"Maybe we should stay right here and brainstorm until we come up with a workable solution," Stu shot back. "Plug away at it all night if we have to. Unless this town doesn't mean as much to the rest of you as it does to me."

Doug produced a clean white handkerchief from his breast pocket, took off his glasses, polished them, and replaced the handkerchief before he responded to Stu's taunt. "I, for one, can't think of any way to stop the woman from posting to her blog. If she does, we'll just have to live with the fallout."

"We could threaten to sue her if she writes about us," Stu shot back.

"What good will a threat do?" The normally amiable Angie sounded irritated. "It won't stop her. And once the damage is done, there's no point in taking her to court. The burden of proof is on us. By the time we collect any solid figures, we'll already be hurting financially. We won't have the spare cash to shell out for a lawyer."

"So we just give up and let her write any damned thing she wants?" Stu was no longer just yanking Doug's chain. Genuine outrage turned his face an ugly red. "No way!"

They debated the issue for another hour. Everyone was in agreement that they hoped to profit from the mystery conference and others like it. There was a general consensus that if Jane Nedlinger could be persuaded not to write a blog post that mentioned Liss, murder, and Moosetooka-look in the same piece, she should be. But no one had a workable plan to convince the blogger to alter her plans.

Individual MSBA members gave up one by one and drifted away, heading home to their beds. Finally only Stu, Doug, Nola, Dan, and Liss remained. Nothing had been resolved.

Liss sighed and turned to Nola. "Give me a minute to let the cats up from the cellar and I'll drive you back to the hotel."

"No need for you to bother, Liss," Stu Burroughs cut in. "I can take her."

Nola's cheeks flared pink. "I don't think that's a good idea."

"Oh, come on, Nola. I promise not to try to lure you into the woods to have my wicked way with you." He made obnoxious little kissing noises at her, causing her color to deepen into red.

"Leave her alone, Stu," Doug interrupted. "You always did have a sick sense of humor." He took Nola's hand. She tried to pull free, but his grip was too tight. "You must allow me to see you back to The Spruces. I'm headed that way anyhow."

"You're offering the lady a ride in the hearse?" Stu gave a bleat of laughter.

"I'll be driving my personal vehicle," Doug said in a voice as cold as embalming fluid. "That's a Porsche," he added for Nola's benefit.

If he expected her to be impressed, he was doomed to disappointment. She just looked more rattled. "I don't think that's a good idea, either." She sent a desperate look Liss's way.

"Back off, both of you," Liss told them.

But Doug did not release his grip on Nola's hand. If anything, he tightened his hold, making her wince. "I was so looking forward to reminiscing," he said, "and to telling Nola all about my lovely wife and our fine, upstanding son."

Liss was sorely tempted to tell Doug, then and there, just how carelessly young Frank had handled Lenny Peet's body, but she knew this was not the right moment. "It's up to you, Nola," she said instead.

To Liss's surprise, Nola pulled herself together. She tugged her hand free and poked one finger into Doug's chest. "Since you say you're going my way anyhow, I'll accept a lift from you, but I refuse to look at baby pictures."

Then, while Doug pulled on the thin leather driving gloves he wore year-round, claiming his hands were always cold, Nola turned on Stu.

"As for you, Stu Burroughs, since you've agreed to call the charity auction, I will talk to you tomorrow afternoon. Until then, I've no interest in your company. You'll have to excuse both of them," she added to Liss, sending an apologetic look her way. "They always did snap at each other like a couple of pit bulls."

Wearing a disgruntled expression on his face, Stu watched Nola and Doug leave together. When he glanced Liss's way again, he had the grace to look embarrassed. "I guess I got a little out of line. Sorry."

She patted him on the shoulder, grinning. "No more than usual, Stu."

He chuckled, but sobered again instantly. "About this Nedlinger woman—don't you worry your pretty little head about her. We'll figure something out. Stands to reason there's some way to scotch her story."

Chapter Five

When Dan released Liss's two cats from their prison, he got a snarl from Lumpkin for his trouble.

"You're welcome," he said, and reached down to stroke Glenora. Friendlier than her "brother," she was stropping his ankles in appreciation.

Lumpkin headed for his food bowl. When he found it was empty, he sent an indignant look over his shoulder. Dan obligingly poured out some kibble. After a few more hasty preparations, he returned to the living room. "Alone at last," he said when the door closed behind Stu Burroughs.

Liss turned, smiling. "Not quite." She nodded toward Lumpkin, who had followed Dan into the room.

She scratched the big cat behind the ears, then tried to pet his broad, furry head. She jerked and cried out when he nipped the tip of one finger.

"So much for the theory that cats have a calming effect." Dan took her hand and inspected the indentations Lumpkin's teeth had made. Lucky for Lumpkin there was little damage. Dan had made his share of excuses for the cat in the past, but he drew the line at serious injury to Liss's person. "Apparently he's not in the mood to soothe."

"Being locked up makes him cranky."

"I wonder how he'd like living at the animal shelter?"

"Bite your tongue!"

If Liss could forgive the cat, Dan could do no less. "At least he didn't break the skin," he murmured as he kissed it better. Then, slinging one arm around Liss's shoulders, he steered her into the kitchen. He'd found a bottle of her favorite white wine in the refrigerator and had already poured her a glass.

"This will knock me out," she warned, but she accepted the offering and sipped.

"You could use a good night's sleep." Dan opened the beer he'd extracted for himself and took a long pull from the bottle. For a few minutes, they enjoyed a companionable silence. Then Dan gestured toward the answering machine attached to the kitchen phone. "You've got a message waiting."

"I know. I checked the caller I.D. when I first came home from the hotel. The message is from my mother. I'm ignoring it."

Dan frowned. "Are you sure you want to do that? What if your folks have some kind of emergency?"

"If that were the case, there would be more than one message waiting. And Mom would have called Aunt Margaret and the hotel as well as here. Trust me, whatever she wants, it can wait."

In Dan's world, you didn't ignore family. He regarded her with a steady, uncompromising stare until she relented.

"Okay, okay. But don't say I didn't warn you." She depressed the Play button, and her mother's cheerful voice emerged from the speaker as clearly as if she was in the room with them.

"Hi, sweetie," Violet MacCrimmon said. "I just had the most brilliant idea for your wedding. But first—what did Dan say when you told him you wanted to get married at the Western Maine Highland Games?"

Dan choked on a swallow of beer. *What?*

"It will make things so much easier to have the ceremony there," Violet went on, "since the wedding and the games are scheduled for the same weekend. And it will be more fun for everyone, too."

"When were you going to mention that little detail?" Dan asked.

Liss shushed him, but she had a guilty look on her face.

The message played on.

"Anyway, here's my idea," Violet said. "I've just found out that a medieval Scottish reenactment group is signed up to attend the games this year." She paused to let that nugget of information sink in.

Dan set his beer on the counter. His mind reeled. Get married at the area's annual Scottish festival? That was a far cry from his naïve assumption that they'd tie the knot in a small, quiet ceremony at the little nondenominational church located just two blocks away on Lowe Street.

Liss's mother's voice grew increasingly chipper

as the message continued. "I've mailed you a copy of *Renaissance Magazine*'s bridal issue. It's full of the most gorgeous gowns. Any one of them would look wonderful on you, especially since all the men in the wedding party will be wearing traditional dress. Oh, I just can't wait! Call me when you get a chance. Love you. Bye."

The click of the disconnect sounded abnormally loud in the quiet kitchen.

Dan cleared his throat. "I thought we were getting married in a church."

"Mom had a better idea."

"It's *our* wedding."

"Well, yes, but it's important to my mother, too. As she keeps pointing out, I'm her only child. And the parents of the bride traditionally pay for the wedding."

"We can afford the cost of our own damn wedding!"

"Not unless we elope. You have no idea how expensive—"

"I'm not a pauper!" But money was always tight and he'd been brought up to be frugal. "Elope?" He hoped he didn't sound too eager.

Liss ran her fingers lightly over his cheek. "I know. I'm tempted, too. But Mom and Dad really want to do this for us. The MacCrimmons are big on tradition. It would break their hearts if we deprived them of the opportunity to go all out for the occasion."

"Tradition, huh?" Funny how that word kept cropping up. His eyes narrowed. "Would that be *Scottish* tradition?"

Liss flashed him a grin. "Bagpipes sound much better outdoors. Inside a church, they're really much too loud."

Dan groaned. "I hate bagpipe music."

"But you love me. And it doesn't make all that much sense for us to get married in a church anyway. Neither one of us attends services regularly."

"Is it okay if I wear earplugs?"

She laughed, as if she thought—or hoped—that he was joking. "Not a good idea. You might not be able to hear the vows. You could agree to anything."

Beneath the teasing words, Dan heard her anxiety. He could give her this, he told himself. If bagpipe music and getting married at the Scottish festival were that important to her and her folks, how could he deny her?

He caught her hand in his, turning it so he could plant what he hoped she'd see as a romantic kiss on the backs of her knuckles. "It doesn't matter to me where we get married, as long as it's legal."

"Oh, it will be."

"Anything else I should know about?" he asked.

"Let me get my list."

Of course there was a list, he thought. Liss was a habitual list maker. He followed her back into the living room and watched while she fished this one out of the drawer in the end table. When they were settled on the sofa together, she handed over a 5x8 yellow lined tablet. At the top of the first page she'd written "Three Months Before."

"Complete guest list," he read aloud. "Order

wedding rings. Done and done." The next few
items were equally nonthreatening, ranging from
ordering the wedding cake to booking rooms for
out-of-town guests at The Spruces. Then he hit
number thirteen and he felt a sinking sensation in
his gut. "Select Scottish formalwear for groom and
ushers? Okay. I'll bite. What exactly does *Scottish*
formalwear consist of?"

Liss took a last sip of her wine and set the glass
on the end table. "I've been meaning to talk to you
about that."

"It means a kilt, doesn't it?"

She nodded. "Traditional Scottish wedding,"
she reminded him.

"Liss, I don't—"

"It's no big deal. I know for a fact that you're
not bowlegged or knock-kneed and I doubt your
brother Sam is, either. And I've already seen how
good Pete Campbell looks in a kilt." Sherri's husband regularly competed in athletic contests at the
highland games.

Dan chose his words carefully. "I guess I'm okay
with getting married at the Western Maine Highland Games, and I promise I won't wear earplugs
to block out the screeching—"

"Skirling," she corrected him. "Bagpipes skirl."

"I won't wear earplugs," he repeated, "but you'll
have to be the one to compromise on what I wear."
He took both her hands in his. "I love you, Liss
MacCrimmon, but there is no way in hell that you
are getting me into a skirt."

Liss sighed. "I knew I didn't want to listen to
Mom's phone message tonight."

Dan saw an out and grabbed it like a lifeline. "We're both too tired to get into all this now. Let's leave any discussion about the wedding until after the weekend, okay?"

Dan figured time was on his side. Although Moose-tookalook Scottish Emporium sold kilts off the rack, Liss undoubtedly wanted something custom-made for him to wear at their wedding. A kilt she'd expect him to wear to other Scottish events. He repressed a shudder. If he could just stall her long enough to make ordering such a kilt impossible, maybe he'd have a shot at convincing her that a tux was the better option.

"You're right," Liss agreed. "I've got too many other things on my mind just now. We'll let the wedding ride for the next couple of days."

"Show me your list of other things. Maybe there's something I can help with there."

She tapped her forehead. "That one is all up here. I haven't had time to write anything down."

"First item?"

"Stop blog."

"Moving right along. . . ."

His grimace coaxed a chuckle out of her. "Let's see. Oh—talk to Doug about his son." She described what she'd witnessed that morning.

"You can't do that tonight," Dan said. "Next?"

"Open mail and look at bridal gowns." She gestured toward the hall table where she'd tossed bills, letters, and a bulky mailer that was clearly the magazine her mother had mentioned.

"Nope. That's wedding related. It's on hold until after the weekend."

"Then that leaves just three items: work in the dealers' room; attend conference events; and find a good home for Lenny Peet's dog."

Dan shook his head over the number and variety of her tasks, but he couldn't help but smile at the last item. "I guess I was right," he said, giving her a quick peck on the cheek before he left the sofa and headed for the door. "You definitely need a good night's sleep."

"You're going home?"

Her obvious disappointment pleased Dan no end. He had a hard time keeping his feet moving away from her. "Tomorrow is going to be a long day for me, too." He came back long enough to claim one last kiss, but then stuck to his resolve to leave. "If I stay here any longer," he muttered on his way out the door, "neither one of us will get any rest."

Sherri was in the office early. It was barely six in the morning when she started the coffeepot and settled in at her desk in the P.D. She'd left her son Adam sound asleep, but neither of them had gotten a lot of shut-eye the previous night. The break in his arm was a clean one, but Adam's cast seemed huge to her. And for the next little while, he was going to need someone with him 24/7, if only to distract and pamper him.

Pete could stay in the apartment until two o'clock. Then he had to go to work. The town authorized paid time off for parents to nurse their sick kids, but Sherri didn't feel right just abandoning her post and leaving the department shorthanded.

She figured that she had until two to find someone to cover for her. With luck, one of the part-timers who filled in from time to time would be available to work her day shifts during the weekend.

She reached for the phone, knowing that her most likely prospect was an early riser. Her hand stilled when a red light went on. It indicated an incoming call to the fire department. Sherri was on her feet and running toward the front of the municipal building before the overhead door of the garage that held the fire truck had time to open all the way.

"What've you got?" she shouted to Greg Holstein, the volunteer fireman who was just climbing into the cab. No alarms were sounding. That meant it wasn't a fire.

"Accident out at Lover's Leap," he yelled back. "Someone spotted a body at the bottom."

"Teenager?" The spot was prime make-out territory.

"No idea!"

He took off in the truck in the direction of Spruce Avenue. Sherri raced to the police cruiser parked in the lot behind the municipal building and in a matter of minutes had caught up with him. Loaded with search and rescue equipment and medical supplies, as well as the wherewithal to put out house and car fires, the town's fire truck did triple duty for their small community. A car driven by a local woman who had been trained as an emergency medical technician fell into line behind Sherri's vehicle.

There was no ambulance in Moosetookalook. One had to be dispatched from the hospital in

Fallstown, a twenty-minute drive at legal speeds. Sherri wondered if she should start it on its way. Greg had said there was a body, but there was always a chance that the victim wasn't dead yet. Check first, she decided. With the added complication that Lover's Leap was a good half-mile walk from the nearest point where any vehicle but an ATV or snowmobile could go, it might make more sense to request a LifeFlight helicopter.

Two more members of the volunteer fire and rescue squad reached the parking lot at the hotel at the same time as the fire truck, Sherri's cruiser, and the EMT's car. Joe Ruskin was waiting for them there.

They set out together toward the spot at the edge of the woods that marked the start of the cliff path. "An early-morning jogger spotted the body," Joe reported. "He damn near killed himself scrambling down the goat track, and there wasn't a thing he could do when he got to the bottom. Close up, it was pretty obvious she'd broken her neck."

Joe was puffing slightly from the brisk pace Sherri and the others set.

"Any I.D.?" she asked.

"The kid who spotted her body is named Kline. Davy Kline. He says she's another guest, that he saw her at the reception last night. She must have gone out jogging as soon as the sun came up. Kline says that's what she's dressed for."

"Did you go out there yourself?"

Joe shook his head. "I figured I'd better wait for you. Kline is in my office if you want to talk to him. He's pretty shook up."

They'd reached the break in the trees. "Tell him

he can return to his room if he wants to," Sherri said. She felt sorry for the poor guy. Finding a corpse was not a good way to start the day.

Relieved that he didn't have to go look at the body, Joe headed back to the hotel. Sherri and the rescue team, armed with ropes and other equipment, followed the path into the woods. It seemed this was going to be a recovery rather than a rescue. With a little luck, the victim would have I.D. on her. If not, Joe or one of his employees might be able to supply a name once they'd brought up the body.

Lover's Leap was on town property, part of a small park adjacent to The Spruces. A sturdy rail fence stood between the jogging path and the drop-off. The cliff was of substantial height for this part of the world, rising about fifty feet above rocky terrain. That was small potatoes, Sherri supposed, compared to cliffs and escarpments found in the Rockies or in Europe, but it was high enough to be dangerous . . . and to provide a terrific view. From this "scenic outlook," she could see tree-covered mountains rising in the distance, dark green against a cloudless blue sky. The tallest of them still had a fringe of snow at its peak.

Too bad she wasn't there to sightsee.

The rescue team had already begun its descent. What Joe had called the goat track wasn't really a trail, just a natural route, narrow and overgrown, off to the side of the height of land. Someone had to want to reach the base of Lover's Leap very badly to scramble down that way.

A shout, quickly followed by a curse, told Sherri that the EMT had slipped and covered the last few yards on her backside. Last night's scattered rain showers had left the goat track muddy.

Gingerly, Sherri climbed over the fence to stand on the dew-laden grass at the edge of the cliff. At the bottom she saw what the jogger, Kline, had—a body, dressed in a jogging suit, lay sprawled face-down, the neck bent at an unnatural angle. Even from this distance, Sherri had no doubt but that she was staring at a corpse.

At the EMT's signal verifying that conclusion, Sherri punched a number into her cell phone. This was an unattended death. That meant they needed permission from a medical examiner before they could move the body.

"Looks like some poor silly woman was trying to get a better look at the view and lost her balance," Sherri said into the phone. It was tragic, but things like that happened all too often when people got careless.

Assured by George Henderson, the local M.E., that he'd be there directly, Sherri climbed back over to the safe side of the fence. This was pretty clearly an accident, but it was her job to consider the other possibilities.

She made a careful visual survey of the area in the clearing. She saw no scuff marks that might indicate a struggle. Neither was there a suicide note held in place by a rock. The only thing in the immediate vicinity of the scenic outlook that wasn't there compliments of Mother Nature was a plastic name badge holder. Sherri squatted down for a closer look but did not touch it. It had been lying by the side of the path long enough to be thoroughly soaked by the rain, and it no longer contained a name badge.

It could have been dropped by the victim or by an attendee at some other conference days earlier. The Spruces had hosted one small gathering after another for the last couple of months. Margaret Boyd had turned out to be very good at the job of attracting business to the hotel.

With nothing better to do, Sherri followed the cliff path a little way into the trees at the other side of the clearing. She knew that the trail made several large loops through a thickly wooded area and covered the best part of another mile before it came out on Spruce Avenue, just short of the entrance to the hotel's long, winding driveway. Within the first hundred feet, she found litter enough to fill a small trash bag, but only of the sort she'd expected—used condoms, tissues, empty beer cans, and a couple of gum wrappers. Leaving the items where they were, she returned to Lover's Leap to wait for the M.E.

Dr. Henderson and Jeff Thibodeau, Moosetookalook's chief of police and Sherri's boss, arrived together. The two men were about the same age but otherwise provided a study in contrasts. Jeff, portly enough to play Santa Claus every Christmas and nearly bald, was puffing like a steam engine as he loped into the clearing. George Henderson, thin as a whippet, had not only retained all of his hair but had it in abundance—a shock of dark brown atop his head and eyebrows so bushy they would have dominated his face had it not been for the handlebar mustache that was his pride and joy.

"What are you doing out here?" Jeff demanded when he'd caught his breath. "Go on home to your kid."

"I haven't found anyone to work for me yet."

"I'll call someone in. Go on. Get a move on. That little tyke needs his mom."

Sherri's sense of responsibility to her job warred with the knowledge that Jeff was right. Adam and Pete got along just fine, but Pete was still new at the stepfather gig. She'd have called her mother in to babysit, but Ida Willett had gone on a bus tour to Graceland with some of her cronies. Sherri's father, Ernie, was likewise unavailable. He worked twelve-hour days to keep his combination gas station and convenience store open.

"You still here?" Jeff asked. Below them, George, who had to be fifty if he was a day, had just reached the bottom of the cliff. Sherri hoped she'd still be that spry at his age.

"What about that book signing at Angie's to-morrow?" Sherri asked. "There might be crowds. If you need extra manpower—"

"If I do—and that's a big if—I'll call in the sher-iff's deputies." He chuckled. "It'll give Pete some-thing to do for a change. Now shoo!"

George's brusque voice drifted up to them, faint but clear. "Injuries consistent with a fall from this height. Just another damn fool accident."

"*Now* will you go home?" Jeff asked.

Sherri rolled her eyes, but she went.

She returned to her apartment less than two hours after she'd left to get an early start on her day. It wasn't even eight o'clock yet, and Adam and Pete were both still asleep. She smoothed a hand

over her son's forehead to make sure he wasn't
running a fever, then changed from her uniform
to jeans and a loose top. Both of her men would
appreciate a hearty breakfast when they woke up.
She could stand to eat something substantial herself. French toast, she decided. And sausage.

She didn't give the unfortunate jogger or her
fatal fall another thought.

When Liss's alarm clock went off at eight, Lumpkin had her legs pinned at the bottom of the bed.
The kitten, Glenora, had draped herself over the
top of Liss's head like a pair of furry black ear-
muffs.

"Off," she ordered, but she was not surprised
when neither cat moved.

With an effort, she extricated herself, made a
quick stop in the bathroom, and stumbled downstairs to start the coffee brewing. Lumpkin nearly
tripped her as he dashed past, determined to be
the first one to reach the kitchen and his food
bowl. Glenora gamboled after him, fetching up by
the water dish and nearly upsetting it.

When Liss began to run water into a large glass
measuring cup, Glenora was right there, batting at
the stream coming out of the faucet. Liss pushed
her off the counter. Three times. The little cat was
back by the time Liss stuck the container in the
microwave. At that point, Liss gave up. She left the
water running in a thin trickle so that Glenora
could play with it.

Still half-asleep, she measured scoops of coffee
into her French press, popped two slices of bread

into the toaster, fed the cats, turned the faucet off, poured hot water over the grounds, and set the timer for four minutes of brewing time. Her plan was to drink one cup in the kitchen and a second upstairs while she dressed, and put the remainder in a thermos to take with her to The Spruces. She had nibblies ready to go into a small cooler, too, just in case business was so brisk in the dealers' room that she couldn't get away for lunch.

Halfway through the first reviving sip of caffeine, the phone rang. Since the caller I.D. told her it was Patsy from the coffee shop, she picked up.

"I'm just back from delivering pastries to the hotel for the author breakfast," Patsy said. "Good news. Our little problem has resolved itself."

"What problem?" Still groggy, Liss struggled to recall if there had been a crisis over the baked goods. She couldn't remember one.

"This morning one of the hotel guests went out for an early-morning jog along the cliff path," Patsy continued.

Liss's hand clenched on the phone. With a sick certainty, she knew she wasn't going to like what she heard next.

"We don't have to worry about the evil blogger anymore," Patsy announced. "Jane Nedlinger took a header off Lover's Leap. Broke her danged fool neck in the fall."

Chapter Six

The dealers' room opened promptly at nine. It had been arranged so that a large open area in the middle was surrounded by long tables. They had been set up about two feet out from the wall, so that the dealers had room to move around behind them. As the only bookseller at a conference for readers, Angie had the most prominent spot, to the right as people came through the door. She was also the only one who had three tables. Today she was working them alone, but her ten-year-old daughter, Beth, would help out on Saturday and Sunday.

Liss stood behind the two tables to Angie's right. She had a variety of items from Moosetookalook Scottish Emporium displayed in front of her. To her right was an empty space, room for the lines they hoped would form at the signing tables. These took up the entire wall opposite the entrance.

There was only one other dealer at the Cozy

Con. A T-shirt vendor displayed a variety of brightly colored offerings on two tables set up just across from Liss. Most bore book-related slogans and graphics. Next to him were two tables holding the items to be auctioned off at the charity auction that evening. A third, where attending authors were encouraged to put out promotional material for their newest titles, was rapidly filling up with post-cards, flyers, bookmarks, newsletters, pens, pencils, key rings, bowls of candy, and refrigerator magnets.

From her vantage point, Liss had a good view of the entire room. The first panel didn't start until 9:30, so they had attracted a good number of people, including several of the guest authors. Yvonne Quinlan was at the center of a small group of adoring fans.

Solo and in groups of two and three, attendees wandered from table to table, examining the merchandise and chattering excitedly among themselves. The mood was upbeat, even though word of an accidental death near the hotel had clearly gotten around. "That's the young man who found the body," someone whispered.

Liss followed her gaze to a young man pushing an older woman in a wheelchair, but she barely had time to think that he looked to be no more than twenty years old when she was distracted by a loud "Well, really!" from Angie's direction.

The woman who had been trying to get Dorothy Cannell's autograph the previous evening tossed the book she'd been examining back onto Angie's table and turned away, looking affronted. The book, a hardcover, grazed a nearby stack of paper-backs with enough force to send the entire pile topping. Angie only just managed to catch them before they tumbled to the floor.

"What was the matter with it?" the woman's friend asked as they walked past Liss's tables. Neither seemed aware that they'd very nearly left a mini-disaster in their wake.

"It was written in that god-awful present tense. I can't stand reading books written that way."

The second woman shrugged. "Oh, that doesn't bother me if the writing is good enough. But I hate it when an author head-hops. That constant switching back and forth will drive you crazy. Do you remember that one book where the author even included the point of view of the detective's dog?"

When the two moved out of carshot, Liss and Angie exchanged exasperated looks. "At least they read," Angie muttered.

Liss caught other bits and pieces of other conversations as she watched over her stock.

One woman said, laughing, "And she shoved the book right up under the bathroom stall! Can you imagine? And she actually expected the author to sign it while she was—"

A deeper voice obscured the first: "When does the first panel start?"

A woman wearing a purple T-shirt dashed up to another sporting a bright red tunic and trim black slacks. The second woman had on one of the green name tags, identifying her as a panelist. "You're Kathy, aren't you?" the first woman gushed. "Oh, I'm so excited to meet you. I just love your historical mysteries. I'm writing one myself. Do you think you could introduce me to your agent? I'm sure—"

Liss had to smile. Good luck with that one, she thought.

Just before nine-thirty, Nola came in, clipboard in hand. She was hotly pursued by a pale-haired young woman in an identical outfit—conference T-shirt and jeans.

"You haven't told me yet who next year's guest of honor is going to be," the blonde whined. "How am I supposed to talk up the second Cozy Con if I don't know that?"

"Keep your voice down, Phoebe," Nola snapped. "Nothing's settled yet."

"The conference committee voted a week ago," the younger woman persisted. "You must know by now who won and if they've agreed to do it."

"Phoebe, this is not the time or the place for this discussion. Go back to the registration table where you belong."

Phoebe turned sulky. "I'm going to be stuck there all day. It's not fair. I'll miss all the panels."

"Someone has to remain on duty, Phoebe." Nola sounded exasperated.

"Why?"

"Because there are a few registrants who haven't checked in yet. And there will be other attendees who have questions. About next year's conference, as you suggested. You can assure them there will be one and give them the dates, even if you can't yet reveal the next guest of honor's name. Besides, what if someone got an extra-large conference T-shirt in their goodie bag and wants to know if it comes in a smaller size?"

"But it doesn't," Phoebe objected.

"Exactly. That's why a representative of the Cozy

Con needs to be at the registration desk all the time. To tell people that."

"But why does it have to be me? Susie could do it."

Nola looked as if she wanted to hit Phoebe upside the head with her clipboard. "You're my second in command. It's your responsibility," she said through clenched teeth.

"Second in command, my ass," Phoebe muttered as she stomped past Liss on her way to the door. "Slave labor is more like it!"

Soon after that, the room began to clear out. It was almost time for the first two panels to begin. According to the program, they'd run from 9:30 to 10:30 and be followed by a signing session for the participating panelists from 10:30 to 11:30.

"I wish you'd stop talking about it, Davy," the woman in the wheelchair said as she and the young man pushing her passed Liss's tables. "I get palpitations every time I think about you climbing down that cliff to check that poor woman's pulse. You could have fallen to your death yourself, and then where would I be?"

"I was perfectly safe, Mother," the young man said, and shoved her chair out into the corridor with just a little more force than seemed absolutely necessary. Liss had a feeling it wasn't the first time he'd been obliged to reassure her.

With the first rush of business over, Angie began to tidy the piles of books on the tables in front of her. Dozens of people had picked up titles and read back cover copy and even the first page, but from what Liss had seen, few had actually bought anything.

"What on earth was that woman doing out at Lover's Leap in the first place?" Angie asked as she worked.

"Apparently, she was out jogging," Liss said. Her stock, too, had been pawed through. She refolded a tartan scarf and straightened a stack of boxes that contained pins in the shape of bagpipes. "That's what Joe Ruskin told me when I got here."

Angie's brows shot up. "Jane Nedlinger didn't sound to me like the type for early-morning exercise, but I guess you never know."

"You can't judge a book by its cover," Liss quipped, then winced at her own misplaced sense of humor. A woman was dead. That was nothing to joke about. Or to be glad of, either, even if it did mean that she, along with the hotel and the town, were now unlikely to be written up in *The Nedlinger Report.*

Liss hadn't had much time to gather information. She'd already been running late by the time she'd arrived at The Spruces. "All he said was that one of the guests—apparently that young man, Davy—found Jane Nedlinger dead at the foot of the cliff this morning. He said it looks as if she went out there, jogging, at the crack of dawn, got too close to the edge while admiring the view, and took a fatal fall."

"Still strikes me as some peculiar," Angie said.

"Be glad it's so cut and dried. The last thing we need around here is another murder."

The sound of a throat clearing made Liss look up. Yvonne Quinlan stood on the other side of the display table. Liss and Angie had been so intent on their conversation that neither of them had heard her approach. The only other person left in the dealers' room, besides the three vendors, was Nola Ventress. She was on the opposite side of the room, fussing with the display of auction items.

"Perhaps," Yvonne suggested with a faint smile, "Ms. Nedlinger was lured into the woods by a vampire. It's well known that vampires have the power to compel obedience from mere mortals."

"Uh-huh," Liss said. Looking past Yvonne, she saw Nola start to walk toward them.

"I'm sorry," Yvonne said with a rueful little chuckle. "I meant no disrespect for the dead. You know writers. We just can't resist spinning stories. I'm always startling the people around me by saying things like, 'Oh, look! Wouldn't that be a great place to hide a body?'"

The twinkle in Yvonne Quinlan's eyes was difficult to resist. Liss found herself responding to it, but she couldn't help but notice that Nola didn't appear to be at all pleased by what she'd overheard. She looked, in fact, as if she'd just bitten into something extremely sour.

"Sorry to disappoint you," Liss said to the author, "but the vampire explanation won't work. Apparently the fall took place after the sun came up."

Yvonne's smile widened into a grin. "What a pity! And I guess that means it really was an accident. After all, few humans would have the brute strength to toss someone as hefty as Jane Nedlinger off a cliff. I suppose there was a fence to haul her over first, yes?"

Liss had to think about it. She hadn't been up to Lover's Leap in years, not since she was a teenager.

It had been considered a daring make-out spot when she was in high school.

"Lover's Leap is on town land and the selectmen are cautious people, so I'm sure there's a barrier of some kind." There had been a dozen years ago—a sturdy structure with log rails.

"You don't seem real upset over her death," Angie said to Yvonne. "Knew her well, did you?"

"Hardly at all." The actress examined one of the thistle pins Liss had for sale, the thistle being the symbol of Scotland. "I talked to her a few times at events like this one. That's about it. Put this aside for me, will you?" She passed Liss the pin. "I'll send Bill by to pick it up and pay you for it later."

When Yvonne had left, Liss closed the box the pin came in and stashed it in one of the empty cartons she'd stored beneath her table. While she was down there, she thought about fishing out a notebook and a pen. The temptation was strong to start making lists of suspects, motives, and alibis.

She resisted, telling herself that she mustn't let her imagination run away with her. Jane's death had been a terrible accident, nothing more. It was only the influence of all the murder mysteries stacked on Angie's tables that was making her remember just how many people would benefit from Jane Nedlinger's sudden demise.

You're here as a dealer, not a detective, she told herself firmly, *and there has been no crime.*

Some two hours later, Bill Stoltz wandered in. "Yvonne tells me you're holding something for her," he said.

Liss produced the box with the pin in it and an

invoice. "Terrible about Jane Nedlinger, isn't it?" she asked as she swathed the little box containing the thistle pin in tissue paper and placed it in a small Moosetookalook Scottish Emporium bag, then added one of her business cards.

"Who?" Bill handed over a credit card—his, not Yvonne's.

"The woman who fell off the cliff."

"Oh, yes. I did hear something about that. Didn't catch the name. As you say, a terrible thing."

"What were you two talking about last evening?"

"I didn't talk to her. I didn't know her."

His denial set off alarm bells. "Perhaps you didn't catch her name then, either," Liss said smoothly as she passed him the gift bag. "As I recall, she wasn't wearing a name badge. Jane Nedlinger was the woman who cornered you at the opening reception, at right about the time Nola Ventress was introducing Yvonne."

Bill blinked a few times, then apparently decided that Liss wasn't going to be put off by repeated denials. "Oh, *that* woman," he said. "I suppose I've been trying to repress the memory."

"So? What did she say to you?" Liss wasn't sure why she persisted, except that Bill had lied to her. He had to have known all along who Jane was. He'd been right there with them last night when Yvonne had been telling them about her own encounter with the blogger. Since they'd been discussing Jane Nedlinger's negative review of Yvonne's latest book, Liss was certain Bill had been paying attention. After all, he *was* Yvonne's manager.

"She was angling for an in-depth interview with

Yvonne," Bill said, his reluctance to share the information almost palpable. "That's it." He shrugged. "I told her no. Why would I do any favors for that barracuda after she trashed Yvonne's novel?"

Bill's explanation made sense, but Liss couldn't help but think there'd been more to his encounter with Jane. She had seen the expression of sheer panic on his face when Jane latched onto him at the reception.

Bill glanced at his watch. "I must go." He started to scurry off without reclaiming his credit card.

"Mr. Stotz. Wait."

For a moment, she thought he intended to keep going, but when she waved the plastic rectangle at him, he came back.

"Thanks," he said, grabbing it. "Sorry, but I've got to run. There's, um, a panel I need to be at." On his way out, he nearly bowled over a small, round person just coming in.

"Hi, there," the woman said, coming straight to Liss but nodding at Angie, too. "Are either of you two ladies working on a novel of your own?"

Liss laughed and shook her head.

Angie said, "Not a chance. Too much work involved."

"And that's exactly how I stay in business. I'm Ruth Merchason. My friends call me Ruthie." She pulled a stack of business cards out of her purse and handed one to each of them. "If you ever need my services, just give me a call."

She abandoned them for a group of conference-goers who'd just entered the dealers' room, passing out more cards and brightening when one of them admitted she'd been trying to write a mystery

of her own. Liss glanced at the card in her hand. It
read: RUTH MERCHASON, BOOK DOCTOR.

"What the heck is a book doctor?" Angie wanted
to know.

"I think she edits manuscripts. Fixes them up so
they'll sell to a publisher."

"Huh. And here I thought the people who
wrote books knew how to do all that stuff for themselves."

Liss thought she detected a hint of sarcasm in
the comment, but a potential customer appeared
and she let it go.

Many of those who stopped to look at Liss's
wares and shop at the adjacent tables, where Angie's
selection of mystery novels was displayed, seemed
unaware of Jane Nedlinger's sudden death. Or, if
they had heard about an accident, they weren't
discussing it. All the talk was of panels, writers, and
books. Liss supposed that a few of the attendees
must have read Jane's blog, and some might miss
her daily dose of vitriol, but her presence at the
First Annual Maine-ly Cozy Con had not been general knowledge, and her absence appeared to create nary a ripple of concern in the convivial
atmosphere of the conference.

Nola stopped by the dealers' room again just before three o'clock that afternoon.

"I never did think to ask you last night," Liss said
after the other woman had admired the offerings
spread out on the Emporium's tables—everything
from clan crest badges to canned haggis. "What
exactly did Jane Nedlinger say to you at the reception to upset you so much?"

To Liss's dismay, Nola's eyes instantly filled with

tears. "I can't talk about it," she whispered. "It's just too awful!" Without another word, she turned and fled.

"Nice going, Liss," Angie hissed.

Liss would have gone after Nola to apologize and make sure she was okay, but the two o'clock panels had just let out and there was a sudden influx of conference-goers. Fastening a professional salesperson smile on her face, Liss silently reviewed what she knew about Nola Ventress. It did not take her long to realize that all the facts did not add up. Here was a woman who had single-handedly organized an entire conference and yet, last night at the MSBA meeting, she'd acted like a timid little mouse . . . until she got her second wind and decided to put both Doug and Stu in their places. And now—tears for Jane Nedlinger? Something very odd was going on.

Liss's gaze fell on one of the books on Angie's tables, a used copy of *The Body in the Library*. Liss frowned at the classic Miss Marple title. Agatha Christie's famous sleuth appeared to be a dithery old lady on first acquaintance, but she had a sharp mind and inevitably solved the murder before the police did. It followed that people in real life could be just as contradictory, so maybe Nola wasn't really that unusual, after all.

Besides, she reminded herself, Jane Nedlinger might be dead, but she hadn't been murdered. Her death had been nothing more sinister than a convenient accident.

But some people were certainly reacting to it strangely! Nola wasn't the only one. Bill Stotz had tried to deny knowing Jane. Had the blogger threatened him—or his client—in some way, as she had Liss? Surely a piece on murder in Moose-tookalook hadn't been the only story Jane was working on.

Liss was glad when a customer with a question about tartans distracted her. She did not want to think about real murders. Only the fictional kind.

At a little before four in the afternoon, Margaret shooed Liss out of the dealers' room. "You've been stuck here all day. I'll take over for you until we close at five-thirty."

"You don't have to—"

"Of course I don't have to. I want to. And we've already discussed my spelling you when I can so that you can attend a few of the panels. So go. Enjoy yourself."

"You'd better take her up on the offer," Angie advised, glancing up from making change. "If you don't, I will."

"I could use a break," Liss admitted. She and Angie had traded off minding each other's tables to allow for visits to the restroom, but other than that, they'd both been behind their tables in the dealers' room for the last seven hours straight.

Liss glanced around. The place was already emptying out again, as it did every time a new set of panels began. "I'll be back," she promised, "to help with the final book-signing session and to close up."

While Liss tried to decide which of two panel offerings to attend, she detoured into the fan lounge, where coffee was available. Little clumps of people were gathered there. Extra chairs had been pulled up to one table so that a full dozen conference-goers could share the same conversation. Laughter issued from the group in loud, staccato bursts. If those people hadn't been fast friends before the conference, Liss had a feeling that they were now.

She recognized a few faces, but she wasn't in the mood to join anyone. She selected an unoccupied table and sat down with her coffee to study the program. One of the four o'clock panels was a discussion of short stories. Since she didn't read many of those, having a strong preference for novels, her decision was easy to make.

With a few minutes to spare, Liss flipped through the program to the panelist bios. They were brief, only a paragraph in length and therefore much too short to be very useful. Liss thought the authors looked very glamorous in their publicity photos. Some had done so much with hair and makeup before they had their pictures taken that she'd never have recognized them in real life.

She was just polishing off her coffee and watching fellow attendees drift off toward the meeting rooms when a flash of color caught her eye. There, off in the corner, unnoticed until the room began to clear out, sat Stu Burroughs. It had been his bright red tie that had attracted her attention.

Stu didn't notice her. He was too intent upon his conversation with Nola Ventress. Stu was going to be the auctioneer for the charity auction that evening, Liss remembered, but she didn't think that was what the two of them were discussing. Stu was rigid with tension, shoulders stiff and hands clenched into fists on the tabletop. Nola's face was devoid of expression, but very pale. Whatever Stu was saying to her, she didn't like hearing it.

This is none of your business, Liss told herself, but she couldn't make herself leave the fan lounge, not even after everyone else had gone.

"Never going to happen, Stu," Nola said, and abruptly rose from the table.

"You'll regret it, Nola."

She turned her back on him and walked rapidly to the exit.

"I'm telling you, you will regret it!" Stu started to follow Nola, then checked when he caught sight of Liss. His steps faltered. Looking embarrassed, he nodded to her. "Afternoon, neighbor."

"Stu, is something wrong?"

"Of course not. Nola and I were just clarifying some last-minute details for tonight's festivities." He sauntered closer, adopting a casual attitude that didn't fool her for a minute. "Are you coming to the auction? We've got some dandy items up for sale. You can bid on the chance to have a character in a book named after you. You could end up as the murder victim. Or the killer."

"Thanks, but no thanks." She frowned as she realized that something Stu had said at last night's meeting had been nagging at her all day. When he'd promised her that they'd scotch Jane Nedlinger's plans to trash the town, he'd almost sounded as if he'd come up with a plan to accomplish that feat. "Stu, can I ask you a question?"

"Fire away." He flashed the good-natured grin he usually reserved for ski shop customers.

"Had you ever heard of Jane Nedlinger before last night?"

The grin vanished. "What are you really asking me, Liss?"

"Well, Stu, you were pretty determined to put a stop to her blog. It almost seemed . . . personal."

"So—what? You're wondering if I came up here to the hotel after the meeting, kidnapped her, and threw her off a cliff? Do I look like an idiot?"

She had to smile at the expression of outrage on his face. "No, of course not. And when you put it that way, it does sound ridiculous. I'm sorry. I'm just trying to piece things together in my head. I mean, the last thing we needed here in Moose-tookalook was another death, even an accidental one, and her fall was just so . . . opportune."

He glowered at her. "Trust me, as much as I wanted to find a way to get rid of that Nedlinger woman, I wouldn't have murdered her." With a harsh laugh, he added, "And give me some credit. If I ever do decide to kill somebody, I'll have the decency to hide the body where it will never be found."

His casual promise gave Liss a bone-deep chill. As she watched him leave, she wondered if she really knew him as well as she thought she did.

What does it matter? she asked herself. *There was no murder. Jane Nedlinger's death was an accident. She fell.*

But for some reason she seemed to be having trouble remembering that.

In desperate need of distraction, Liss headed for the panel she'd selected. Unfortunately, listening to Yvonne Quinlan and three other panelists talk about "How to Choose Your Victim—The Fine Art of Taking Revenge on Real Life Irritants," did nothing for her peace of mind.

* * *

Dan entered the lobby of The Spruces forty-five minutes after leaving the Ruskin Construction work site at four-thirty. He'd stopped off at home long enough to shower and change his clothes. He had an evening free of responsibilities to the hotel and he planned to waylay Liss before the dealers' room closed and whisk her away for a couple of hours. Feeding her would also cheer her up, or so he hoped.

She had called him at work that morning to tell him about Jane Nedlinger's fatal accident. He'd felt nothing but relief at hearing that news. By the time he'd disconnected, however, he'd sensed that something about the situation was eating at his fiancée. If he knew Liss at all, she'd spent half the day brooding over the unexpected twist of fate.

Just to make sure of his facts, Dan took a moment to slip into his father's office and phone Jeff Thibodeau.

"What—you think we can't have a plain old accident in this town?" the chief of police asked, chuckling.

"Call me a pessimist, but in light of what's happened in the past . . ." He let his voice trail off.

"There were no signs of anything off-kilter at the scene," Jeff said, suddenly serious. "Do you have any reason to believe there was foul play?"

Dan hesitated, wondering if he did. Would someone he knew have committed murder just to save the town's reputation? It didn't seem likely. "Not really. She was just the sort of woman who rubbed people the wrong way."

"Met her, did you?"

"Briefly. Last night. I didn't like her."

"You push her off the cliff?" Jeff's light tone made it clear he was kidding.

"Not hardly."

"Know anyone who did?"

"No, Jeff." Shaking his head at his own foolishness in making this call, Dan changed the subject and asked Jeff how his vacation had been—the chief had only just returned from a week spent visiting his wife's family in Pennsylvania. After hearing far more than he wanted to about mother-in-law troubles, Dan ended the call.

He returned to the lobby and headed for the stairs to the mezzanine, but the sound of raised voices at the check-in desk stopped him cold. His father looked and sounded royally pissed off, an indulgence Joe rarely allowed himself, especially when he was on duty.

"She's not in her room and we do not give out room numbers, let alone allow people into those rooms to wait for the occupant." From Joe's tone of voice, this was not the first time he had explained this policy. "The best I can do is let you leave a message."

"But this is important. And it's not as if we aren't old friends."

Belatedly, Dan recognized the woman glaring across the desk at his father and sounding just as ticked off as Joe was. It was Dolores Mayfield, the town librarian. Hands on her hips, feet firmly planted, she didn't look like she intended to budge until she got her way.

"Problem?" Dan asked, coming up beside her.

Dolores's voice shifted abruptly from angry to wheedling. "Oh, Dan, can't you reason with your father? He knows perfectly well that Nola Ventress and I were like this"—she held two fingers aloft, pressed tightly together—"all through high school. And I have a perfectly legitimate reason for wanting to see her. We have a class reunion coming up."

"Oh, yeah?" Dan asked, affecting interest. "Which one?"

"It's our forty-first," his father answered. "Big whoop. No one was interested in getting together for our fortieth. I very much doubt there will be any more takers this year."

"We can but try." Dolores was at her snooty best. "Now, are you going to let me into Nola's room to wait for her or not?"

"Not," Joe said.

Dan wondered why his father was being so protective of Nola's privacy. He could have picked up the phone and asked Margaret Boyd—another member of that same high school class, if Dan remembered rightly—to find Nola and tell her she had someone waiting to see her in the lobby. Instead he seemed hell-bent on getting Dolores off hotel property before she could make contact with her old classmate.

Dolores let out an exasperated huff. "If that's the way you want it, so be it. You let Nola know that a woman named Jane Nedlinger stopped by at the library yesterday. She had a lot of questions about this town, *and about Nola.*"

Dan and his father exchanged a look. For once Dolores, the town's biggest gossip, appeared to be out of the loop. Clearly, she hadn't yet heard about Jane Nedlinger's accident. Neither Dan nor Joe volunteered any information.

Joe dutifully wrote down the message. "Anything else?" he asked.

Dolores was really fuming now. "Yes," she snapped. "Tell Nola that I told Ms. Nedlinger *everything*! I can hardly wait to see what she does with it." Nose in the air, a militant gleam in her eyes, she turned on her heel and swept out of the hotel.

"What was that all about?" Dan asked.

"Nothing," Joe said.

"Right."

He shrugged. "Just old business. Very old business and none of yours."

Holding his hands in front of him in surrender, Dan backed away from the desk. "Okay. Okay. I can take a hint. If you're looking for me between now and the auction tonight . . . don't. I'm taking Liss out for a bite to eat."

"Have fun," Joe called after him as Dan once more headed for the stairs that led to the mezzanine.

Chapter Seven

As Dan climbed one set of stairs, Liss and her aunt descended another. Taking the back way used by hotel employees, they bypassed the lobby and went directly to the office Margaret used as events coordinator.

Margaret MacCrimmon Boyd had made the small room, painted a pretty pale green, even more cheerful and welcoming with the addition of a love seat upholstered in a bright floral pattern and a glass-topped coffee table. A set of three Carrabassett County landscapes, done in pen and ink by local artists, decorated the wall opposite.

Liss plopped herself down on the love seat and gave her aunt a direct look. "What's the story on Nola Ventress?"

"She organized the conference."

Liss made a face. "I know that. I mean before. You knew her when she lived here, right?"

"Yes, I did." Margaret turned off the desk lamp, leaving only the soft glow from the computer monitor and the indirect light of a late-afternoon sun shining through her north-facing window to illuminate the room. She collected her purse and was clearly ready to leave for the day, but Liss stayed put. With a sigh, Margaret came around to the front of the desk and rested a hip on the edge. "Nola and I were in the same class in school. That was a long time ago."

"But you stayed in touch."

"On and off. It took some persuading to get her to come back here, but she couldn't find a better deal anywhere else on room rates or food."

"She told me she didn't much like rural living. Or camping," Liss said.

Margaret's quick smile spoke of a memory.

"What?"

But Margaret only shook her head. "If you want to know anything about Nola Ventress's past, you'll have to ask Nola herself. You know I'm not one to gossip."

Unlike so many who made that statement, in Margaret Boyd's case it was true. Still, Liss persisted. "Are you close friends? Were you then?"

"Not particularly, no. But you know small towns. There are few secrets. Still, if she prefers to keep her youthful indiscretions safely buried, then you and I both should honor her wishes."

Liss's eyebrows shot up at the hint that Nola had a scandal in her past. She couldn't help but wonder if Jane Nedlinger had unearthed the details during her short stay in Moosetookalook. Had Nola felt threatened on a personal as well as on a professional level?

Margaret grimaced at her niece's expression. "It's nothing all that bad, Liss. Just something Nola isn't likely to want to rehash more than thirty years later. And no, I won't say another word. I already feel guilty for pressuring her to come back here in the first place. I just wanted to bring business to the hotel. That's my job, after all. But I let her down. I promised her she could stay right in the hotel the whole time she was here and that she wouldn't have to go into the village at all."

"I was the one who took her to the MSBA meeting."

"She doesn't have good memories of Moosetookalook," Margaret said, ignoring Liss's attempt to absolve her of guilt. "I was hoping she'd leave here with better ones. And bring the conference back to The Spruces in future years."

"There's no reason she shouldn't," Liss said. "She's just upset right now over Jane Nedlinger's death."

"That was an accident," Margaret said in a firm voice.

"A convenient accident."

"Don't go making something out of nothing, Liss."

Liss shrugged and tried once again to shake off the uneasy feeling that had haunted her throughout her day. "You're right. I'm letting my imagination run away with me. I'm sure it's just the influence of all the talk of murder and mayhem at this conference." She forced a smile. "The next thing you know, I'll be blaming Jane's death on vampires." She told her aunt about Yvonne Quinlan's extemporaneous bit of plotting.

"I suppose a mystery writer would make a murder out of it, with or without the paranormal elements," Margaret conceded. "Thank goodness this is real life."

"Still, Jane's death has made me curious about Nola." Liss held up a hand to silence Margaret before her aunt could interrupt with an objection. "And no, I'm not imagining that Nola pushed Jane off that cliff. For one thing, she wouldn't have the strength to do it. Jane was twice her size."

"Thank goodness for small favors," Margaret muttered under her breath.

"But Nola seemed very emotional today. I asked her about her encounter with Jane and she burst into tears. And earlier, she had the most peculiar expression on her face when I was talking to Yvonne Quinlan."

"Are you worried about Nola? Or just nosy?"

"A little of both," Liss admitted. And she was not, despite her protests, completely convinced that Jane had fallen to her death without help.

After Margaret left, Liss detoured to the check-in desk. It took a bit of persuading to convince Joe Ruskin to give her Nola's room number, but in the end he relented when she said she was worried about how the conference organizer was taking Jane Nedlinger's death.

"Did Dan find you?" Joe asked.

"Not yet," she told him, and kept going in the direction of the elevator.

On the second floor, she rapped on Nola's door. The conference schedule called for "meal on your own" this evening, but the charity auction was scheduled to begin at seven. Liss expected to find Nola in her room, either resting or changing her clothes.

When Nola opened the door, she looked as if she'd been crying again.

"Are you okay?" Liss asked, genuinely concerned.

"I'm fine. I'm just . . . it's so upsetting. Last night we were all plotting against her and now she's dead."

"She was plotting against us first," Liss reminded her. "Maybe it would help to talk about it. If you told me—"

Harsh red color flooded into Nola's face. "If you're going to badger me with questions, you can just go away. I won't be harassed."

Liss backed off at once. "I don't mean to pry, Nola, but Jane Nedlinger's death is preying on my mind, too. I just thought—"

"I've heard about you, Liss MacCrimmon. You make a habit of sticking your nose into other people's business. You just stay away from me." With that, she slammed the door in Liss's face.

The click of the lock engaging sounded very loud in the quiet corridor.

Time to go home, have some supper, and feed the cats, Liss decided. Maybe Nola wasn't the only one who needed a little alone time.

A brisk knock at the back door of Sherri's apartment had her scurrying to answer it. Although it was only a little after six in the evening, Adam had just drifted off to sleep. She didn't want the noise to wake him. Even so, she was cautious enough to take the time to peek through the window beside the door to make certain she knew who was standing on the other side.

Liss and Dan were faced off on the small landing at the top of the outside staircase. They looked to be having words, if the expression on Liss's face was any indication. "Uh-oh," Sherri muttered under her breath. "Trouble in paradise."

When the door swung open, they turned to face her. She lifted a finger to her lips to shush them. "Adam's sleeping. You'll have to keep it down." Only after they both nodded did she let them in and lead them through to the kitchen.

"How's the little guy doing?" Dan whispered, stepping over a toy dump truck Sherri had missed picking up off the floor.

"He's cranky. So is his mom." She was ready for a nap herself, but she knew she wouldn't rest until Pete came home at ten. Thank goodness he'd put in for a sick day for tomorrow! "I was going to fix myself something to eat. Do you want coffee? A hot dog?"

"We'll get something later, thanks."

"Not so you'd notice," Dan grumbled, giving Sherri a clue to the problem between them.

"Let me guess. You wanted to take Liss out for a nice meal. She's planning to nuke something in the microwave."

"Got it in one. Plus I just had to chase all over the hotel to find her."

"I did not know you were looking for me," Liss said in the aggrieved tone of someone who has said the same thing several times already.

Sherri made the time-out sign. "Truce, you guys. Is there a reason you came by?" She popped two hot dogs into the microwave, set the cook time, and punched the start button.

"I wanted to see how Adam was doing and ask if you need anything," Liss said promptly.

"He's got a humongous cast on his arm and can't go out and play. Other than that, he's fine. His mother, however, feels like a wrung-out dish-rag. And this is only day one."

"As soon as the conference is over I'll be able to give you a hand," Liss promised. "If nothing else, I can sit with Adam so you can escape for a bit."

"I appreciate that, but Pete and I can handle it. Now, tell me what you've been up to. Take my mind off mothering for a while." The microwave dinged and she extracted the hot dogs, slid them into buns, and added mustard.

"Well, there is something I'd like to run past you."

"Liss," Dan said, a warning clear in the tone of his voice.

"What? It'll give her something to think about other than her son."

"Spill it," Sherri told her. "Ever since Adam's accident I've been so focused on him that nothing else has made any impression." She gave a short, humorless laugh. "I had an unattended death this morning, and even that couldn't distract me for long."

Liss stared at her. "You already know about Jane Nedlinger?"

Surprised, Sherri stared at her friend. "Is that who the body was? The one out at Lover's Leap?" At Liss's nod, she gave a low whistle. "I didn't know. Jeff relieved me before we had an I.D. for her."

"But you'd met her," Dan said. "You called out

to the hotel to ask if we had a J. Nedlinger registered."

"And Joe said you didn't." Sherri sent a questioning look Dan's way.

"He did a little more digging. It turned out that
she used her own credit card, but she signed in
under the name Jane Smoot."

"Why?"

"Hard to say. Maybe she was trying to keep a low
profile. She showed up at the conference's opening reception, but she wasn't wearing any name
tag."

"Maybe not," Liss cut in, "but she wasn't shy
about introducing herself, or telling people that
she was the force behind *The Nedlinger Report.* By
any name, she was a very nasty piece of work. She
came to Moosetookalook looking for dirt."

"Well, yes. I did suspect that." While she poured
herself a glass of diet root beer, Sherri gave them a
quick recap of her own encounter with Jane
Nedlinger at the P.D. "I have to admit I didn't take
to the woman," she added when she'd filled them
in on the pertinent details.

"She was going to write about the murders in
Moosetookalook, and she intended to make it
seem like Liss was responsible for them," Dan said.
"What was that phrase she came up with? A lightning rod for murder?"

"Something like that," Liss agreed with a grimace. "You were at the hospital with Adam, Sherri,
or you'd have known that we called an emergency
meeting of the MSBA last night. Everyone was
pretty upset about what she planned to write. And
we weren't the only ones. There were several peo-

ple at the conference, including Nola Ventress, the organizer, who also had run-ins with Jane Nedlinger. I've no idea what she might have intended to write about any of them, but she wasn't known for singing anyone's praises."

Sherri put two and two together and didn't like the total. "Are you trying to tell me that you suspect her death was something other than an accident?"

"The thought had crossed my mind," Liss said.

"Too much exposure to murder mysteries can rot the brain," Dan muttered. "There was nothing at the scene to suggest foul play, was there?"

"Not that I saw," Sherri said, "and I did take a look around. I didn't notice anything particularly suspicious." She cracked a wry smile. "Same old Lover's Leap—but at least kids today use condoms."

"That's all you found?" Liss asked.

"Pretty much." She thought back while she munched on her hot dog. "Tissues. A couple of gum wrappers. That's—" At Liss's sudden increase in interest, she broke off. "What?"

"It's probably nothing. But one of the people at the conference, the guest of honor's manager, is a gum chewer. And a litterer. And he's one of those Jane Nedlinger talked to last night. I wasn't close enough to overhear what she said to him, but it looked to me as if she was trying to scare him. Succeeding, too."

As much as Sherri longed to dismiss Liss's information as irrelevant, she had to wonder if she'd missed something at the scene. If she'd known at the time who it was at the bottom of the cliff, she might have done things a little differently. Even without being aware of the MSBA meeting, or that other people had felt threatened by the woman, her own experience alone would have been enough to make her wonder if Jane Nedlinger's sudden death wasn't just a bit too fortuitous. The more she recalled of her own initial reaction to Jane, the less difficult it became to think that someone could cheerfully have murdered her.

"Gum wrappers?" Dan made a derisive sound. "Like that would hold up in court."

"Maybe Jane was blackmailing Bill Stotz—that's his name. And when he went out there to Lover's Leap, to pay her, they quarreled and he pushed her off the cliff instead."

"Jeff is satisfied it was an accident," Dan said.

"You talked to him?" Temper sparked in Liss's eyes. "You didn't tell me that."

They glared at each other.

Shaking her head, Sherri polished off the second hot dog before she spoke. "You're giving me a lot of speculation and not a shred of proof."

"There's just something *off* about all of this," Liss insisted.

"The M.E. doesn't think so," Sherri said.

At least she didn't believe that he did. She hadn't stuck around once George Henderson had declared the death an accident. Had he changed his assessment on a closer examination of the body? There was only one way to find out. She reached for the phone.

Sherri had gotten to know George fairly well over the last year. She'd first encountered him when she was going through the state's Criminal

Justice Academy. He'd been one of their guest lecturers. They'd talked one day over lunch and discovered that they were actually distantly related on her father's side of the family, and that George lived less than a mile from the trailer she and Adam had shared with her mother until her marriage to Pete. Of course, George's residence was considerably more posh.

"Hi, George," she said when he answered. "It's Sherri Campbell. I hope I'm not taking you away from your supper, but I'm calling about that accidental death this morning."

"How's that boy of yours?" George interrupted.

"He's doing better. Thanks for asking. Listen, George, this is just me being curious, since Jeff took over for me up at Lover's Leap, but I was wondering if everything checked out on the victim. It was the fall that killed her, right?"

"Sure did," he said cheerfully.

"And she *was* already dead when that jogger found her?"

"Oh, yeah. Been dead a couple of hours by then."

Sherri's hand clenched on the phone. "A couple of *hours*?" she repeated. "Are you sure?"

"Well, you know time of death is never exact, but yeah. My best guess is that she died between midnight and four in the morning."

"Uh, George—I think you'd better give the attorney general's office a call."

"Why? She was out jogging. She stopped to look at the view. She . . . oh, crap! It was overcast last night."

"Yeah. No view."

A few minutes later, she hung up and turned to

face the two civilians who'd been hanging on her every word. "The M.E. says she didn't die shortly after five o'clock sunrise, as we assumed. He estimates time of death at between midnight and four. He can't be more exact than that, but it makes it highly unlikely that she was out jogging, tried to get a better look at the view, and fell."

Dan frowned. "Why on earth would she—"

"Go out there at night?" Liss finished for him. "Not to make out with a boyfriend. That's for sure. Personally, I like my blackmail theory." She turned to Sherri. "So, now what?"

"Now the M.E. reports his findings and things get official. I'm out of it. Permanently out of it if they decide I messed up the scene of the crime."

"It's hardly your fault that it didn't look like murder." Liss rose from the table to give her a hug.

"But if I'd stuck around to find out who was dead, I might have asked more questions at the time."

"Why didn't you?" Dan asked.

Sherri managed another small smile. "Jeff told me to go home and take care of my kid."

"Bingo. You're off the hook."

Sherri wasn't so sure about that, but she appreciated the thought. "Be that as it may, you two mustn't get any more involved in my mess. You both know who will be sent to investigate." It would be Gordon Tandy, who had once been Dan's rival for Liss's affections.

Dan grimaced.

Liss sighed. Then she pulled herself together, glanced at her watch, and gave Sherri another hug. "I've got to get back to the hotel. The charity

auction will be starting at seven, and I promised
Aunt Margaret I'd meet her there."

"Go," Sherri told her. "But try to stay out of
trouble."

Dan dropped Liss off at the hotel as a crowd
started to gather for the auction. Since he didn't
have to work, he wasn't sticking around. He was
still annoyed with her, she supposed, for putting
the kibosh on his plans for a romantic evening.
They'd gulped down leftovers reheated in haste
and washed the two-day-old pasta dish down with
bottled water they'd guzzled on the way back to
the hotel. She would definitely have to find a way
to make things up to him.

She'd start, she decided, by keeping out of Gordon Tandy's way when he showed up to investigate
Jane Nedlinger's death. She'd done her bit by
voicing her suspicions to Sherri. Truthfully, she'd
been hoping she was wrong. The last thing anyone
needed was another murder in Moosetookalook.

Determined to focus on fictional crime for the
rest of the evening, to be just another fan attending the First Annual Maine-ly Cozy Con, Liss entered the hotel ballroom. She was pleased to see
that the event had drawn so many people. The
place was packed, not only with conference attendees, but also with members of the community.
Betsy Twining was there with her husband. So
were Dolores and Moose Mayfield. Liss spotted
Doug, too, and wondered why the funeral director
hadn't brought his wife along. Lorelei Preston was
always complaining that there wasn't enough to do
in Moosetookalook in the evenings.

A woman jostled Liss, belatedly making her aware that she was blocking the entrance.

"That guy's got some nerve," the woman said to her companion. "He wouldn't let me give Yvonne a book to sign. He said I should bring it to one of the signings she's got scheduled and not just go thrusting it at her willy-nilly."

"Who is he, anyway? Her husband?"

"Nah. He's her manager. Anyway, then Yvonne herself steps in and she's just as nice and polite as he was rude. She signed the book with a sweet little personal note. I'll show it to you later."

The two women moved out of range of Liss's hearing, leaving her to wonder why Bill Stotz was so protective of his client. She told herself that, like so many other things, it was none of her business, but she couldn't help but notice that neither Yvonne nor Bill was in the audience gathered for the auction.

Stu Burroughs barreled into the room, apparently running late, and headed straight for the podium. Liss was about to pick up a bidding paddle and find a seat when Margaret appeared at her elbow.

"Have you seen Nola anywhere?" she asked.

"She was in her room earlier."

"I've already checked there." Margaret looked worried. "I even used my passkey to make sure she wasn't just asleep or something. Do me a favor and take a look around the rest of the hotel? I know she wanted to be here. One of the auction items is a free registration for next year's Cozy Con, and she planned to make a pitch for people to register for it before they leave this year's conference. She's offering an early-bird rate."

"I'll see if I can find her," Liss promised, although she didn't intend to look very hard. She had her eye on a hand-crocheted throw decorated with cats. It was the sixth item on the list of auction items and she didn't want to miss her chance to bid on it.

She went back down to the lobby and asked at the check-in desk, peeked into the lounge and the hotel library, and then waylaid Fran Pertwee, who was just closing up the gift shop.

"Working kind of late, aren't you?" she asked the other woman.

"I had inventory to check."

"Were you open while you were doing it?"

"Sure. I figured I might as well be, since I was there. Did you need something?"

"Someone. Do you know Nola Ventress?"

"The woman who organized the conference? Sure. She's been in a couple of times. Including this evening."

"I'm been trying to locate her. When was it that you saw her?"

Fran checked her watch. "About an hour ago. She came in and bought one of those dried flower arrangements we started carrying a month or so back."

"She bought *flowers*?" Liss's first thought was that Nola intended to put them in the auction, although she couldn't think of a good reason why she would. "Did you see which way she went when she left?"

"Outside, I think," Fran said. "She had a sweater with her, and she stopped to put it on before she left the gift shop."

After thanking Fran, Liss went back across the lobby and out of the hotel. Sunset wasn't until around eight o'clock at this time of year, and several hotel guests were still ensconced in the omnipresent Adirondack chairs, enjoying the evening breeze. Liss had no trouble finding one who remembered seeing a woman carrying flowers. According to him, Nola had crossed a swath of green lawn, heading in the direction of the break in the tree line—the start of the cliff path.

She'd taken the flower arrangement up to Lover's Leap.

The idea struck Liss as a very odd thing for Nola to do, especially when she recalled Nola's remarks about her dislike of wooded areas. It wasn't as if she and Jane had been friends. Then again, people had been known to set up impromptu memorials at accident sites. It was common in rural Maine to see a cross or a mound of flowers at the side of a road, marking the spot where a car had crashed, killing those inside.

At least Liss now knew where she'd find Nola. She considered going back inside. Surely it wouldn't take Nola long to complete her mission. She'd certainly return before sunset, since she'd claimed to have such a phobia about "the great outdoors" after dark. On the other hand, if what Sherri had heard from the medical examiner was right, Lover's Leap was now a crime scene. Liss was a little surprised that the state police hadn't yet shown up to cordon off the area.

That meant Nola might inadvertently disturb evidence.

Liss set off across the lawn, thinking that perhaps she could catch up with Nola before the other woman reached the clearing by the cliff. If she wasn't in time to warn her off, then she could at least get Nola away from the scene before she got herself into trouble with the authorities.

Liss suspected that there was a flaw in her logic, but she did not stop to examine it.

The path was easy to find. It had been groomed to remove hazards to walkers, runners, and joggers. At first she was able to move along it at a good clip, but she slowed her pace when the trail abruptly narrowed and began to wind and twist through thick woods. With twilight coming on, the shadows of the trees gave her the creeps, especially once she passed off hotel property and into the public park owned by the town. What on earth had Nola been thinking to come out this way so close to dusk?

A small wooden sign told Liss when she was halfway to her goal: SCENIC VIEW 1/4 MILE AHEAD. Once again, she considered turning back. Then she shrugged and continued. Since she'd come this far, she might as well go all the way.

While Liss appreciated the area's natural beauty, a walk in the woods wasn't really her thing. In fact, she always felt a little edgy when she completely lost sight of civilization. In the intense quiet of the forest, she could no longer hear voices, or cars passing on the road. The only sounds were the soft thumps of her own footfalls as she strode along the path.

Although it hadn't bothered her as a teenager, when she'd come up here with a boyfriend and two other couples, she couldn't imagine making such a trek alone in the middle of the night. What on earth had possessed Jane Nedlinger to do so? Then again, maybe she hadn't been alone.

If she hadn't fallen, then someone had pushed her. That meant two people had been at Lover's Leap in the dark of night. The mind boggled. Had Jane agreed to meet someone in the clearing? Or taken this walk with someone? Who? More to the point, why? Liss knew high school kids did it all the time on a dare or because they were desperate for privacy. But it made no sense for a grown woman with her own hotel room to come out here, not even if—and that was a big, fanciful if—she had been hitting someone up for blackmail money.

Liss breathed a sigh of relief when she finally came out into the clearing. It looked much as it had when she'd been sixteen. The fence that stood between the path and the drop-off had been rebuilt since she'd last seen it. It appeared to be even sturdier than the old one.

Liss spotted the flowers at once. Nola's tribute to Jane had been placed on the far side of the fence atop a small boulder. But where was Nola? The trail continued on. After leaving her offering, Nola could have gone off in that direction, instead of returning the way she'd come. Perhaps she'd thought it would be shorter.

Liss didn't want to consider the only other possibility, but she couldn't ignore it, either. Hesitantly, telling herself with every step that it was only her too-vivid and somewhat ghoulish imagi-

nation that was driving her, she approached the
fence. When she reached it, she took a deep,
strengthening breath. Then she looked down.

The body lay roughly fifty feet below. In the
light of the setting sun, Liss could see the blood
pooled beneath the head and the unnatural angle
of the neck. And she could see the features of the
ravaged face well enough to make an identification.

She'd found Nola Ventress.

Chapter Eight

Liss sat down with her back against the rail fence and fumbled in her pocket for her cell phone. Then she just stared at it. Call the Moosetookalook Police Department? Hit 911? Or just speed-dial Sherri at her apartment? Given the turmoil of her thoughts, the latter made more sense.

"She's dead," Liss blurted when Sherri picked up. "Nola Ventress. She's at the bottom of the cliff."

A dead silence that lasted a full minute greeted this announcement. When Sherri finally spoke, her voice was tight. "Are you certain?"

"That it's Nola? Or that she's dead?" A bubble of hysterical laughter, totally inappropriate to the situation, threatened to erupt. Liss quelled it with an effort, but her voice was still unsteady. "She can't be alive. Not with all that blood."

But the possibility nagged at her. Could Nola have survived? There was a track that led down the cliff, but in the lengthening twilight it would be suicide to try to descend that way.

"Liss, why did you call me?"

"I . . . I don't know." Liss's thoughts refused to settle. At first Sherri's question made no sense. Of course she'd call Sherri. Sherri was the local law. Then she remembered Adam, and that Sherri wasn't at the P.D. She was at home with a small boy who couldn't be left alone. "Oh, God. Oh, Sherri, I'm so sorry. I didn't think."

Sherri had to be conflicted for other reasons, too. She'd been at the scene when it was Jane Nedlinger lying down there on the cold, gray rocks. And she'd failed to see that Jane's death might have been something other than an accident.

Jane's death had to have been murder, Liss thought as she clutched the cell phone more tightly. Jane's death and Nola's death both had to be. Two deaths at the same spot from the same cause in two days—that simply could not be coincidence.

"Are you alone there?" asked Sherri's voice in her ear.

"Yes. And it's getting dark." Why, oh why hadn't she thought to bring a flashlight?

"I need you to get off the phone so I can call the state police." Sherri's tension remained evident in her voice, but she was calmer than Liss was and she knew the procedure she had to follow. "When I disconnect, call someone at the hotel to come out there and wait with you. Okay?"

Liss nodded, only realizing that Sherri couldn't see her when her friend's voice rose an octave.

"Liss? Okay?"

"Yes. Yes, I will." But as soon as Sherri broke the connection, the number Liss dialed was Dan's. He'd planned to go back home after he dropped her off. She could only hope he was still there and hadn't decided to go out for a beer at the local pub or over to his brother's to mooch dessert.

Dan picked up on the first ring. "Hey, Liss. What's up? The auction can't be over already."

"Dan." Her voice shook so on that single word that he knew at once something terrible had happened.

"What's wrong?"

"N-n-nola. She's dead, too."

He swore colorfully, then asked, "Where are you?"

"At Lover's Leap. Please come."

His expletives became considerably more forceful, but he knew she needed him. There was never any question but that he'd come. "Hang in there," he said just before he broke the connection. "I'll be there as quick as I can."

The wait seemed endless. Liss hated feeling weak and frightened, but finding Nola had been a shock. Nola had to be dead. No one could have survived that fall, or landing that way. Liss was sure Nola's neck was broken. But what if she still had a spark of life left? Liss glanced over her shoulder toward the edge of the cliff. She'd be risking her own life to try to climb down there. And what could she do when she got there? She knew only rudimentary first aid. No, Sherri had said to stay put, hadn't she? Besides, if she fell and broke her own neck, or an arm or a leg, that wouldn't help anyone.

She gasped at a rustling sound in the underbrush. A squirrel, she told herself. Or a chipmunk. Or a rabbit. Or a bird. But it belatedly occurred to her that, if Nola had indeed been murdered, her killer could still be lurking nearby. Liss pulled her knees up beneath her chin and wrapped her arms around them, partly to control her shivering and partly to make herself as small as possible.

The sun had fully set, leaving only pink streaks on the horizon, before Liss heard running footsteps on the path. She staggered to her feet. Her heart leapt into her throat when a man's shape emerged from the darker shadows of the forest. The silhouette was big and solid, but it wasn't Dan. A scream welled up inside her. A fraction of a second before it could escape, the beam of a flashlight hit her full in the face and the newcomer spoke her name.

Or rather, State Police Detective Gordon Tandy said, "Damn it, Liss! Why can't you stay out of trouble?"

Liss flung herself into his arms, embarrassingly close to tears but filled with relief that she was no longer alone in the gathering darkness. "I just wanted to talk to her. Nola Ventress. Someone said she'd headed out this way, so I followed her, and then I found her. She's dead. She went over the cliff."

"Did you push her?" Gordon's voice was cold and official-sounding. His hands tightened on her shoulders.

Liss jerked back and out of his grasp just as Dan burst into the clearing. "How can you even think such a thing?" she demanded. "Of course I didn't push her!"

Dan came directly to Liss and enveloped her in a bear hug. After a moment, he eased back far enough to lift his hands to the sides of her face and stare deep into her eyes. It was getting too dark for him to see much there, but he seemed satisfied that she wasn't hurt or in shock. "God, Liss. You scared me half to death."

"It's okay. I'm okay. I was just so upset to see her down there. And then the light was going and I started imagining all kinds of things." She shook her head to clear it and realized that Gordon had gone to the rail and was playing the powerful beam of his flashlight over the scene at the foot of the cliff.

Clinging to her fiancé, Liss watched Gordon detach a portable police radio from his belt and call for assistance. Soon the place would be swarming with forensics people. When Gordon was through barking orders into the portable, he spared Liss one quick, assessing glance, then spoke to Dan. "Take her back to the hotel and keep her there. I'll talk to her after the team from the state police crime lab takes over here."

Liss didn't argue. She was glad to get away. But she knew she could not escape from what had happened at Lover's Leap. Nola's image was imprinted on her brain. And Gordon—Gordon had all but accused her of pushing Nola over the edge. Did he already know that she'd benefitted from Jane Nedlinger's death? He probably did. That had to be why he was suspicious of her. And because she'd been the one to discover Nola's body. The mystery novels got that much of real life right. Gordon would have questions for her, all right. Liss just wished she had a few answers.

"We can wait in your aunt's office," Dan said

when they emerged from the woods and stepped onto the hotel lawn.

Unlike the dark path behind them, this area was illuminated by both ornamental lanterns and subtle floodlights. Dan kept one arm around her, as he had all the way back from Lover's Leap. He hadn't asked any questions, not even why she'd gone looking for Nola in the first place.

"I need to tell Aunt Margaret what's happened," Liss murmured.

"No, you don't."

But Liss shook him off. "I have to. And she'll need to tell Nola's assistant. Phoebe something. Someone has to decide whether to keep the conference going or send everyone home."

Dan frowned. "It has two more days to run."

"Exactly my point." Besides, Liss needed to *do* something. If she had to sit in a chair and wait for Gordon to come and question her, she'd go crazy.

Although it seemed to her as if hours had passed since she'd left the hotel, in reality less than one had elapsed. The auction was still going strong. When Liss and Dan entered the ballroom, a stocky, hatchet-faced woman had just made the winning bid on a set of signed first editions by the late Charlotte MacLeod, a Maine author Liss had loved for years.

"Jane Nedlinger talked to that woman last night," Dan said.

Liss took a hard look at the bidder. She didn't know her and wasn't close enough to read her name badge, but if the Nedlinger woman had singled her out, that automatically put her in the running as a suspect. She looked husky enough to have gone one-on-one with Jane. Tossing Nola over the edge would have been a piece of cake.

Appalled by the way her mind was working, Liss nevertheless set a course for her aunt that passed close enough to the woman in question to read the name so prominently displayed on her chest— Eleanor Ogilvie. By the color of her badge, she was a speaker at the conference. Liss didn't think she was an author, but she remembered that there was at least one panel made up of "industry professionals." Ms. Ogilvie was probably an editor or an agent. Or maybe another book doctor, like that woman who'd left her card in the dealers' room. The program book would give her the answer to that question.

Aunt Margaret took one look at Liss's face and knew at once that something was wrong. The fact that Dan was hovering protectively behind her niece provided confirmation, if she'd needed any, that there was bad news in the offing.

"Did you . . . find Nola?" she asked.

As gently as she could, Liss told her what she'd discovered out at Lover's Leap. Margaret closed her eyes for a moment. When she opened them, unshed tears glinted. "Another accident?"

Liss and Dan exchanged a look.

"It's too early to say," Dan said. "Gordon Tandy will be in shortly. I expect he'll want to talk to people."

Margaret pulled herself together with an effort. "Then we have a lot to do first. I need to locate the two women who were Nola's lieutenants. She had a committee. One of them will have to take over, to make sure everything runs smoothly for the rest of the weekend."

"You don't think they'll decide to cancel the rest of the events and send everyone home?" Dan asked.

"I don't see how they can. There will have to be some sort of announcement, though. Jane Nedlinger's passing had no particular impact on the other attendees, but everyone knows . . . everyone *knew* Nola. Her disappearance will be noticed even if we try to keep the circumstances quiet."

"Now that the police are involved, the press will catch wind of a story," Liss predicted.

"Oh, Lord, yes. Well, we'll just have to make the best of it. I'll hunt up Phoebe and Susan. You'd better tell Doug, Liss. And Stu. But wait until after the auction is over with."

In the background, they could hear Stu Burroughs trying to up the bidding on a theme basket provided by one of the attending authors. He seemed to think the T-shirt alone was worth fifty dollars.

Margaret took off before Liss could ask why Doug and Stu, in particular, needed to be told of Nola's death. They'd known her, of course, but so had several other people. Joe, for example. She voiced her question to Dan, but he had no more idea of the answer than she did.

"In any case," he said, "it's up to the police to decide who's told what and when. And you need to go to Margaret's office and stay there."

"You're siding with Gordon?"

Her attempt to tease him fell flatter than a soufflé after a buffalo stampede. Dan's expression remained grim.

"In this, I am. You're in enough trouble with the law already. If Gordon hears you've been running around talking to potential witnesses, telling them about Nola before he can, he'll pitch a fit."

"I only told Margaret!" she objected.

But Margaret was even now taking Phoebe aside to break the bad news. Dan was right. Gordon would not be pleased with her. She wasn't supposed to do anything but wait quietly for him to come and interrogate her. And there was that whole thing about not releasing the name of the victim before next of kin had been notified, too.

All of a sudden, the events of the evening hit her with the force of a wrecking ball. Without further protest, she headed for her aunt's office. At Dan's urging, she curled up on the love seat. He found an afghan in the closet and draped it over her as she squeezed her eyes shut and tried to block the memory of finding Nola's body.

It did no good. The image continued to play across the backs of her eyelids.

Liss wished she'd never followed Nola out to Lover's Leap. It would have been far more sensible of her to go back to the auction, tell Margaret where Nola had gone, and wait patiently for the conference organizer to return.

Except that Nola would not have come back.

But I wouldn't have been the one to find her, Liss thought.

"I need to tell my father what's going on," Dan said. "Will you be okay alone for a little bit?"

"Go ahead," Liss said, and flipped the corner of

the afghan up over her face, blocking out the light from the desk lamp he'd turned on.

She heard the door close softly behind him and then, remarkably, felt herself slide into an exhausted sleep.

Liss had no idea how much time passed before someone awakened her by gripping her shoulder and giving her a shake. Groggily, she sat up and opened her eyes to find Gordon Tandy's gaze boring into her.

Gordon's eyes were a dark, deep brown. If it hadn't been for a scattering of light golden flecks, they would have looked black. She'd always found them fascinating.

He stepped back, bringing the rest of his face into focus. He wore his thick, reddish brown hair close-cropped. That hadn't changed since she'd last seen him. But the set of his jaw had. His lips were pursed in a thin, hard line. He looked almost angry with her.

Abruptly, the reason Gordon Tandy was at The Spruces, looming over her and scowling, came back to Liss in a rush. Once again she saw Nola Ventress at the bottom of the cliff, blood pooled beneath her head, neck twisted at an impossible angle. She tasted bile and swallowed convulsively.

"I don't suppose—" Her words came out as a hoarse croak and she had to stop and clear her throat before she could finish the sentence. "I don't suppose finding Nola was just a nightmare?"

"Not hardly," Gordon said.

He still looked formidable, six-foot-plus of solid

muscle and bone, but there was a little more warmth in his expression. They'd had a good relationship once. They'd liked each other. But up there at Lover's Leap had been the first time she'd seen him since she'd accepted Dan's marriage proposal. She let Gordon's brother break the news to him while Gordon had been out of state taking some sort of special law-enforcement training. Ever since he'd come back to Maine, he'd avoided her. Now that he had to deal with her on official business, neither of them knew quite how to handle the situation.

Liss scrubbed at her face with her hands, then ran her fingers through her hair, trying to restore some semblance of order. Aunt Margaret had a small refrigerator tucked in behind her desk. Liss crossed the room to forage for cold caffeine. The only soda she found was of the diet and decaffeinated persuasion. She snagged a bottle of Poland Spring water instead.

Gordon waited patiently, leaning against the front of Margaret's desk. He'd fished a notebook and pen out of his pocket and flipped to a blank page.

Liss sighed as she reclaimed the love seat. "Let the interrogation begin."

"This is no joke, Liss."

She twisted the cap off her water bottle with more force than was strictly necessary. "I know that, Gordon. I was the one who found her. Remember?"

"A fact impossible to forget. Why were you out there?"

"Margaret asked me to look for Nola. Fran Pertwee from the gift shop said she'd bought a flower arrangement. One of the guests saw her heading for the cliff path. I assumed that the flowers were a memorial for Jane Nedlinger, although why Nola would bother with a tribute to that woman is beyond me. She didn't much like her when she was alive."

"So I'm told."

Something in Gordon's voice made Liss think he'd already been filled in on the trouble Jane Nedlinger had intended to make for the town and on her activities at the opening reception, as well. She sighed again.

"So," Gordon said, head bent over his notes, "you decided that Nola Ventress went out to Lover's Leap to make a memorial for Jane Nedlinger?"

As Liss had long since learned was the norm in a criminal investigation, the police asked the same damned questions multiple times. "It looked that way to me," she replied, "and you must have seen the flowers on the rock for yourself."

At the asperity in her voice, Gordon cocked an eyebrow. "I did. Clearly, she climbed over the fence to leave them there."

"You can't think she fell? Two identical accidents in less than two days?" There was no way anyone, let alone a trained detective, would buy that explanation.

Gordon hesitated. "There are three choices, Liss. She fell. She was pushed. Or she jumped."

Before she could respond, he asked another question, this one about the MSBA meeting. As the interrogation continued, she gave him the names of everyone who had been at her house on

Thursday night and also those of the conference attendees who'd been harassed by Jane Nedlinger, including Eleanor Ogilvie.

"But Nola Ventress was the one who seemed most upset by her encounter with Ms. Nedlinger?" Gordon asked.

"Yes. And by her death, too." Liss described Nola's behavior in the dealers' room and later, when Liss had tried to talk to her in her hotel room.

"So you spent time with Nola, both before and after Jane Nedlinger died?"

"A little. Aunt Margaret was with her more than I was."

"Can you think of anyone who'd want to murder her?"

"No, I can't. *Was* she murdered?"

He shrugged. "Pushing someone off a cliff is an awfully chancy way to kill. In a fall like that, Nola could have been horribly injured but still able to tell the authorities who pushed her."

Although Liss knew this was a nonanswer, she badly wanted to believe that both Nola and Jane could have fallen by accident. Unfortunately, that solution wouldn't fly. "Coincidences happen," she said, "but an accidental fall doesn't make sense if the medical examiner is right about Jane's death taking place *before* dawn."

Gordon's already somber expression turned positively grim. The hard glint in his eyes promised retribution to someone. "And how," he said in a much-too-soft voice, "do you know that?"

"I . . . uh . . . overheard Sherri's side of a phone conversation."

Too late, it dawned on her that the M.E. had dealt only with Sherri. He didn't know that a visit from Liss and Dan had prompted the Moose-tookalook police officer's request for more information. And Sherri, good friend that she was, would have soft-pedaled the role they'd played in her decision to follow up on the circumstances of Jane Nedlinger's death.

Gordon snapped his notebook closed. "I'll want to talk to you again later, after I've had a chance to investigate further."

"I'm not planning to leave town."

Her sarcasm did not go over well.

"Make no mistake, Liss. I won't stand for civilians meddling in police business." With that warning, Gordon abruptly left the office.

It was almost, Liss thought, as if he was afraid he'd lose the tight control he always kept on his temper if he stayed in her presence a moment longer. She didn't know whether to be chagrined or relieved.

Although she had been up late the night before and did not sleep well, Liss was wide awake at a little after six on Saturday morning. She left Dan snoring softly to get up, feed the cats, and start the coffee. A few minutes later, she heard light footsteps on her back stoop. She was not at all surprised to look through the glass panel of the door and see Margaret lifting her hand to knock.

Keeping an eye on Lumpkin, who'd been known to make a dash for freedom, she opened the door.

Glenora was attracted by what lay beyond the house, too, but she was easier to recapture. On the rare occasions when she did escape, she headed straight for a small patch of grass at the corner of the back porch and settled in to graze.

"Is Dan still here?" Margaret asked in a whisper. "I saw him bring you home last night but I didn't see him leave."

"He's sound asleep. An earthquake wouldn't wake him, and I could use some company." She waved Margaret over to the table and reached for another coffee mug.

"Must be nice, being able to sleep soundly."

Liss chuckled. "There are times I outright resent his ability to fall asleep so easily. He never tosses and turns the way I do when I have something preying on my mind."

"I didn't sleep well last night, either." Margaret settled into one of Liss's kitchen chairs and accepted with equanimity the addition of a small black cat to her lap. She began to stroke Glenora's soft fur. Lumpkin, having been foiled at the door, had returned to his food bowl to console himself with kibble.

"Every time I talked myself out of worrying about one thing, another would crop up," Liss admitted.

"I wonder if there will be reporters in town today," Margaret said. "Even if the press hasn't yet twigged to the news value of our two unattended deaths"—she put air quotes around the last two words—"they may show up for Yvonne Quinlan's book signing."

"She brought her manager with her," Liss said

slowly, putting the pieces together. "Bill Stotz came along to make sure she gets as much publicity out of this gig as possible."

"That's my theory," Margaret said, accepting the steaming mug Liss handed her. "A few days ago, I was all for it."

"Maybe only a reporter or two will show up. They'll talk to Yvonne and leave before they hear rumors about Lover's Leap."

"Don't count on it." Margaret sipped and gave a sigh of pleasure before she turned serious once again. "I took a look at that woman's blog—*The Nedlinger Report?* There's a place for readers to post their comments. There are already dozens of queries asking where she is and why she hasn't blogged since Thursday morning. The consensus seems to be that she's ill, but it won't take long before some enterprising soul discovers that she's dead."

"And news of the suspicious circumstances surrounding her death won't be far behind." Liss all but inhaled her first cup of coffee. Her brain slowly began to defog, but she couldn't for the life of her think what they could do to keep things quiet.

"It would be nice if both deaths could be ruled accidental," Margaret mused, "but we'll still have to deal with the press. And someone will be sure to bring up last January's murder, if not the ones before."

Liss wrapped both hands around her ceramic mug, needing the warmth and comfort nearly as much as she did the caffeine. "And if it was murder? Who would want Nola dead? I can see someone killing Jane, but Nola seemed to be a nice enough woman."

"She'd still be alive if I hadn't convinced her to hold her conference at The Spruces," Margaret whispered. Her face worked, and for a moment Liss thought her aunt was going to cry. She regained control of herself at the last second and took another healthy swig of coffee instead.

Liss sat opposite her at the small table and reached across to touch Margaret's hand. "Nothing that happened was your fault."

"But none of it would have happened," Margaret said with a tremor in her voice, "if Nola had gone somewhere else. She didn't want to come here, you know. When she left Moosetookalook, more than thirty years ago, she swore she'd never come back."

Liss frowned. A bit of mental arithmetic had her wondering if she was missing something. She'd been thinking that Nola had left town right after high school, but if Nola and her aunt had been in the same class, that would make it a little more than forty years back, not thirty. Nola had remained in Moosetookalook for the best part of another decade.

"You aren't to blame," she said aloud, hoping repetition would eventually convince Margaret to stop beating herself up over events that had been well beyond her control.

"I should have expected trouble," Margaret insisted, "especially when I went and involved Stu in the conference. But he's so good at running auctions. He was a logical choice."

"What does Stu have to do with anything?" Liss

asked. "He's too young to have been in your class at school."

"Yes. He's a few years younger than we are. Your mother and Dan's mother were a bit younger, too. And your father and my late husband and Moose Mayfield, they were all a few years older."

That Margaret hadn't answered her question disturbed Liss. What was her aunt hiding? Clearly something was preying on her mind. Something from the past.

"Who was in *your* class?" she asked. Who, she wondered, had Nola wanted to avoid?

"Joe Ruskin. Dolores Mayfield. Ernie Willett."

Ernie was Sherri's father and Margaret's beau, so that news didn't surprise Liss.

"Doug graduated the year before we did," Margaret added. She slumped dispiritedly in the chair, a shadow of her usual cheerful self.

Liss sipped coffee and studied her aunt. "Don't you think it's about time you spilled the beans?" she asked. "It's only a matter of time before the press is involved. When everything comes out, I'd just as soon not have some reporter know more about the situation than I do. What's the connection? Why did Nola behave so peculiarly around both Stu and Doug at the MSBA meeting? Why did you want those two, in particular, to be informed of her death last night?"

"I hardly know where to begin," Margaret said. "It was all such a long time ago and yet, I suppose, it isn't the kind of thing anyone can forget. Or forgive." She stroked Glenora's sleek black fur and avoided looking directly at Liss.

"I know you don't like to gossip, but it can

hardly matter now." The more Margaret hesitated, the more importance Liss began to attach to the information she was holding back. "I tried to talk to Nola yesterday. She literally shut the door in my face."

Margaret took another sip of coffee, still trying to delay the inevitable.

Patience had never been Liss's strong suit, but for once, she simply waited. After a long silence, Margaret began to speak in a low voice. "It was over thirty years ago when it all happened. It would have been . . . 1973. That's far too long to hold a grudge, don't you think?"

"It probably is, but I can't say until I've heard the details."

"Nola appeared to be a happily married woman. She had a lovely house and a handsome husband. He had a thriving business. My husband and I saw a lot of them socially. Well, we would, wouldn't we, given the size of the town and the fact that we were all around the same age? Your parents knew them, too. And there were other couples they were friendly with—Moose and Dolores Mayfield; Ernie and Ida Willett. Ernie and Ida were newlyweds then."

Liss tried to imagine Sherri's parents newly married and happy together. She failed miserably. "That was all well before I was born," she reminded Margaret. "You'll have to tell me who Nola was married to." But she had a suspicion she already knew.

"Oh. Nola married Doug, of course. They were sweethearts all through high school. It wasn't long after their marriage that he took over the funeral home from his father. They seemed very happy together."

"But?"

"Well, it all goes back to Lover's Leap. I'm afraid Nola took up with someone else. An extramarital affair. Doug never suspected a thing until they were caught together up at the Leap. Apparently her lover dared her to go there with him."

"I thought Nola was afraid of the woods at night."

"Nola never liked being outdoors after dark," Margaret agreed, "but if the incentive is great enough, a person can overcome fear. She was young—younger than you are now—and a little wild, and she was crazy about him. And they figured they'd be alone at the Leap. Unfortunately, the police chief we had back then decided to crack down on teenagers going up there to drink and smoke pot. He caught Nola and her lover, buck naked and going at it like rabbits."

"Good grief."

"Yes," Margaret agreed. "The whole town was scandalized. Moosetookalook had its fair share of sex and sin. We even had a commune nearby during the late sixties. But Doug and Nola had dated all through high school, and there had never been any hint of trouble in their marriage until Stu moved to town and opened the ski shop."

Liss almost swallowed her tongue. "Stu Burroughs?"

"Yes. Didn't I say? Stu was Nola's lover."

Chapter Nine

That piece of the puzzle fell into place with a resounding thunk.

Nola Ventress—no, Nola *Preston*—had cheated on her husband with Stu Burroughs. No wonder the tension in the room had gone through the roof when Doug walked into the MSBA meeting and saw his ex-wife sitting in Liss's Canadian rocker. And no wonder Stu had been so determined to pick a fight with Doug.

"Moosetookalook is starting to sound way too much like Peyton Place," Liss muttered.

"They were young," Margaret said. "We all were. Twenty-four, Nola would have been. Stu was barely twenty-two."

"That's hardly an excuse."

"Yes, well, there was a divorce, of course, and we all expected Nola would marry Stu. Instead, she left town. It was years before anyone heard from her again. Eventually, I started to get Christmas cards from her. After that, we kept in touch with once-a-year letters. Hers were always interesting.

She moved around a lot. New York. Los Angeles. Even Vancouver for a while."

"What did she do for a living?"

"I've no idea. She never said. I assumed she'd taken early retirement when she moved back to Maine a few years ago. She wouldn't come here, so we didn't see each other, but she sent me pictures of her house in South Portland and we occasionally talked on the phone." Margaret's voice had a catch in it. "I didn't see her again in person until I made her an offer she couldn't refuse to hold the Cozy Con at The Spruces."

"Don't start playing the blame game again," Liss warned her. "None of this was your fault. And I very much doubt that a thirty-year-old love triangle had anything to do with what happened up at Lover's Leap. Maybe if Nola had died first . . . but she didn't, did she? And there's no way that anyone could have mistaken Jane Nedlinger for Nola. So it's all just an old scandal. Nothing to do with the present." Or so she hoped.

"It will be raked up again," Margaret predicted. "People have long memories. And Dolores Mayfield is a terrible old gossip. She'll talk to the press, even if no one else will."

"Did Dolores have a grudge against Nola?" Liss asked. "If they were friends, maybe—"

"Hah! Dolores was a friend of the fair-weather kind. Moose is the one who was close to Nola when we were kids. I don't think he ever asked her out, but everybody knew he had a major crush on her." Margaret shrugged. "He only took up with Dolores after it was clear Nola and Doug were an item."

"So Dolores knew she was his second choice."

Margaret nodded.

"Well, no matter what comes out, it will all blow over." Making her voice as bracing as she could, Liss urged her aunt to go home, get dressed for work, and head out to the hotel. "I'll be there at nine," she promised, "when the dealers' room opens."

"The show must go on?" Margaret managed a wry smile as she set Glenora on the kitchen floor.

"Something like that."

After her aunt left, Liss toasted two slices of rye bread and refilled her mug with coffee. Then, moving quietly so as not to wake her sleeping fiancé, she readied herself for the day.

She saw Margaret's car pass by from her bedroom window, which was situated directly over the living room. Liss had a good view of the town square and could also see Moosetookalook Scottish Emporium next door. Her aunt's apartment was on the second floor. And just beyond the front of the Emporium, the edge of a sign stuck out. It was held aloft by a life-sized figure of a skier mounted on the roof of Stu Burroughs's front porch.

The curtain Liss had pulled aside fell from her limp hand. Stu and Nola had been lovers. They'd had an affair that had broken up Nola's marriage to Doug. And Nola had taken off after the divorce. Liss wondered why she hadn't married Stu. As far as she knew, he'd never had a wife.

She frowned. Had anyone told Stu that Nola was dead? Margaret had wanted to last night, but they'd stopped her. The authorities would have had no reason to notify him. And since the story

probably hadn't aired yet, and news reports wouldn't
have released Nola's name even if it had, then Stu
still might not know.

A glance at the clock told Liss that it was only
half past eight. It would take her less than ten minutes to drive to the hotel. On impulse, she left the
house and walked the short distance to Stu's place.
Like most of the other buildings around the
square, it was a white clapboard Victorian. It was,
however, the only one with purple shutters on the
windows.

It was too early for the ski shop to be open, so
Liss headed for the outside staircase that led to the
second-floor apartment that was Stu's home. She
rapped lightly on the door.

"It's open!" The invitation sounded halfhearted
and the words were muffled.

Liss went in anyway. She found Stu in his living
room. There were no lamps burning, but the
early-morning sun provided enough light to show
her a lumpy shape in an overstuffed chair. Stu
clenched a half-empty bottle of beer in one hand.
It wasn't his first. A dozen dead soldiers lay scattered across the floor.

"I guess you heard about Nola," Liss said.

"She was a good woman." He sounded defensive.

"I liked her."

"Some surprise, seeing her again after all this
time."

"Thirty years, huh?" Liss perched on the edge of
Stu's sofa, facing him. She watched in silence as he
guzzled more beer.

"More than thirty. I was barely legal. She was the

older woman. Experienced." He dragged out each syllable of the last word. The expression on his face suggested especially fond, and possibly lewd and explicit, memories.

Liss did not want to hear details of Stu's sex life. Eeew! But she was curious about something else. "Why did she leave town?"

"Wanted to *find* herself." Stu gave a derisive snort. "That was a bigger deal back then than it is now. Women had been liberated for a while, but they were still trying to figure out how to have it all."

They still are, Liss thought, but she kept her opinion to herself.

"Had you been friends with her and Doug? As a couple?"

"Naw. Doug was a stuck-up prick even back then. I've got no idea why Nola married him in the first place."

"Still, it was kind of hard on him, wasn't it? Finding out his wife was fooling around with one of their neighbors?"

"Don't think he cared all that much. Oh, he was embarrassed, sure. And he didn't like going through a divorce. He'd counted on having the little woman around to take care of the office and smile at the bereaved clients. Doug doesn't have what you'd call a real reassuring manner. He looks too much like a ghoul."

Liss fought a smile, since she was inclined to agree, but she didn't interrupt.

"Nola said he was stiff in bed, too, and not in a good way."

Way too much information, Liss thought. "I

guess you weren't happy to see her again, then, since she abandoned you?"

Stu shrugged. "It was over thirty years ago, Liss. Nobody holds a grudge that long."

"Not even a husband who's been betrayed by his wife?"

He started to laugh and then lost control. Tears streamed down his round red cheeks as he chortled. Liss handed him a tissue from a conveniently placed box.

Stu wiped his eyes, then swallowed the dregs of his beer. "That's a good one, Liss. What are you thinking? That Doug shoved Nola off a cliff because she walked out on him? Have you *seen* wife number two? Lorelei's a real stunner. And she keeps that business running like a Swiss watch. Plus she popped out a son and heir. Trust me, Doug came out way ahead of the game and he knows it."

"And you, Stu? How did you really feel when Nola left town?"

He heaved himself out of the chair before he answered, heading for the kitchen to get another beer. "Damned woman broke my heart . . . for about a week."

Liss scrambled up and followed him. "And when you saw her again?"

"I was surprised, like I said." He foraged in the refrigerator and came up with another bottle of a local brew. "I never expected she'd come back here. She said she was leaving to become rich and famous. She was going to be a best-selling novelist."

"A novelist?" That was news to Liss. "Did she ever get anything published?"

"I doubt it. Looked to me like she turned into fangirl instead." He laughed again, and not in a nice way.

"So, if you didn't care anything about Nola anymore, why did you and Doug almost come to blows over who was going to drive her back to the hotel on Thursday night? I'd have thought neither one of you would want anything to do with her."

Stu laughed again, but this time only a short bark. "Old habits die hard. And old rivalries. I guess we both wanted to know which one of us she'd pick." He turned, drank, and frowned. "Geez, Liss. I don't know. Maybe we all had a few regrets. But she didn't want to reminisce with me, did she? Or rekindle any old flames. The next day, she acted like she barely remembered the good times we had."

"I'm sorry, Stu," Liss said, and meant it, but there was nothing she could do for him while he was in this maudlin frame of mind.

"Yeah, yeah." He collapsed into the nearest kitchen chair. His head fell forward to rest on his folded arms. The beer tilted. Liss rescued it before it could spill out all over the floor and set the bottle upright just out of Stu's reach.

"Very confusing," Stu mumbled. "All the memories. Nola ruined Doug's life. That's what he thought then. He blamed me for it, too. For a while. Till he saw sense. Why blame me? By that time I wasn't too happy with her either. Not after she ran off and left us both flat."

"Seeing each other again at the meeting could have given all of you a sense of closure," Liss murmured. She edged toward the door. She really had to get a move on if she didn't want to be late opening the dealers' room.

Stu's head lifted. His bleary eyes met hers. "Nola got old and lost her looks, just like the rest of us." He sounded as if he found this fact extremely satisfying.

"Nola was nervous about attending the meeting," Liss told him. "Maybe she had a guilty conscience." Then another thought struck her and she blurted out a question before she thought it through. "Did either you or Doug threaten her all those years ago?"

"Oh, yeah. Right. Can you picture Doug swearing to kill her if she ever came back to Moosetookalook?"

Put that way, the idea did sound absurd. Besides, Doug would have to be an idiot to risk everything he'd built in this community for the sake of revenge on his ex-wife. And Stu? Liss sent a pitying look his way as she left. She had a feeling he was grieving as much for his own lost youth as he was over Nola's death.

Dan was waiting for her the bottom of the staircase. "Want to tell me what you were doing at Stu's?"

"Jealous?"

"Hardly." But he stayed put, arms folded across his chest, until she answered his question.

"If you must know, I was paying a condolence call. Stu and Nola used to be lovers."

"You've got to be kidding!" He fell into step beside her, frowning when she headed across the town square toward the funeral home.

"No joke. And the affair took place while Nola was married to Doug."

"No way."

"That's what Aunt Margaret told earlier me this morning, and Stu just confirmed it."

"Huh," Dan said. "That must be what Dolores Mayfield was going on about yesterday. She came out to the hotel looking for Nola. Dad sent her away with a flea in her ear. It was like he was protecting Nola or something."

Liss momentarily broke stride. Just how many people had been in love with Nola Ventress back in the good old days in Moosetookalook? No—she wasn't going to go there. But she heard herself saying, "They all knew each other. They were in school together."

"Yeah, so I gathered. Dolores said she wanted to talk to Nola about a reunion, but Dad wasn't buying it. Anyway, on her way out, Dolores said she'd told Jane Nedlinger everything."

"Maybe she was just talking about the murders here in town."

"That wasn't the impression I got. It sounded more like Dolores told Jane something personal about Nola. I guess this thing with Doug and Stu would qualify."

"You wouldn't think such an old scandal would still matter to anyone."

Dan caught her arm as they reached the funeral home. "You're going to talk to Doug. Why?" His eyes narrowed. "Please tell me you don't think our highly respected town selectman murdered his ex-wife."

"The thought barely crossed my mind. He's too straitlaced. I just want to tell him about Nola's death, in case he doesn't know yet. Do you want him to find out from some news report on television?" She started up the steps with Dan right behind her.

Liss had been inside Preston's Mortuary before, more times than she liked to remember. Moose-tookalook had held funerals in these rooms for decades. The main parlor lay dead ahead, always redolent of lilies and lemon furniture polish. There were viewing rooms on each side, but only one of them was currently occupied. She felt a moment's guilt as she remembered Lenny Peet. She hadn't done anything yet about finding a home for his dog. Or about Frank Preston.

Doug's office was to their right off the vestibule, before they reached the parlor, but Doug wasn't there. It was Lorelei Preston who sat behind the big oak desk. She rose when they walked in.

Lorelei was a striking woman, years younger than Doug but possessed of an austere beauty that would last until she was as old as he was. She glanced pointedly at her watch. "If you're here for the viewing, you're too early," she said in clipped tones.

"I was hoping to talk to Doug for a moment," Liss said.

"About a funeral? Well, it's never to early for pre-planning."

"About Nola Ventress."

Lorelei's hands clenched involuntarily on the edge of the desk. "I don't believe he cares to discuss that subject."

"So you know who she was."

"Was?" Lorelei sat down abruptly. "What do you mean *was*? Did something happen to her?"

"She's dead," Liss said bluntly. "She died . . . unexpectedly . . . last night."

Lorelei's eyes narrowed. "Find a different funeral home. My Dugie wanted nothing to do with her while she was alive and he'll have nothing to do with her now that she's dead. It's been years since he last heard from her. He doesn't need her coming back into his life, not even as a client."

"He saw Nola Thursday night at the MSBA meeting," Dan said. "He drove her back to the hotel afterward."

"That's impossible!" Lorelei looked stricken. "He'd have told me."

Apparently not, Liss thought. "Look, we didn't come here to cause trouble, but I think Doug would want to know about Nola's death. No matter how badly their marriage ended, he shouldn't have to hear that kind of news on the *Six O'Clock Report*."

"I . . . I'll tell him." Again Lorelei stood and this time remained on her feet, clearly expecting them to leave.

Liss saw no point in sticking around. Besides, it was already nine. She was officially running late. Once outside, she headed straight for her car, then stopped short. It was in her driveway and, now that she thought about it, she realized that it shouldn't have been. After her uncomfortable interview with Gordon Tandy, Dan had driven her home.

"My brother Sam ran it into town for you," Dan said, catching up with her. He took her elbow again and steered her toward his house instead of hers. "There's no point in taking two vehicles when we're both going to the hotel. I'll drive."

She might have argued, but she didn't want to take the time.

An hour after the dealers' room opened, the hairs on the back of Liss's neck prickled. Someone was watching her. Slowly, she shifted her gaze toward the entrance. The man standing in the doorway, staring at her with chilling intensity, was State Police Detective Gordon Tandy.

He sauntered over to her display tables. On the surface, he was just another conference-goer. He did not wear a uniform and neither his badge nor his gun was obviously displayed. But he did have that distinctive quasi-military bearing and an air of authority. Somehow, even in civvies, he was easy to spot as a cop.

"Liss," he said in the deceptively pleasant voice she knew so well.

She forced herself to smile. "Gordon."

"A word with you? Somewhere private would be good."

"Of course. Beth, can you mind the store?"

Angie's ten-year-old daughter was thrilled to be asked. Helping in the bookstore was a frequent occurrence, but being responsible for the many and varied gift items sold at Moosetookalook Scottish Emporium was a treat for her.

"Isn't that kid a little young to hold a job?" Gordon asked as they left the dealers' room. Liss could hear laughter coming out of one of the larger meeting rooms where a session was in progress. The sign outside the door said it was a panel of Maine writers—Dorothy Cannell, Julia Spencer-Fleming, Susan Vaughan, and Lea Wait.

"Didn't you ever help out in your father's store when you were a kid?" Like the Emporium, Tandy's Gifts and Music was a family business, handed down to Gordon's brother, Russ, by their father.

"There's a fine line between that and child labor."

"Trust me, there won't be much labor involved. Scottish-themed items do not appear to be big sellers at this conference, except for the few that also feature cats. I sold out of T-shirts picturing bagpipe-playing felines."

"No market for kilt pins? What's the world coming to?" They entered the elevator to go down to the lobby level.

Liss stared at him. Was he actually trying to joke with her? She doubted it. He was probably just trying to soften her up before he hit her with the tough questions and gave her another lecture on the dangers of meddling in a murder investigation. To get a little of her own back, she made her voice as casual as possible and said, "My other big sellers are skean dhus."

Gordon looked puzzled. He knew what they were, of course, being a piper himself. They were the little knives kilt-wearing Scots wore tucked into

the top of their hose. But he appeared to be unaware that a skean dhu had been the murder
weapon the last time there was a murder in Moosetookalook. Although he'd been away then, Liss
was surprised he hadn't been filled in on all the
details as soon as he got back to Maine. After all,
his brother had been one of those present at the
hotel that weekend.

That had been the same weekend Dan proposed to her.

"They make good souvenirs," she blurted, then
winced at her own inane comment.

Just shut up, Liss, she ordered herself.

Gordon opened the door to the hotel library
and waved her in ahead of him. The room was furnished with shelves full of books that hotel guests
were welcome to borrow and also housed jigsaw
puzzles and board games for their amusement. An
audio recorder, notebook, and several pens had
been set out on a small table. A uniformed officer
sat behind it, apparently waiting to take notes.

"So, what's on the agenda?" Liss asked, knowing
she sounded much too cheerful. "More questions
about Nola?"

"First I have a few questions about Jane Nedlinger," Gordon said, and indicated that she should
take a chair.

Liss perched on the edge of her seat, hands
folded primly in her lap. "What about her?"

Gordon grabbed a straight chair, turned it
around, and straddled it. He gave her a hard stare.
"You tell me. You said that you met her for the first
time on Thursday evening."

"That's right. At the opening reception. With about a hundred other people around."

"And then you rushed right out to call an emergency meeting with all the other businesspeople in town."

"Not *all* of them."

"Jane Nedlinger left behind notes she'd made for a blog post she was writing."

Liss waited.

"Those were the only notes I found when I searched her room. It looks to me as if you were the only person at this entire conference who interested her."

Liss frowned. That couldn't be right.

"Liss?"

"She asked to interview me, but later she told Dan that she was going to write the story without my input."

In painstaking detail, Gordon took her through the events of Thursday evening. Liss tried to confine her answers to a simple recitation of the facts. After all, she hadn't known Nola's history at the time of the meeting. There was no point in dwelling on the antagonism between Stu and Doug. She was certain that it hadn't had any bearing on *Jane's* death, and she doubted there was a connection to Nola's, either. Besides, as Gordon kept telling her, it wasn't her place to teach the police their business.

"What did you do after the MSBA meeting broke up?" he asked.

"I had a glass of wine to relax me and went to bed. Trust me, I did not come out here to the hotel, lure Jane Nedlinger out to Lover's Leap, and push her off the cliff."

Her denial didn't get the reaction she'd expected. Gordon should have found her sarcasm mildly amusing. Instead, he kept his cop face on.

The silence stretched until she almost burst into random speech just to fill it. Just as she was about to give in to the urge, he asked another question.

"Can Ruskin give you an alibi?"

Liss wished she could attribute the coldness in his voice to resentment over the fact that she'd chosen Dan instead of him. But this conversation wasn't personal. He was all business, and his business was murder.

"No, he can't," Liss said. She realized she was twisting her engagement ring around and around on her finger and forced herself to stop.

It was Gordon's job to suspect everyone, she reminded herself. But surely he couldn't believe she was capable of murder! He knew her better than that.

Gordon hesitated, then rephrased his question. "He didn't spend the night?" His tone of voice had changed, ever so slightly.

She blinked, then narrowed her eyes to stare at him. Was she wrong about his ability to separate the personal from the professional? She didn't suppose it mattered. Neither the man nor the cop would like her answer.

"Dan and I are engaged to be married," she said in a voice as bland and matter-of-fact as she could make it. "Sometimes he stays over, but we're not living together. The only ones who slept with me on Thursday night were Lumpkin and Glenora."

"Glenora?"

"The black kitten who adopted me last Christmas."

He nodded, remembering, and almost smiled.

"I was planning on talking to Jane Nedlinger yesterday, Gordon, but the only time I actually saw her or spoke to her before she died was at that reception. I didn't care much for what she had to say, but I certainly didn't kill her to stop her from writing about me."

"And yet you admit she threatened you. That makes you a logical suspect in her death."

"Yeah, I had that figured out."

"A pity cats can't testify in court."

"Was that an attempt at humor?"

"Only if you found it funny."

Liss rolled her eyes. "At least tell me that *you* don't believe I killed anyone."

Gordon stood up, swinging the chair around to return it to the exact place he'd taken it from. His expression was as unreadable as ever. "I don't think you're a killer, but I can't play favorites. I'll go where the investigation takes me. Right now it's forcing me to take a very close look at you."

"Okay." She didn't like what he was saying, but she understood where he was coming from.

"I'll have more questions for you later, about Nola Ventress's death, but that's it for now."

He signaled to his associate to turn off the recorder and stop taking notes. Liss had all but forgotten the other officer was there, he'd effaced himself so completely from the interview. She felt her cheeks heat. She hadn't been all that comfortable talking to Gordon about Dan. The knowledge that a complete stranger had heard what she'd said—and recorded every word, too—left her feeling even more flustered.

"You can do yourself a big favor," Gordon said, "by going back to the dealers' room and staying there. Let me do my job and clear you of suspicion. Do not try to help."

"Fine. I get the message." Fuming, both embarrassed and annoyed, Liss headed for the door. "The last thing I want," she flung over her shoulder, "is to become involved in another murder investigation!"

Chapter Ten

Sherri arrived at The Spruces just in time to see a flatbed truck leaving with what looked like an entire tree aboard. She grimaced. That wasn't the kind of evidence anyone collected for an accident or a suicide. Nope. They were looking for clues in a homicide. And that meant she'd blown it, big time, over Jane Nedlinger's death.

A crime lab mobile unit was parked in the hotel's back lot. Sherri ignored it and headed for the path into the woods. It was the crime scene she needed to see again. With any luck, she'd find someone there who'd be willing to talk to her. After all, she was in uniform, even if it wasn't the right shade of blue.

At least she was officially on duty. She hadn't intended to work, but Jeff hadn't been able to find anyone to take her place. He'd been all set to put in a double shift himself when she'd called in to get his okay to make contact with the state police at the hotel in a semi-official capacity. Since Pete had taken a sick day to help her look after Adam, she was determined not to feel guilty about insisting to Jeff that she work her own shift. There was no need for her to stay at her injured son's side every moment of the day. Besides, no one would mind if she made a few stops at the apartment during the next eight hours, just to make sure Adam was okay.

Although Liss had found Nola's body nearly sixteen hours earlier, the site was still swarming with people. Sherri knew the routine. Last night, Gordon would have done a walk-through to get an overview of the situation and Sherri's friend George, as M.E., would have come back out to view yet another body in situ at the foot of the cliff. Then they'd have taken photographs. Lots of photographs. It wasn't uncommon to take a hundred, even two hundred shots of a crime scene. They'd have made a video of the scene, too.

These days the state police did their "chalk outline" with florescent orange tongue depressors stuck in at the head, crotch, arms, and legs. Sherri was glad the body had long since been taken away, safely wrapped in a clean white sheet the state police had brought to the scene themselves. They'd have put brown paper bags over the hands and feet, since plastic destroyed evidence, before they put the remains in a body bag.

Gordon Tandy had been designated the primary for the case. It was his area, after all. That meant he and other officers would talk to everyone and then re-interview many of them two or three more times to verify every detail, tease out anything that might have been overlooked the first time around, and cross-check all the facts. He wouldn't necessarily be looking for a motive. One wasn't required for arrest or prosecution. But he couldn't be happy about Liss's involvement in the case. He'd have to suspect her in both murders. She'd clashed with Jane and she'd been the one to find Nola, both damning circumstances. Sherri felt sorry for both Gordon and Liss, especially if Gordon was still carrying a torch for her.

The first person she saw when she came out into the clearing at the top of the cliff was Gordon Tandy. She steeled herself to face his disapproval and kept going, ignoring the scowl he sent her way when he caught sight of her. His team was still in the process of going over the terrain, inch by inch, picking up and recording the location of everything they found. There was no way to tell at this stage what might turn out to be important

"Is there a reason you're here?" Gordon demanded. If she hadn't known him so well, she might have been intimidated by his brusque manner.

She felt warmth creep into her cheeks, but she answered him with the truth. "I wanted to be sure the forensics team found everything I saw here Friday morning—condoms, tissues, and especially gum wrappers. Those might be important. Bill Stotz is a compulsive gum chewer. He's one of the people Jane Nedlinger talked to at the reception. There was a name-badge holder, too."

Even as she spoke, she saw one of the officers drop the badge holder into an evidence bag.

"We've got it covered," Gordon said.

"The way I hear it, everyone at the MSBA meeting was pretty het up over the threat of bad publicity for the town."

That caught Gordon's interest. "You weren't there?"

"I was home with my kid." When he looked blank, she filled him in on Adam's broken arm.

He softened a fraction. "I'm sorry to hear that. Maybe you should get back to him."

"Pete's there. Look, Gordon, Jane Nedlinger annoyed a lot of people. Me, for instance."

"You talked to the victim?" She had his full attention at last, and wished she didn't.

Feeling like a pinned butterfly, Sherri gave him a succinct report on Jane Nedlinger's visit to the P.D. "I didn't much like her, but I had no idea how much trouble she meant to cause."

"You were the first officer on the scene when she was found. Didn't you recognize her?"

"Well, that's the thing. I never saw her face, just a body dressed in jogging clothes. I know this sounds like I'm making excuses, but I only went into the office yesterday morning to find a replacement so I could stay home with Adam. As soon as Jeff arrived on the scene, he sent me home. That was after the M.E. said the injuries were consistent with a fall but before anyone identified her."

Gordon gave her a searching look. "You feeling guilty?"

"Well, yeah. I should have—"

"Get over it. Yes, the call was a bad one, but you weren't the one who screwed things up. Jeff relieved you before the body was brought up. You had no reason to think anything but what you did. George and the rescue team saw things the same way. If anyone blew it, it was George, for not noticing the discrepancy in the time of death sooner than he did."

"So it's not Jeff's fault, either?"

"Trust me, no one's going to blame Jeff."

Sherri started to say more, then thought better of it. She doubted that Gordon had a very high opinion of Moosetookalook's home-grown chief of police. Jeff had been given the job because he was willing to accept the ridiculously low salary that was all the town selectmen would authorize for the job.

She started to leave, then turned back. "Gordon? Did Jane Nedlinger contact anyone in your outfit about her story? I told her the state police had a public relations office."

"She didn't get hold of them," Gordon said.

But something in his tone made Sherri wonder if Jane had talked to *him*.

At the check-in desk in the lobby, Joe Ruskin was once again on duty.

"Did you get any rest last night?" Dan asked him. "You look done in." Dan sometimes wondered if his father ever slept.

"I'm okay, but I wouldn't mind it if you spelled me here for an hour or two."

Backed into a corner, Dan assured his father that he'd be glad to take over at the front desk. He wasn't happy at the prospect of being trapped there. He'd planned to spend time with Liss, on and off, throughout the day. With everything that was going on, he felt uneasy about leaving her to her own devices. He knew her too well.

Once Dan was ensconced behind the check-in desk, Joe didn't immediately take off. "Something on your mind, Dad?"

"It's hell getting old, son."

"Old!" Dan scoffed. "You're not even sixty yet."

"Yeah, that's me. A real spring chicken." But his expression remained solemn. "Nola will never make it to sixty."

"So, you knew her well?" Dan was still trying to wrap his head around the Doug-Nola-Stu triangle. It was hard for him to imagine either of those men as young and in love, let alone part of a sex scandal.

Joe shrugged. "You know this town. It was even smaller back then. Everybody knew everybody, or thought they did. Besides, I saw Nola once after she divorced Doug and left Maine."

"Oh, yeah?" Dan wasn't sure he wanted to hear this.

"You know I went into the navy right after high school." Joe snorted. "Smart-ass kid that I was, I called myself a draft dodger. There was still a draft back then, you see, and I was afraid I'd end up in Vietnam if I waited for the army to grab me. Anyway, I was young and carefree and I liked the life pretty well. I did two tours of duty as an aviation electrician's mate, mostly stationed on aircraft carriers. That's how I learned I could work with my hands. When I wasn't at sea, a friend of mine got me helping to build sets for a local little theater.

That got me thinking I might be pretty good at putting houses together, too."

Dan leaned his elbows on the counter, fascinated by this glimpse of his father as a young man. Joe wasn't much given to reminiscing. As if he'd just realized that himself, he shrugged and looked self-conscious, but he continued his story.

"I was stationed stateside when one day, out of the blue, I got this phone call from Nola. She was in town, attending a writer's conference, and she'd decided to look me up. I already knew what had happened back home." His lips twisted into an ironic smile. "Your grandmother was still alive back then and she kept me in the loop. Anyway, I agreed to meet Nola for a drink. By that time, your mother and I were planning to get married. I wasn't going to re-up when my tour of duty was over. I was ready to come home, settle down, and start a family. That was why, at first, I was too dumb to catch on to what Nola wanted."

Dan couldn't help grinning. "She tried to put the moves on you?"

"That she did, son." He shook his head. "And all the while she was telling me about the big plans she had now that she'd shaken the dust of Moosetookalook off her feet."

"Plans other than scoring with you?" Dan couldn't resist ribbing his father.

"Oh, yeah. She was more of a dreamer than I am. She was going to be a famous writer. Make a fortune at it. Hit all the bestseller lists." Sadness replaced the twinkle in his eyes as he made a gesture that encompassed the entire hotel. "I was lucky.

Some dreams do come true. Others don't. Poor Nola. Seems to me that organizing this conference and inviting all her favorite authors to attend was the closest she ever got."

Liss passed the registration table on her way back to the dealers' room after a bathroom break. Nola's second in command, Phoebe, sent a brilliant smile her way and waved a flyer at her. "Want to sign up now for next year? Special early-bird registration fee," she called out. "And our guest of honor has just confirmed."

"That's great," Liss called back, but she didn't take the time to stop and find out who that person might be.

She did wonder if she should suspect Phoebe of murdering Nola. The woman certainly seemed to have come into her own since she'd taken charge of the conference. She might have pondered the possibility further if she'd had time at first to think about anything but business, but for once she had customers waiting. In rapid succession, she sold two more skean dhus.

"This is just like the one used in that murder, right?" her second customer asked.

"Close enough." She told herself that a small business owner could not afford to be squeamish and took his money, but the reminder that her hometown might really become infamous as the "murder capital of Maine" had her stomach twisted into knots.

After the next set of panels got under way, Liss once more had too much time to think. She replayed her session with Gordon in her mind. Had there really been no notes in Jane's room except those relating to Moosetookalook? Surely she'd been working on more than one story. She'd blogged daily, and her piece on Liss hadn't been scheduled to run until after the weekend.

Liss could think of several people at the conference who might have wanted to stop Jane from writing bad things about them. She'd already given Gordon their names. Surely it wouldn't be interfering in his investigation if she just jotted down a few questions. They might even trigger an idea that would help him. She burrowed in her tote for a notepad and a felt-tip pen and began to write.

Who was Jane Nedlinger?
Where did she come from?
Why did she hate mystery novels?
Did she come to Moosetookalook only because of the previous murders?

Liss paused to tap her pen against the table. It seemed likely that Jane had found out about the murders *because* of the conference. In that case, she might have had an interest in the First Annual Maine-ly Cozy Con other than talking to townspeople. She wrote:

Who else was Jane after at the conference?

On a separate page she listed names of all the people she knew of who'd had conversations with Jane:

Bill Stotz
Yvonne Quinlan
Dan
Eleanor Ogilvie
Nola

There might have been others. There probably were. She'd have to remember to ask Dan and Margaret if they'd seen Jane talking with anyone else at the reception.

Her third list contained the names of everyone who'd been at the MSBA meeting. She listed Dan and Nola again, then added Stu, Patsy, Betsy, Doug, Joe, Margaret, the couple from the jewelry store, and the craft store woman. Everyone had been pretty riled up, but Liss doubted that any of them had been mad enough at Jane to kill her. Besides, only Nola and Dan, Joe and Margaret had ever met Jane, and Joe and Margaret's contact with her had been ephemeral at best.

Liss flipped back to the first page. There was one other question she needed to add, one that had no sensible answer. It had been the middle of the night—pitch dark and overcast after a rain storm—when Jane had gone over the edge of Lover's Leap to her death. Why had she been out there in the first place?

She started a new page for Nola. It was possible that Nola had fallen by accident, but why had she taken flowers to the scene? She'd certainly had no love for Jane Nedlinger.

Liss filled two more pages in her notebook with questions and speculation, but for once writing things down did not help her think more clearly. All it did was raise more questions. She started doodling, a clear reflection of the way her thoughts were circling round and round without reaching any conclusions. She really wished she'd managed to talk to Nola Ventress before the other woman's death.

"I'm giving myself a headache," Liss muttered, and was glad when the next influx of conference-goers distracted her. Most of them got in line to have their books signed by the authors who'd been panelists during the last hour. Very few bought anything. The T-shirt vendor across the way was doing a far better business than either Liss or Angie.

Just before noon, Margaret turned up with an offer to take over the Emporium tables so that Liss could attend the luncheon. The guest of honor interview would take place while attendees ate. Liss accepted. She'd already agreed to be responsible for Angie's tables, as well as her own, when Angie went back into town to manage Yvonne Quinlan's signing at the bookstore.

Sherri intercepted Liss on her way to the ballroom. "Can I tempt you with a quick meal in the hotel restaurant?" she asked.

"Come with me to the luncheon instead and tell me why you're in uniform."

"Don't I need a ticket?"

"I think we can take it for granted that there will be two no-shows. And I can't believe I was just heartless enough to say that."

"You're just displaying cop humor. Perfectly nat-

ural under the circumstances. And yes, I'd be delighted to join you. Fictional murders will make a
nice change."

"I do not want to start finding cop humor
funny," Liss muttered, but Sherri didn't hear her.
The babble of a hundred voices, all talking at
once, drowned out her words.

They found a table just as the waitstaff started to
serve the meal. By the time Sherri had explained
how she came to be working, shouting directly
into Liss's ear, Nola's former second in command
mounted the podium to address the crowd. She
had to use a microphone to be heard over the
clink of glasses and the rattle of cutlery.

"Welcome to our guest of honor interview," she
greeted them. "I'm Phoebe Lewis. I'm filling in for
Nola Ventress, who is unable to be here this afternoon."

Liss exchanged a puzzled glance with Sherri.
Phoebe knew that Nola was dead. So did a lot of
other people. Did she really think word wouldn't
get out? True, they were hoping the press wouldn't
get hold of the story quite yet, but Liss was certain
the news had already begun to spread through the
hotel by word of mouth.

When no one challenged her statement, Phoebe
introduced Sandy Lynn Sechrest, who would conduct the interview with Yvonne Quinlan. "I give you
our talented toastmistress," Phoebe said, handing
over the microphone.

"Thank you," Sandy Lynn said in her soft,
Southern drawl, "but if you'll recall, we decided
on toast-chick. Now, I will admit that I thought
about calling myself a toast-kitty or a toast-puppy,

since I write about pets, but those didn't seem quite right. Neither did toast-hamster!" She waited for the laughter to die down, then added, "So, there's no alternative. Toast-chick it is."

Liss ate a forkful of pasta salad and glanced at her watch. If Yvonne was going to be interviewed and still get to Angie's Books by two, Sandy Lynn had better get a move on.

As if she'd heard the thought, Sandy Lynn introduced Yvonne. Her first few questions were routine ones about Yvonne's life and her career as an actress. Then Sandy Lynn zeroed in on the books Yvonne had written.

"One of the things that fascinates readers is the insider's glimpse you give them into the world of making movies and television shows. You poke fun at the industry you work in. Isn't that risky?"

Yvonne's gentle laugh drifted out over the room. "Not really. Everyone knows how much more accurate novels are than screenplays. Hollywood . . . and Vancouver . . . are notorious for repeating the same mistakes over and over again. How many times have you seen a cop, who should know better, taste an unknown powder to determine whether or not it's an illegal drug? And don't even get me started on the smell of cordite."

This got a laugh, since most mystery readers knew that substance was no longer used in gunpowder and hadn't been for decades. Whatever someone might smell after a modern gun was fired, it wasn't cordite.

"I've called attention to numerous theatrical bloopers in my books. A couple of my favorites are cars that *always* explode when they crash and female detectives who chase the bad guys while wearing high heels and short, tight skirts."

They went on in that vein for a few more minutes before Sandy Lynn grinned and switched subjects. "You know I have to ask," she said. "Is Simon really a vampire?"

Yvonne gave her a variant of the same answer she'd given Liss at the opening reception—"I'll never tell."

Since Liss and Sherri were seated at a table near the exit, Liss heard the door when it creaked open behind her. Heavy footsteps approached and stopped beside her chair. She wasn't surprised to look up and find Gordon Tandy staring down at her.

"I need to talk to you again," he said.

"Now?"

"Yes. Now." He waited, expecting her immediate compliance.

He got it, but not without a disgruntled look.

"It's just a re-interview," Sherri whispered as Liss stood. "Nothing to worry about."

"Easy for you to say."

As far as she knew, she was still Gordon's prime suspect. And if he decided he had a personal bone to pick with her, he might just be vindictive enough to arrest her. Although he had to know she wasn't a murderer, when there was a volatile emotion like jealousy involved, anything could happen.

Liss followed Gordon out into the hall.

Sherri was right behind them.

"I should get back to work," she said.

"Or you could sit in on the interview. I'd like you there, and I'm sure Gordon won't have any objections." She sent him a look that said he'd better not.

He wisely agreed to the suggestion and once again led the way to the hotel library, this time descending the stairs from the mezzanine and crossing the lobby to reach that large, comfortable room that was situated in the west wing near the gift shop. When Liss saw that Dan was the one working behind the check-in desk, she gave him a little wave and forced herself to smile brightly. If his glower was any indication, he didn't buy her nonchalant attitude.

This time, Liss made the mistake of taking the first chair she came to. The oversized, upholstered wing chair almost swallowed her whole. She'd have fought her way free and chosen another seat had Gordon not already repeated his maneuver with the straight-back chair and settled in, facing her. His big body blocked her escape.

Sherri eased herself down onto the arm of Liss's chair and put a comforting hand on her arm. That reassurance helped calm Liss's jittery nerves, but she still felt nervous. Once she'd thought she knew Gordon Tandy well. Now he was a stranger to her—a stranger who appeared to suspect her of murder.

They were just getting started, with her name and address and occupation, when the door to the library opened and Dan came in. Apparently he'd found someone to take over at the front desk.

"This isn't an open house," Gordon snapped.

The silent, unobtrusive officer who'd once again been manning the recorder and notebook shot to his feet, ready to toss Dan out.

"In this case, I represent the owner of this hotel."

"I could have you evicted," Gordon said. "Sherri, too."

"Not if you want me to answer your questions," Liss cut in. Sadly, she had some familiarity with this part of Maine's criminal law. "I don't have to talk to you at all. I'm willing to do so only if they both stay."

That got Gordon's full attention and stopped the other officer from laying hands on Dan.

"Do you think you need protection from me?" Gordon asked. There was a peculiar quality to his voice, but Liss couldn't decide if he was hurt or offended or both.

"I don't know," Liss said. "Are you planning to arrest me?"

"No."

"I'm no longer a suspect in Jane Nedlinger's death?"

"You're not at the top of the list anymore."

"Is she a suspect in Nola Ventress's death?" Sherri asked before Liss could.

"No."

"Then why do you want to talk to me again?" Liss demanded. "And don't give me any more one-word answers. It's very irritating."

Gordon looked ready to chew nails. "Turn off the recorder." As soon as the other officer did so, Gordon burst into speech. "Liss MacCrimmon, you are the most aggravating, exasperating woman

I've ever met. In my saner moments, I consider myself well rid of you."

Liss didn't know what to say to that. Dan went stiff with outrage. Sherri seemed to be trying to hold back a laugh.

"Okay," Liss said. "Well . . . good."

Gordon got himself back under control. "Let's stick to business, shall we?"

Liss nodded, but she put her hand over his before he could signal his colleague to turn the recorder back on. "I want to do all I can to help, Gordon. The sight of Nola Ventress at the bottom of that cliff is going to haunt me for a very long time. I need to know how she ended up there."

He stared at her, long and hard, then abruptly stood and grabbed her hand, pulling her out of the chair and away from the others in the room. "Stay put," he ordered them, and led Liss to a secluded corner that offered a modicum of privacy. He lowered his voice to a whisper. "I don't have an official answer for you. Not yet."

"But you have a theory?" She kept her voice as low as his.

"It's *just* a theory," he warned. "Nothing official," he repeated, stressing that word. "Not yet. And I shouldn't be talking to you about it. I wouldn't if I could think of any other way to keep you out of the investigation."

"Oh, thank you very much!" He was breaking the rules in an attempt to keep her from interfering. Wasn't there anyone who thought she was capable of minding her own business?

"I know you, Liss. You have trouble letting go.

Well, there's no need for you to get involved this time. We have things well in hand."

"How do I know you aren't just saying that to—?"

"What? Protect you? Keep you out of trouble?"

"Well . . . yes."

For just an instant, his expression softened. The old affection was there in his dark, gold-flecked eyes. He still cared about her. "This information is not for public consumption," he warned, "but right now the deaths of Jane Nedlinger and Nola Ventress are looking like a case of murder/suicide."

Liss gasped so loudly that Dan took a step toward them. He stopped when Liss motioned for him to stay back. She needed a few seconds before she could manage to ask the obvious question: "You think Nola killed Jane and then herself? But why?"

Gordon shrugged. "I'm not at liberty to say, since the investigation is ongoing, but I will tell you this much. After I talked to you earlier today, I made an interesting discovery in Nola Ventress's room. I found more of Jane Nedlinger's notes hidden under Nola's mattress. And just a few minutes ago, the results came through on a fingerprint we found in Jane's room. It belonged to Nola."

"So Nola went in there after Jane was dead and stole her notes." Liss's brow furrowed. If Nola had done that, it had been after she knew Jane was dead, but it didn't mean she had been the one who'd killed her. All it meant was that Nola had left other notes behind, notes relating to Jane's story on Liss. Had that been deliberate? Had Nola hoped to focus suspicion on her old friend Margaret's niece?

"Our working theory is that Nola Ventress pushed Jane Nedlinger off that cliff," Gordon said.

"No," Liss said. "No, I don't buy it. How could Nola kill Jane? She was half her size."

"The larger woman could have been off balance. In that case, a good shove wouldn't necessarily take a lot of strength."

"And what were they doing on the cliff side of the fence in the first place? Don't tell me you think a little bit of a thing like Nola lifted Jane up and tossed her over!"

The three other people in the room were looking very interested in their conversation. Gordon sent Liss an exasperated look. "Lower your voice. I'm not supposed to be telling you any of this."

"I'm sorry, but it's a preposterous idea, and you're being pretty stingy with details. You know a great deal more than you're sharing."

"There's a lot about this case that's absurd," he said, admitting nothing more.

That was certainly an understatement!

"Why did Jane go out to Lover's Leap?" Liss asked. "Was she asked to meet someone there? Even if she was, why would she go? Only the heroines of Gothic novels are that foolish, running into the woods when anyone with any sense would hide under the bed. And if the old book covers are to be believed, they're usually wearing flowing white nightgowns as they flee the looming castle in the background. Jane was dressed for a run."

And if Jane had been a character in a Gothic

novel, Liss decided, she would not have been the virginal heroine. She'd been more the sinister housekeeper type. The murderer, not the victim. She'd been a nasty piece of work, but she'd also seemed to be a sensible, organized sort of woman, one who undoubtedly knew she'd made enemies and would have been prepared to deal with them.

Who would she have agreed to meet there? A lover? Liss shook her head. In spite of Margaret's story about Nola and Stu, a romantic or sexual rendezvous seemed unlikely. Liss knew she'd never agree to meet Dan out there, and she was crazy about him. Then again, Dan would never suggest such a stupid thing. When Liss tried to imagine Jane with a lover, planning to meet him in a remote spot after midnight, she just couldn't picture it. Why bother when Jane had a perfectly good bedroom in the hotel?

"Jane may have been the one to suggest the meeting spot," Gordon offered. Then he clammed up, reluctant to say more.

Liss hadn't been serious when she'd quipped— had it only been yesterday?—that Jane might have gone to Lover's Leap to collect a blackmail payment, but the more she thought about that scenario, the more plausible it seemed, especially when stacked against even less likely explanations. Jane had appeared to enjoy taunting her victims. Perhaps she'd chosen that spot for its intimidation factor.

Her silent ruminations seemed to annoy Gordon. "As you pointed out," he said, "Jane Nedlinger was a large, imposing woman. If the person she planned to meet was much smaller, she may have felt she had no reason to fear for her own safety."

"Fear," Liss echoed. "Well, then, it couldn't have been Nola. Nola was scared of the woods, day or night. She'd never have agreed to go up there after dark."

"What about the notes under her mattress?"

"Were they about Nola?"

"No," Gordon admitted. "I expect she destroyed any that were."

But she'd kept Jane's notes about other people, except for the ones that concerned Liss. She'd deliberately left those behind in Jane's room for Gordon to find. What kind of sense did that make?

"At least you must have other suspects now. Besides me, and besides Nola, too. And at least now Moosetookalook won't be fodder for Jane's blog." Frowning, Liss replayed what she'd just said to Gordon. "Wait a minute. You said notes. Didn't Jane Nedlinger have a laptop in her room? I mean, she made her living writing a blog. Weren't those notes—?"

"Electronic? No. Everything we found was handwritten. She did have a laptop and we confiscated it, but she hadn't added anything to her files since before she arrived in Moosetookalook. Maybe she thought pen and paper were more secure. Less likely to be stolen, at any rate. That means Nola knew what to look for. What to take. She left the computer because she knew it wouldn't have anything on it to incriminate her."

"That implies she knew Jane well. I don't think they ever met before Thursday evening."

"Is that what Nola told you?"

To herself, Liss conceded that Nola might have lied. She'd certainly been up to something if she'd searched Jane's room. But *murder* Jane? That was still hard to believe, especially given Nola's physical size and her phobia. Unless she'd been lying about that, too.

"This is all very confusing," Liss admitted aloud.

"Tell me about it."

"But you said murder/suicide. You think Nola killed herself. Why? Even if she did murder Jane, she must have thought she got away with it."

He shrugged. "Maybe she couldn't live with the guilt. We're still working on it, Liss. Give us a little time and we'll tie up all the loose ends."

But Liss shook her head. "Nola's death was not suicide. The First Annual Maine-ly Cozy Con was her brainchild. Her baby. She'd have wanted to participate in every moment of it. If she was going to kill herself—and I'm not convinced she was, or that she was responsible for Jane's death—then she'd at least have waited until after the conference was over."

"Murder/suicide makes more sense than double murder."

"I didn't know Nola well enough to say what she was capable of, but I do know how much this conference meant to her. Unless she thought you were close to arresting her . . . ?" He shook his head in the negative. "Then she'd never have taken a leap off that cliff earlier than late Sunday afternoon, after the closing ceremonies."

"I'll take your opinion into consideration." Without giving her the chance to say more, Gordon took her arm and led her back to the others.

When she'd once more been swallowed whole by the wing chair, Gordon's associate turned the recorder on and Gordon repeated the same questions he'd asked her earlier in the day. Liss gave him the same answers. He added a few new ones, most of them regarding Nola and her interaction with various attendees at the conference.

"If you want to talk to any of the Cozy Con people," Liss pointed out after she'd replied, "you'll have to do it soon. Another twenty-four hours and they'll be scattered all over Maine and beyond."

"I know my job." Gordon sounded testy. "I'd appreciate it if you'd let me do it."

"I'll see to it that she stays out of your way," Dan said, speaking for the first time since he'd insisted on sitting in on the interrogation.

Liss glared at him. She had no plans to interfere in Gordon's investigation, but she didn't like Dan answering for her.

"Just clear things up quickly, Tandy," Dan continued, his stance as aggressive as that of a guard dog defending his territory. "That's all I ask. The longer this goes on, the worse it is for everyone in the community."

Sherri hopped off the arm of Liss's chair and stepped in front of Dan, preventing him from getting any closer to his rival. "Can I send someone else in for questioning?" she asked Gordon.

"We'll handle it." He appeared unaffected by Dan's belligerent display.

The other officer, however, had been braced to

step in. Liss fancied that he looked a little disappointed when he didn't have to.

She stood and headed for the door, relieved
when Dan followed her out. It was ridiculous for
Dan and Gordon to act this way around each
other. She'd made her choice. They both knew
and accepted it. But no amount of talk seemed to
make any impression on either of them. Was this
what Nola had faced with Stu and Doug? No wonder she'd taken off on her own and left them both
behind.

Liss felt drained, as limp as a wet dishrag. "I've
got to get back to the dealers' room," she said,
glancing at her watch. "It's nearly one-thirty, and
Angie needs me to cover for her during Yvonne
Quinlan's signing in town."

But instead of heading up the stairs to the mezzanine, she came to an abrupt halt in the middle
of the lobby. Suddenly, she wanted nothing more
than to go home, crawl into bed, and pull the covers over her head. The thought of smiling and
dealing with customers or, worse, being stuck behind her tables with nothing to occupy her mind
except thoughts she didn't want to dwell on made
her cringe.

Angie's daughter, ten-year-old Beth, couldn't
handle things in the dealers' room alone, but Margaret was already working at the Emporium's tables. If she could be persuaded—

Ten minutes later, Liss was on her way out of the
hotel with Sherri, who had offered her a lift into
town.

Bill Stotz intercepted them just short of the exit.

"What the hell is going on out there? There are police all over the place and someone said that Nola Ventress is dead." Although Bill's manner was combative and his voice loud, his face was ashen. "Is it true?" he demanded.

"I'm afraid so," Liss said. "Last night."

"Why wasn't I told at once? How am I supposed to look after my client's interests if I'm kept in the dark?"

"You're Yvonne Quinlan's manager?" Sherri asked.

"That's right." His gaze sharpened as he took in her uniform.

"Nola appears to have gone up to the cliff to leave flowers in Jane Nedlinger's memory," Sherri said before Liss could blurt out anything more sensational.

"You mean she fell off, too? Stupid women."

Bill had no sooner made that insensitive remark than he caught sight of something behind Liss and Sherri and took off in that direction. Liss turned to see Yvonne just exiting the elevator and watched Bill corral her, whisper in her ear, and then hurry her outside by way of the verandah doors. Liss and Sherri circled around to the parking lot in time to see Bill hustle his client into a waiting limo.

"They're on their way to the book signing," Liss said. "Unless he was the one who left those gum wrappers up at Lover's Leap and he's really going on the lam. I still think he makes a good suspect in Jane's death. Too bad I can't come up with a reason for him to have killed Nola."

"I wonder if he meant Nola was stupid to fall or stupid to want to honor Jane," Sherri mused.

"He said women," Liss reminded her as she got into the police cruiser. "Plural."

During the short drive down the hill and into Moosetookalook proper, Liss said nothing more. In fact, she was trying very hard not to think about murder or suspects or suicide at all. She wanted to focus on putting her feet up, petting the cats, and vegging out.

Halfway home, they passed the gas station / convenience store Sherri's father owned. Odd, Liss thought. There were three cars lined up at the single pump. She couldn't remember the last time Ernie Willett had been obliged to deal with more than one customer at a time.

As they drew closer to the town square, she realized that there were also more cars than usual parked along both sides of the narrow road. "What on earth is going on?" she wondered aloud.

Then the square came into view and she gasped. There had to be a hundred people milling about and—even stranger—almost all of them were dressed in black.

"Funeral?" she asked.

Sherri shook her head. "The only body at Preston's Mortuary is Lenny Peet. Jane and Nola were sent to Augusta for autopsy."

"I'm pretty sure Lenny didn't have this many friends."

"His send-off isn't until tomorrow, anyway," Sherri said, "and there's something off about the clothing. It's not funeral black."

Liss started to laugh, causing Sherri to gawk at her.

"I just figured it out," she said. "These people are here for the book signing. They aren't mourners. They're fans of Yvonne Quinlan—the actress who played Caroline Sweet, the undead heroine of *Vamped*."

Chapter Eleven

Liss sat in the Canadian rocker in her bow window, feet up on a stool and a mug of herbal tea—mostly ginger—in her hand. From this vantage point, she had a clear view of the line of fans trailing out of Angie's Books and winding around through the town square. Angie had opened the door twenty minutes earlier, and those waiting to meet Yvonne Quinlan had inched forward at a slow but steady rate ever since. The book signing was supposed to last two hours. Liss had a feeling it was going to run longer.

She was glad for Angie's sake. A big crowd meant good sales.

She closed her eyes, but as soon as she did, she saw Nola's body again. She swore crossly. So much for putting murder out of her mind!

Resigned, she tried to reorganize her thoughts and envision Gordon's scenario. Little Nola did not succeed in defeating massive Jane. David might have slain Goliath, but he'd had a slingshot. Liss just couldn't picture what Gordon proposed. She hoped he was also looking into other possibilities.

"I will not interfere," Liss said aloud. But that didn't mean she couldn't satisfy her curiosity about a few minor points of interest.

Off the living room, Liss had a combination library and home office. A computer sat on her desk, recently upgraded for high-speed access and tricked out with a wireless router so she could download e-books to a newly acquired reader. She still preferred the feel and smell of a real book, but she had to admit that the instant gratification was nice. It took about two seconds to order a new title from the online bookseller. Being able to enlarge the font was a nice bonus, too.

Liss wasn't sure what she expected to find on the Internet. Maybe there was nothing to find. But she could see no harm in typing Nola's name into her favorite search engine. A moment later, she started scrolling through the hits.

There weren't many. The First Annual Maine-ly Cozy Con had a website. There had been little advance coverage in Maine newspapers, but a couple of mystery-oriented organizations listed upcoming events and named Nola as contact person. Another link led to an e-book store. Without much hope of discovering anything new, Liss clicked on it.

What came up surprised her. She glanced at the author bio and saw that, yes, it was Nola. An ad to buy an e-book subscription popped up and she quickly deleted it. Returning to the book page, she read the description of the unoriginally titled *Con-*

tract for Murder, then selected the button that would take her to a free sample chapter and began to read.

Stu had mentioned Nola's goal of becoming a best-selling novelist, but he'd also seemed to think she'd never sold anything, let alone made money at it. *Contract for Murder* read well, even though the blurb at the e-book site indicated it had never been published in print format. The copyright date was 1988.

Liss finished reading the free sample, bought the rest of the book online, downloaded the electronic file to her e-reader, and carried the device back to the rocker in the window. She was vaguely aware that the crowd in the town square was smaller, but her attention remained fixed on the words on the screen in front of her. Nola's book was a mystery, and it wasn't half-bad. In fact, the more Liss read, the more familiar it seemed. Not the plot. She was sure she hadn't read this particular story before. But there was something about the writing style that rang a bell.

Liss frowned. Nola had written only this one book. It had said so right there in the author bio on the website. In fact, that had been the only information in Nola's bio. There hadn't even been a photo. Liss read to the end of the next chapter and stopped again, trying to puzzle out what she was feeling.

Her gaze shifted to the view from her window in time to see a news van from one of the Portland television stations pull up in front of Angie's Books. Liss swore under her breath. It was probably too much to hope for that they were just there to cover the book signing. Had word already leaked out about the suspicious deaths of two women staying at the hotel?

She kept watching. A reporter and cameraman went inside. Ten minutes later, they came back out, moving at a good clip, got into the van, and drove off. It was impossible to tell if they were heading for the hotel or back to the studio.

At least the book signing seemed to be going well. Perhaps a dozen fans were still waiting to get into the store to have Yvonne sign their books. Angie would be ecstatic. She'd been so worried that she'd ordered too many of Yvonne's titles. Now she was probably wondering if she'd run out. Liss was glad she already owned her own copies of all of them. She'd been a fan of the series since the first book. Yvonne's writing style was—

Struck, Liss swiveled her head around to stare at the door of her library/office. "Huh," she said aloud.

Taking the e-book reader with her, she left chair and living room in favor of shelves packed with mystery novels, including Yvonne Quinlan's. It took only a few minutes of reading first one novel, then another, to confirm the incredible theory that had popped, full blown, into her head.

Nola's book, *Contract for Murder,* had seemed familiar to her for a good reason. The writing style was identical to that in Yvonne Quinlan's work. The two women shared the same voice. It wasn't easy to describe exactly what that meant, but Liss was sure of one thing—one person had written *all* the books.

She wandered back into the living room and once more stood staring out through her bow window. Only three people remained on the porch of Angie's Books. The signing was almost over.

There were two possible explanations for what she'd found. But which was correct? Either Nola had plagiarized an early work by Yvonne Quinlan. Or Yvonne Quinlan hadn't written any of her mysteries—Nola had. Maybe Nola Ventress had become a successful, best-selling author, after all—as a ghostwriter.

That would explain the sour look on Nola's face in the dealers' room when she'd overheard Yvonne talking about what inspired her to write and how she went about plotting her novels. It must have been hard enough not to be able to take credit for her creations, but to have to listen to someone else claim them—that would have been infuriating.

As soon as Liss accepted that her theory was valid, subsequent events fell easily into place. Ghostwriters were nothing new. Celebrities often hired other people to write books for them, then insisted they'd done all the work themselves. But that nugget of information, in the hands of someone like Jane Nedlinger, could have been made into an explosive exposé.

The threat that she would reveal all had given more than one person a motive for murder.

Sherri had been providing crowd control for Yvonne Quinlan's book signing ever since she dropped Liss off at home. She was inside Angie's

Books when Liss walked in. At almost the same moment, the last customer left. Angie flipped her OPEN sign to CLOSED. Yvonne Quinlan, seated at a cloth-covered table near the back of the store, paid no attention. She was too busy signing the few copies of her books that remained. Bill Stotz stood next to her, also oblivious, intent on something he was doing on his BlackBerry.

Angie beamed at Liss. "The signing was a huge success. I'm so glad I agreed to host it. This was the best day I've had since I opened the store."

"I'm glad you're pleased," Liss murmured, but she was already moving past Angie toward Yvonne and Bill.

Yvonne finished signing stock and carefully flexed the fingers of her right hand—to relieve the cramping, Sherri supposed. She'd stacked the books she'd just autographed in a neat pile, but the rest of the table was in disarray. In addition to a scattering of pens, it was littered with discarded Post-it Notes with the names of fans written on them—a practice that had ensured that Yvonne would spell them correctly.

Sherri cleared her throat before she spoke, knowing that her friend hadn't seen her standing in the shadows, but Liss didn't even glance her way. "Liss? What are you doing here?"

Liss ignored Sherri's question. She had a strange look on her face.

Although Sherri had been about to leave, anxious to get home to Adam and Pete, she stayed put. Every instinct told her there was trouble brewing, but she had no idea what kind.

When Liss reached the signing table, she flattened both hands on the cloth-covered surface and fixed Yvonne Quinlan with a cold-eyed stare. Momentarily startled, the actress-turned-author made a quick recovery and reached for one of the hardcover books in front of her.

"Lisa, isn't it?" she asked. "I'm sorry. I thought everyone had gone, but I can add a personal inscription above my signature."

"It's Liss, not Lisa, and I'm not here to buy an Yvonne Quinlan novel. I have, however, always enjoyed reading mysteries written by Nola Ventress."

Yvonne blinked at her. Her hands fluttered, as if she didn't know quite what to do with them. Then, very carefully, she placed her signing pen beside the open book and stood up. "If you don't want an autograph, then I guess I'm through here."

"Not so fast." Liss grabbed Yvonne's arm, preventing her escape.

"Hey, now!" Bill Stotz objected. "You're out of line."

Sherri stepped closer. Such behavior was very unlike Liss. Something had clearly gotten under her skin but, for the life of her, Sherri couldn't guess what it might be.

Very slowly, Liss released Yvonne, but she continued to hold her gaze. "I just want the answer to one question. Was Nola Ventress your ghost-writer?"

Again, Bill stepped in to protect his client. "Don't dignify that with an answer," he barked at Yvonne, and gave her a little push in the direction of Angie's back door. He sent a formidable glower over his shoulder at Liss. "Where do you come off making an accusation like that?"

"Is it false, then?" There was a clear challenge in Liss's tone of voice.

Yvonne turned back halfway to the exit, the fight-or-flight conflict plain on her heart-shaped face. "Of course it is."

"And if it *were* true, you'd deny it anyway," Liss muttered.

Bill chewed harder on his gum, as if that action might aid in his thinking. Sherri had seen ball-players use the same trick to concentrate on a pitch.

"I never even met Nola Ventress until I arrived at The Spruces," Yvonne declared.

"Then why did you agree to be guest of honor at a conference no one had ever heard of?"

Bill slid an arm around Yvonne's shoulders. "I set it up. Yvonne goes to at least one small conference every year, to showcase how accessible she is—a 'real person' mingling with her fans. These occasions aren't easy to schedule, let me tell you, what with all her film and television commitments."

"I wouldn't think an acting career leaves much time to write novels, either."

Yvonne's look shot daggers. Liss should have resembled a porcupine. "I write my own stuff," she insisted, her words clipped and cold. "All by myself. The only one who has a hand in the process is my editor, and she has to listen to me if I don't like one of her changes. That's in my contract." On that exit line, she gave a haughty toss of her head and left the building.

Bill was right on her heels. "That's my girl," he murmured, sounding proud as a new papa.

"Your girl and Nola Ventress have a writing style that's extremely similar," Liss called after him. "Nola's novel is online as an e-book. Read it for yourself."

Bill turned back again, this time framed in the doorway. "That won't be necessary. I don't know what you think you'll accomplish by this absurd accusation, but you should know that even if Yvonne did use a ghostwriter—which she does not!—there's nothing illegal about that practice. There are, however, confidentiality considerations. I have no personal experience with this, you understand, but I do know that ghostwriters customarily sign contracts that forbid them to reveal their part in the process. Ever. If Nola Ventress earned her living that way, she'd be in a lot of trouble—financial and legal trouble—if she decided to talk about her clients."

Lecture delivered, he went to join Yvonne in the back of the waiting limo.

"Whew," Sherri said. "Did you hit a raw nerve or what?" Bill Stotz had come across all outraged and huffy, but he'd been sweating bullets.

"A fat lot of good it did me," Liss grumbled. "I didn't get anything out of either of them."

"What were you expecting, a confession of murder?" Sherri's eyes widened when she caught sight of Liss's expression. "Geez, Liss! How stupid is that?"

"It's only stupid if one of them really did murder Jane and Nola. And you were right here to protect me and make an arrest. You've got a gun and everything."

"You didn't know I was here when you came in."

Sometimes her friend's impulsive behavior scared Sherri to death.

"I had to try, Sherri. When was I going to get another chance to confront Yvonne?"

"Yvonne? Or Bill. Because if this is about that gum wrapper again—"

"It's not. That is, I wasn't thinking of that." She hesitated. "Maybe it is."

"Uh-huh." Either way, this wasn't the time or place to discuss it. Giving Angie a friendly wave, Sherri strong-armed Liss out of the bookstore, across the street, and into the town square.

"Don't you want to hear what I found out?" Liss asked as Sherri hustled her along the now-deserted path.

"I suspect you're going to tell me whether I want you to or not." Sherri was resigned to the inevitable.

Once they were inside Liss's cozy, inviting kitchen, Liss started talking, first sharing the theory Gordon had confided to her, along with her reasons for rejecting Nola as either murderess or suicide, and then revealing what she'd just discovered online and in her own library.

"You thought Yvonne killed both Jane and Nola so no one would find out she didn't write her own books?"

"Made sense to me." Liss began to cobble together a meal out of leftovers.

"Only if you think killing the goose that lays the golden eggs makes sense. If you're right, then without Nola there would be no more Yvonne Quinlan novels."

"She'll hire someone to replace Nola."

"Using your logic, it makes more sense for Nola to have killed Jane. After all, if this ghostwriting thing came out, she'd lose a major source of income."

Liss frowned.

"Besides, even supposing that Jane Nedlinger did reveal that Nola was the one who really wrote Yvonne's books, who would care? If they're good books, people will still buy them. Heck, throw in a little controversy and sales would probably skyrocket."

"Yvonne's ego would take a hit. Did you hear her?" Liss popped a cube of cheese into her mouth.

"Sure. And she'd be just that ticked off if she really did write her own novels. It could be pure coincidence that Nola's writing seemed similar to you." Sherri didn't say so aloud, but she was skeptical about Liss's ability to identify a writer's voice—whatever *that* was.

"Their styles aren't just similar, Sherri. The phrasing, the word choices . . . it's just too big a coincidence for them not to have been written by the same person. And don't even suggest that Nola might have plagiarized something of Yvonne's. There would be too much chance she'd get caught and prosecuted, since Yvonne is famous and has been for years."

"Still—"

But Liss stubbornly shook her head. "I read a lot, Sherri. The similarities are too striking to miss. I bet if you put Nola's book and one of Yvonne's into that computer program they used to try to determine if Shakespeare wrote some of the plays that scholars weren't sure were his, you could prove the probability is too high for two separate individuals to have written Nola's book and the Toni Starling series."

Sherri held up a hand. "Wait a sec. Who's Toni Starling?"

"The detective in Yvonne's—I mean Nola's—novels. Do you want something to eat?" She gestured toward the food she'd set out on the table.

Sherri didn't even look at the offerings. "No, thanks. I've got to leave in a minute. Adam will be wondering where I am. Pete, too," she added, and couldn't help but smile at the thought. She did enjoy having a husband to go home to. Then she jerked her thoughts back to Liss's accusations against Yvonne Quinlan. "Don't try to distract me. Lacking the scholarly software, I'm going to go with common sense. Let's say you're right about the ghostwriting thing. It still seems highly unlikely to me that Yvonne Quinlan threw two women off Lover's Leap. Just look at the physical aspect. Yvonne might have been able to push Nola around, but she wouldn't have been able to budge a behemoth like Jane."

"That's one of my arguments against Nola killing Jane," Liss reminded her. "But what if Yvonne and Bill were in it together?" She settled in at her kitchen table and popped a grape into her mouth. The two cats miraculously appeared, one on each side of Liss's chair. Lumpkin rapped a paw against her thigh.

Sherri leaned back against the kitchen counter and tried to think of the best way to talk Liss out of doing anything foolish. Not an easy task! "There are easier ways to handle the threat of bad publicity than killing someone," she said at last. "Bill Stotz is her business manager, right? Wouldn't the simplest route have been to threaten to sue Jane if she put the story online?"

Liss's mouth quirked into a rueful smile. "That was Stu's idea, too. At the MSBA meeting," she added when Sherri sent her a questioning look. "Sue Jane to stop her blogging about me being a magnet for murder." She winced at the sobriquet.

"Ah. Figures."

"Someone pointed out that it's hard to sue before the fact, and after—well, it's too late then. The damage is done."

"There are other legal options."

"And no one took them. So, back to Bill. You did say you saw gum wrappers up at the Leap."

"Spearmint," Sherri said. The picture suddenly came clear in her mind—soggy green wrappers lying just off the trail.

"Bingo." Liss stopped with a glass of orange juice halfway to her lips, eyes alight.

"I take it that's the kind Bill Stotz chews?"

"Yes. I'm sure of it. I smelled it on his breath." She set the juice back down, untouched. "So that's it. Bill killed them."

"You'd better hope he didn't," Sherri said. "The way you were throwing accusations around, you may have made yourself his next target."

Liss gave an uneasy laugh. "Then I guess I should hope I'm wrong, but I don't."

"Right or wrong, you need to stay out of the investigation. Let Gordon do his job." Sherri was well aware that she was repeating advice Liss had already heard more than once from Gordon himself. Still, maybe this time she'd listen.

"Gordon seems to be set on Nola as the villain." Liss speared a chunk of cold chicken with her fork, looked at it more closely, and put it back down. What looked like congealed cream of mushroom soup clung to it, along with a few stray grains of white rice. "What if he isn't even looking at any other suspects?"

For herself, Sherri liked Gordon's theory. It wrapped things up in a neat little package. Aloud, she said only, "Gordon Tandy's a good cop, Liss. You know that. And he's not closed-minded."

"Maybe you could steer him toward Bill—tell him that *you* found Nola's book online."

Sherri didn't get a chance to reply. At that moment, the back door opened and Margaret Boyd rushed in. She was out of breath and flushed, as if she'd been running.

"Did you see the news?" Margaret gasped.

Sherri glanced at the clock. It was twenty minutes past five. The first of three local news broadcasts had run at five.

"I saw it at the hotel and came straight home." Margaret looked close to tears. "This is terrible, Liss. Just terrible. We've got to do something about it."

They trooped into the living room so that Liss could turn on the wide-screen television she'd bought herself as a Christmas present. They were in good time to catch the 5:30 report. They watched the camera zoom in on Yvonne Quinlan's tear-streaked but still beautiful face. "Poor Nola," she sobbed—prettily. "She was a wonderful woman. A true devotee of the genre."

Nothing so terrible there, Sherri thought as the camera panned, giving a nice bit of publicity to Angie's Books, before coming back to the reporter. Sherri had been out in the square at the time, riding herd on the last of Yvonne's black-clad fans.

"The state police detective in charge of the case refused to comment on camera," the reporter stated. Behind him, Sherri caught a glimpse of The Spruces. "An official statement will be issued tomorrow. In the meantime, we have learned from other sources that this is the second suspicious death at the same location in as many days, and viewers will recall that the seemingly peaceful little village of Moosetookalook was recently the scene of several other murders."

The spot ended and a close-up of the studio anchorman came on the screen. He lifted one expressive eyebrow at his female cohost. "Makes you wonder, doesn't it? Is there a real-life Cabot Cove in the Western Maine Mountains?"

Margaret buried her head in her hands.

Liss groaned aloud.

Sherri sighed and slipped quietly out of the house, heading home. A quiet evening with her son and her new husband was sounding better by the minute.

Liss's phone started to ring moments after Sherri left. She hung up on three reporters in a row and then let the fourth call go to the answer-

ing machine. In between interruptions, she gave
her aunt the capsule version of her afternoon,
ending with her confrontation with Yvonne and
Bill at the bookstore.

Margaret said nothing, but her face creased into
a deep frown.

"What?" Liss leaned forward in her chair, toward Margaret, who was seated on the sofa.

"I think you're right about that ghostwriting
business. Do you remember that I told you how
Nola lived all over the place before she returned
to Maine? Well, she was in Vancouver for quite a
while. She could easily have met Yvonne there.
That's where her vampire series was shot."

"Did Nola work in the film industry?"

"I don't know, but now that I'm thinking about
it, she was always making up stories when she was
young. Stands to reason she might have tried her
hand at scriptwriting. And she must have had
some connection to Yvonne. How else could she
have gotten such a big name to come to her little
conference?"

"Bill Stotz said he arranged it. Yvonne claimed
she'd never met Nola before she arrived at the
Cozy Con."

"Now, I know that isn't true. I don't remember
exactly what Nola said to me, when we were setting
things up for the conference, but I got the distinct
impression that she and Yvonne were already on
friendly terms. Not bosom buddies or anything,
but more than mere acquaintances."

"That's what I thought, too." Liss leaned back in
her chair, arms folded across her chest. "So Yvonne
lied to me. And it's clearly important to her to keep

the ghostwriting secret. That means she might well have committed murder to hide the truth."

"Does it have to be murder?" Margaret asked. She toyed with the thistle pendant she wore and avoided Liss's eyes. "Why couldn't Nola have fallen by accident, just as that Nedlinger woman did?"

"But Jane Nedlinger didn't just fall." Liss repeated Gordon's theory that Nola had killed Jane and then committed suicide out of guilt over her crime.

"No," Margaret said firmly. "No, that explanation won't wash. Nola put too much effort into this weekend not to see it through. Even being arrested in the middle of the conference would have been preferable to killing herself that way."

"That's what I tried to tell Gordon." She grimaced. "I also promised him that I'd let him handle things."

"Well, you can't," Margaret said. "No matter how much better a verdict of murder/suicide might be for the town and the hotel, the truth needs to come out. I owe Nola that much for talking her into coming here in the first place."

"Finding out that Bill and Yvonne did it wouldn't be a bad outcome," Liss mused. "At least they aren't local people."

Margaret switched her attention to the fringe on the sofa cushion. "It's the local people I'm worried about."

"You aren't seriously suggesting that either Doug or Stu was responsible for Nola's death? We've known both of them forever."

At Margaret's stricken look, Liss could have bitten her tongue. Anyone could kill. They both had reason—more reason than she liked to think about—to know that. But she couldn't apologize for her thoughtless words. That would only make matters worse. Instead, she expanded on her reasoning.

"Nola left Moosetookalook a long time ago. Doug has a new wife and a son. Stu just isn't the type to hold a grudge that long. He loses his temper, explodes, and then it's over."

But that image bothered her. What if he'd exploded up at Lover's Leap? At Nola?

When the phone rang again, both women jumped. Liss grimaced as she listened to the message—another demand for an interview. Muttering to herself, she went from room to room, unplugging every extension in the house. For good measure, she burrowed in her purse for her cell and turned that off, too.

By the time Liss returned to the living room, Margaret had pulled herself together. "You're right, Liss," she said. "Neither Doug nor Stu would have any reason to want to kill Nola now. And, of course, neither one of them knew Jane Nedlinger. But someone committed murder, and I want that person caught and punished. I want Nola's name cleared. And if Gordon Tandy isn't looking in the right place, then we have to help him."

"That's misplaced guilt talking," Liss told her. "It's not up to us." The thought of Margaret meddling in a murder investigation sent cold chills down Liss's spine.

"I understand that. I know full well that Jane Nedlinger might have been killed wherever the conference was held. Nola, too. But the attendees and the guest of honor would have been the same. That makes all of them potential murderers." Margaret glanced at her watch and abruptly rose from her chair. "We'd best get a move on. The banquet starts at seven."

"The banquet? But I wasn't planning to—"

"You bought a ticket, didn't you?"

"Well, yes, but—"

"So did I."

"But I've already had my supper," Liss protested.

"You are going to the banquet," Margaret said in a tone that brooked no disobedience. "We both are. Where else are we going to find all of our suspects conveniently gathered together for questioning?"

Chapter Twelve

Dan Ruskin's plan was to stop off at his house just long enough to grab a shower and then spend the evening, and hopefully the night, at Liss's house. He'd heard something about reporters being turned away from the hotel, but with the state police still there in force, he hadn't actually encountered any. He hadn't had to field phone calls, either. Joe had taken over at the front desk soon after Liss and Sherri headed for town. Dan had spent the rest of his shift in the hotel office doing assorted bookkeeping chores. He'd foolishly assumed that the "unfortunate accidents" story had been accepted by the press, until he turned on the six o'clock edition of the evening news, hoping to catch the weather report.

Even while he was still watching Yvonne Quinlan's tearful performance and listening to the news anchor's snide speculations, Dan tried Liss's number. It just kept ringing. Either she was ignoring it, or she'd unplugged the phone. He slammed the receiver back into its cradle.

From his bedroom window, he could see her house, and there was Margaret, just leaving.

As he hunted for clean socks, he tried her cell from his and was sent straight to voice mail. He supposed he wasn't really surprised. With newshounds on the scene, he'd be avoiding phone calls, too.

He was halfway down the stairs when the landline in the living room rang. He hesitated, glaring at the jangling phone on the end table. He didn't want to talk to the press any more than Liss did, or to some gossipy neighbor. On the other hand, the person on the other end of the line might be Liss herself. She'd probably noticed his truck in the driveway.

He answered on the third ring.

The voice in his ear was a MacCrimmon of the female persuasion, but it wasn't Liss. It was her mother.

"Vi, I'm just on my way out. Can I—"

"What's going on there, Dan?" Violet MacCrimmon interrupted him. "Dolores Mayfield phoned us here in Arizona to say it was all over the news that there'd been two more murders at the hotel."

"And Liss isn't answering her phone," Donald MacCrimmon put in from the extension.

Good old Dolores, Dan thought.

"Dan?" Vi sounded impatient.

"I don't know what to tell you, except that Liss and I are fine and only peripherally involved." It was a lie, but only a white one. Liss had better not be planning to embroil herself in more trouble.

"What does that mean?" MacCrimmon sounded suspicious.

"There was an unfortunate accident at Lover's Leap. It had nothing to do with the hotel or with your daughter." He hoped.

An ominous silence answered this second foray into telling half truths.

Dan didn't say anything more, either. He didn't want them to worry. What was the point? They were too far away to be of any help. For that matter, they wouldn't be much use even if they lived right next door. Look how little impact his presence was having!

"Will you be seeing Liss this evening?" Vi asked.

"I was just heading over to her place when you called." That, at least, was the truth.

"Well, then, give her a message from us, will you?"

"Of course."

"Tell her we're changing our travel plans. We have no real reason to wait until next month to close up the house here and head for Moosetookalook. We're going to load up the car tonight and start your way first thing tomorrow morning."

"Wait! Vi, that's not necessary. I—"

"We were already thinking about an earlier departure before this happened," she interrupted. "We just can't wait to see you and Liss again. And to be on the spot to help my daughter with all the last-minute wedding details."

Phone still to his ear, Dan rested his forehead against the wall. This wasn't a disaster, he told himself. Liss's parents were a nice couple, people he'd known all his life, and they were going to be his in-laws soon. But now that Violet MacCrimmon had abandoned the subject of murder, Dan knew what was coming next.

"Have you ordered your kilt yet?" Vi asked.

After Margaret left, Liss hurried upstairs to change into something suitable for a banquet. It wasn't earmarked as a super-dressy affair, but she felt grubby in the clothes she'd been wearing all day. She slipped into a sleek silk dress that made her feel ultra feminine and took the time to freshen her hair and makeup. She heard the sound of Margaret's car as her aunt headed back to the hotel, but felt no need to rush. She'd be a little late, no matter what.

She'd just come back downstairs when Dan let himself into the house with the key she'd given him. He gave a low whistle of approval when he got a load of her outfit. Liss turned in a circle so he could admire it from all sides. The dress had a demure neckline, but it was red and clingy and he clearly liked what he saw.

"I have to get back to the hotel," she said when she faced him again. "There's a banquet tonight."

Dan frowned. "Can't you give it a pass?"

"I don't want to. After the meal, there's a program. A couple of awards, I think. And a bit of entertainment. There will probably be a tribute to Nola, too. Poor woman. She worked so hard to make this event a reality."

His frown deepened. He wasn't buying her cheerfully given explanation.

"Okay. I confess. I'm not going for the food or entertainment, but I haven't got any plans any-

one—not you, or Gordon, or Sherri—could possibly object to. I just want to observe people's reac-
tions. I imagine everyone knows by now that she's
not just unable to be there." Phoebe Lewis's attempt to keep the news of Nola's death under
wraps had been doomed from the start. "I'll be
like a fly on the wall, and I promise I'll tell Gordon
right away if I notice anything peculiar."

"No, you'll tell me, or Sherri, and one of us will
tell the super trooper."

Liss knew she ought to resent his bossiness, but
she found herself smiling instead. "Fine with me,"
she said. "I'd just as soon not talk to Gordon
again." She went up on her tiptoes to kiss Dan on
the mouth. "So, are you giving me a lift out to The
Spruces or am I driving myself?"

"I'll drive," he said. "And I'm sticking with you
for the evening. Come back to the house with me
while I change clothes." He was wearing jeans and
a sweatshirt, hardly banquet attire.

A few minutes later, Liss was sitting on the bed
in Dan's room while he burrowed in the closet for
dress pants and a good shirt. It was not the first
time she'd been there, but it always seemed a little
strange to her. Dan hadn't always owned this
house. He'd only bought it a few years back. Long
ago, when Liss had been growing up in Moosetookalook, this had been her family's home. Dan's
bedroom had been the one her parents slept in.

"I wonder if I should give Mom and Dad a call.
They both knew Nola when they were young, although Dad was older and Mom was a couple of
classes behind her."

Dan turned, his selections in hand and a peculiar expression on his face. "Uh, no need. They already know what's going on."

She narrowed her eyes at him. "Come again?"

After he'd filled her in on his conversation with her parents, Liss couldn't decide which news bothered her more—that Dolores Mayfield had phoned her parents or that they'd changed their plans and would be arriving in Moosetookalook ahead of schedule.

"I know it's awful of me, but I don't think I can cope with my mother right now."

"Cheer up," Dan said. "It will take them the best part of a week to drive here."

"Still too soon." She loved her parents, but she'd inherited her tendency to meddle from her mother. Long distance, she could tolerate all those helpful suggestions. Dealing with Violet MacCrimmon in person was an entirely different matter.

"At the moment," Dan said, "I'm not particularly interested in what your folks have planned. I'm more concerned about what you're up to. You may say you're just going to observe, but I know you, Liss." Dressed for the evening, even to a necktie, he sat down next to her on the bed. "What are you really hoping to accomplish by going to this banquet?"

Liss sighed and leaned against him. She didn't want to lie to the man she was going to marry. Reluctantly, knowing full well how he'd react, she gave him the same abridged account she'd shared first with Sherri and then with Margaret—Gordon's confidences; her own rationale for rejecting the murder/suicide theory; her recent discoveries about Nola; and the conclusions she'd drawn from those.

Dan put one hand on each of her shoulders and turned her so that they were facing one another. "Let me see if I've got this straight. You think that because Nola was a ghostwriter for Yvonne, something you can't prove, that Yvonne, or maybe her manager, or maybe both of them acting together, killed Jane Nedlinger, then Nola, to keep them from telling anyone? What kind of sense does that make, especially for killing Nola? If you're right, Yvonne needed her to write more books."

"That's what Sherri said, too, but what if Nola found out they'd killed Jane? What if she threatened to tell the authorities?" When another possibility suddenly occurred to her, Liss felt her eyes go wide. "Or maybe Nola was the one who told Jane about the ghostwriting in the first place."

Dan gave her a hard look. "Nope. She appears to be sane. Must be something contagious about the mystery conference. Is there a prize for coming up with the wildest scenario?"

"I'm serious, Dan." He couldn't doubt that she was in earnest, but he might indeed be questioning her sanity. She didn't let that stop her from expanding on her newest theory. "Nola knew what Jane's blog was like, but she sent her information about the First Annual Maine-ly Cozy Con anyway. And a copy of Yvonne's latest book."

"Don't you mean Nola's latest book?"

Liss ignored the sarcasm. "Who's to say Nola didn't do more? It makes a terrible kind of sense. Nola must have been sick and tired of always stay-

ing behind the scenes while Yvonne was in the
spotlight, praised for her writing and raking in
both royalties and honors. It's a really big deal to
make the *New York Times* bestseller list. Maybe that
was the final straw. Nola must have—"

Dan shut her up by the simple expedient of kissing her. Hard.

"What was that for?" Not that she minded. Not
really. Dan was a heck of a good kisser.

"It was either kiss you or tie you up and gag you.
How about we skip the banquet and spend the
evening right here?"

"Nice try, but no." She squirmed out of his embrace and stood. "And now I have a secondary reason for sticking to my plans—I want to impress on
a certain stubborn man that he can't run my life
for me, even if I do love him to distraction. I have
the right to make my own decisions. And my own
mistakes. You should be happy I chose to confide
in you instead of keeping everything to myself!"

She had to give Dan credit. He did not take the
opening to remind her of just where some of her
past mistakes had led her. In her heart, she knew
he was right to worry about her. She had a history
of not leaving things well enough alone. Still, it
galled her to do nothing when she genuinely
thought she might be able to help. And she would
go straight to Gordon with anything she stumbled
across. Or, at the very least, she'd ask Sherri to pass
the information along.

"If we're going to do this," Dan said, "then let's
do it." He heaved himself off the bed but took the
time to look pointedly at his watch. "Are you sure

there's any point in going to the banquet? It must be half over with by now."

"I told Margaret I'd meet her there."

Dan drove her to The Spruces, mostly in silence. He was right on her heels when she reached the ballroom. She entered on a wave of laughter. Apparently the toast-chick had just said something uproariously funny.

Liss located Margaret without difficulty, seated at a table near the middle of the room. She'd saved a chair for Liss, but Dan was out of luck. The round table had places for ten, and the rest of them were occupied by conference attendees.

"You don't have a banquet ticket," she whispered. "You can't stay."

He scanned the immediate area, but there wasn't an empty chair to be seen. "I'll be back," he promised and stalked away.

Liss wondered if she'd find him waiting in the corridor for her at the end of the banquet.

Her first quick visual survey of the ballroom located both Yvonne and Bill. She was onstage with the other luminaries. He occupied a table near the front of the room. Relieved that neither of her suspects had flown the coop, Liss allowed herself to relax and enjoy what was left of the event. She'd missed the meal, but not the entertainment.

Betty Jean Neal, the fan guest of honor, had taken the podium. "I've met a lot of mystery writers," she began, "mostly because I've been high bidder at charity auctions at other conferences. So far, I've won the right to name characters in four books, and one of my best friends is up to three.

This friend, who wants to remain anonymous, doesn't always choose her own name. One time she asked the author to name a character after her mother-in-law. Unfortunately, Ms. Mother-in-Law ended up as a hooker and was killed off on page three. You got your money's worth out of that one, didn't you, Susie?" Betty Jean winked at a woman wearing a yellow name tag and seated at the table closest to the stage. "How long was it before she spoke to you again?"

Good-natured about the ribbing, Susie called out, "Over a year!" When the crowd laughed and applauded, she stood and took a bow.

Aunt Margaret leaned close to Liss to whisper in her ear. "A lot of these people know each other from other fan conferences."

"So it seems."

"More suspects."

"Maybe."

"I've been making a list," Margaret said and pulled a small spiral notebook out of her purse.

Liss wasn't surprised. She'd picked up her list-making habit from spending time with her aunt. Most of the names on Margaret's list were the same ones Liss had written down. As Liss had, Margaret had labeled one page "Jane" and another "Nola." Liss ran a finger down the first list, stopping at "Eleanor Ogilvie."

That was the woman Jane Nedlinger had accosted after she'd talked to Dan at the opening reception. She'd worn a green name tag, indicating that she was a speaker at the conference. Liss had meant to look her up in the program but somehow she'd never gotten around to doing so. Now she tapped Ms. Ogilvie's name with her fingernail and lifted her eyebrows at Margaret in an unspoken question.

The noise level had risen, making conversation in normal voices next to impossible, but Margaret pointed at the next table. Liss recognized the stocky, hard-faced woman sitting there as the same one Dan had pointed out to her, but she was no closer to knowing any more about her.

"Who?" she mouthed at Margaret.

Margaret took back her notebook, fished a pen out of the tiny clutch purse she carried, and wrote, "Agent. Used to be an editor."

Liss wondered what Jane had known about her. After the banquet, she'd try to find out, although the last thing she really wanted was to discover another likely suspect.

She returned her attention to the stage in time to see three of the attending authors rush the podium. To the obvious surprise of the toast-chick, they shouldered her aside and relieved her of the microphone.

"We're here to present the award for worst review of a great book," Blair Somerled announced.

Liss's first reaction, when he held up a napkin-draped object—a statue of some kind, or perhaps a plaque—was to think that this award was in poor taste, considering that Jane Nedlinger, had she lived, might have been a serious contender for the "honor." Then Somerled whipped off the covering to reveal a rather ghastly-looking stuffed pigeon wearing a red hat and a little cape.

A moment of shocked silence was followed by sustained, helpless laughter. The "presentation" was a spoof. Another Maine author, who wrote Elizabethan mysteries—Liss couldn't remember her name—put on a "literary" accent to read the mock review aloud. The text contained every cliché of a badly written negative critique. It even gave away the ending of a fictitious mystery novel titled *Off With Their Bodies!* As soon as she finished reading, the "reviewer"—a scarecrow dressed in a tux—was brought onstage to accept the award.

"A dummy with straw for brains," someone in the audience remarked. "That's appropriate!" And everyone laughed again.

After Blair Somerled made a brief apology to Phoebe, Susie, and the other members of the organizing committee for the high jinks, the third author, someone Liss didn't recognize, turned to the crowd. "Of course this was all in fun," she said, in the manner of a disclaimer. "We're certain any real reviewers among you would never turn out such a feeble attempt at literary criticism." With that, all three left the stage.

"Well, that was the highlight of the conference for me," said a tall redheaded woman sitting at Liss's table. She wiped tears of laughter from her face. "Too funny."

"They'd better hope real reviewers have a sense of humor," Margaret commented.

"The only reviewers likely to be at this conference are those who came here as fans. That means they appreciate humor." The redhead's face split into a broad, toothy grin. "I should know. I am one."

The scheduled program resumed with a brief speech by Yvonne Quinlan as guest of honor. After that, two real awards were presented. One was for service to the local mystery community. It was awarded, posthumously, to Nola Ventress, and accepted on her behalf by a solemn-faced Phoebe. The other was for favorite book by an author attending the conference. Liss vaguely remembered seeing a ballot in her goodie bag but she'd never gotten around to voting. She wasn't surprised when the award went to Yvonne Quinlan for her current best-seller.

Yvonne seemed genuinely surprised and absolutely delighted. "Thank you so much," she gushed. "I've won a few acting awards in the past, but never one for my writing. I'm just so grateful for the recognition, and I promise you that I intend to continue the Toni Starling series for many years to come. I might even reveal a bit about Simon's distant past in the next one."

"Hypocrite," Liss muttered under cover of tumultuous applause.

Her gaze drifted over nearby tables until it came to rest on Eleanor Ogilvie. She looked as if she, too, found Yvonne's claims hard to swallow.

The banquet wound down around ten, but almost everyone in attendance lingered and mingled, chatting with friends or sidling up to authors for one more brush with fame. There were additional panels scheduled for the morning, and a group signing, followed by a tea, but no one seemed in a hurry to call it a night.

"Why do you have Eleanor Ogilvie on your list?" Liss asked Margaret as she set a course to intercept the editor-turned-agent.

"I saw Jane Nedlinger talking to her at the opening reception. They were huddled together when I got back from checking that everything was set to show those classic movies. At that point, of course, I didn't know who she was."

"And who is she?" Margaret's tone of voice made Liss think that Eleanor Ogilvie must be someone important.

"Oh, didn't you know? She's Yvonne Quinlan's literary agent."

Margaret's identification came just as there was a brief diminution in the noise level. Overhearing, Ms. Ogilvie snapped her head around, looking for the person who'd been talking about her. Liss saw no advantage in subtlety.

"I'm Liss MacCrimmon from the dealers' room," she said as she covered the last few feet to Ms. Ogilvie's side, "and this is my aunt, Margaret Boyd, the hotel's events coordinator. I wonder if you'd mind telling us what you talked about with Jane Nedlinger on Thursday evening?"

Her forthrightness earned her a frosty look and an even colder tone of voice. "I don't see where that's any of your business."

"Jane's dead."

"So is Nola, poor woman."

The editor-turned-agent for the actress-turned-writer took another swallow of the drink she carried—a rum and cola by the look of it.

"Can I buy you another drink?" Liss asked. "I'd really like to talk to you."

"I don't discuss my clients. And if you're a writer, I'm not interested in taking on any new ones. I only came here because I owed Nola a favor. I participated in a panel discussion. That paid off my debt."

Margaret stepped in to soothe where Liss had riled. "That was very generous of you and I'm sure that's why Nola always spoke so highly of you."

Liss gave her aunt a sharp look. She hadn't realized Margaret could lie so smoothly.

Eleanor shook her head. "I doubt that. Nola didn't like me much."

"Why not?" Liss asked.

Eleanor drained her glass. "Because back when I was an editor, I rejected her first book."

"*Contract for Murder*?"

"You know it?" Her face was a study in astonishment.

"I read the e-book."

Eleanor's lips pursed in disapproval. Of Nola making her novel available electronically, Liss wondered, or of e-books in general? Then something clicked. "You called it her *first* book. That means you know she wrote others. And I'll bet you know under what name."

The flash of panic in Eleanor's eyes gave her away, although she quickly denied that she had any idea what Liss was talking about.

"So you've had nothing to do with Nola since you left editing to become an agent?"

"I didn't say that." Eleanor's frown turned into a scowl when she lifted her glass and found it empty.

"You were ticked off at Yvonne when she gave her acceptance speech," Liss said. "Did you expect her to acknowledge your contribution?"

Eleanor shrugged and a sardonic smile twisted

her thin lips. "She didn't mention her manager, either."

"And she didn't mention Nola, even though Nola must have been on her mind."

"On her mind? How do you mean?" The panic was back, although once again it was swiftly controlled.

"Nola had just been given an award," Liss reminded her. "It would have been natural to acknowledge her contribution to the conference, if nothing else. Without Nola, Yvonne would not have won that award."

"Yes, I see." Eleanor began to relax. "No conference, no award."

"No Nola, no Yvonne Quinlan novels." Liss leaned in closer and lowered her voice. "I know Nola was Yvonne's ghostwriter. Anyone who reads *Contract for Murder* can see the similarities."

Eleanor drew herself up, looked down a rather large, long nose at Liss, and gave her a withering stare. "I don't know what you're talking about," she said again. Then she turned and strode out of the ballroom.

"Good luck finding a replacement," Liss called after her.

She thought she knew what must have happened. Years ago, for whatever reason, Eleanor Ogilvie had rejected Nola's novel. Later, as an agent, she'd remembered the writing and persuaded Nola, who still hadn't sold anything under her own name, to ghostwrite Yvonne's books. Then Jane had found out about the arrangement. That explained why she'd buttonholed Eleanor, as well as Bill, Yvonne, and Nola, at the opening reception. Jane had been working on two stories simultaneously. One had been about Liss and Moosetookalook. The other had concerned Nola and Yvonne.

"Uh-oh," Margaret murmured. "Your bodyguard is back."

Liss scanned the ballroom for Dan and located him on the far side of the room. He'd been waylaid by Tricia Lynd, one of the hotel employees, but he was staring right at Liss. She waggled her fingers at him and then showed him her back. "This is getting really old, really fast."

"I think it's sweet," Margaret said, "and since he's not keeping an eye on me, I think I'll just slip away and see what I can find."

The look on Margaret's face alarmed Liss. "Find where?"

"In Yvonne Quinlan's suite. I have a passkey."

"Margaret! That's crazy. If you get caught, Joe will fire you."

"It's worth the risk. I've been thinking all evening about what you told me. I won't allow Nola to become a scapegoat. I may be able to find something in Yvonne's belongings that will prove she's the guilty one, just as you suspect."

The crowd was starting to gravitate toward the exit. Margaret joined the herd, working her way closer to the nearest door. Liss looked again for Dan. For the moment, whatever Tricia was telling him had his full attention. Liss seized the opportunity and followed her aunt. The way the conference-goers were milling about, she imagined Dan would have trouble catching up with them, even if he realized right away that they'd left the ballroom.

She found Margaret waiting for the elevator,
surrounded by banquet-goers. Her aunt's inten-
tions alarmed her—and gave her a much better
understanding of why it was that Dan worried
about her so much. And why he tended to turn
bossy when he was concerned about her safety.
Now that she was experiencing some of those
same fears on Margaret's behalf, she was sorely
tempted to order her aunt to cease and desist.
Only the fact that she knew it wouldn't do any
good stopped her. When the elevator doors
opened, they both got in.

Snooping around at the hotel was not new territory for Liss. Her only qualms came from bringing
Aunt Margaret into the mix. Even though Liss
understood that Margaret felt guilty because she'd
been the one to convince Nola to hold the conference in Moosetookalook, she'd never expected
her aunt to show such a determined streak.

For a miracle, they boarded the elevator before
most of the conference-goers left the banquet and
descended on it. And Dan was nowhere in sight as
the doors slid shut. There were eight other people
crowded into the car. Liss didn't know any of
them, but their presence gave her an added reason not to spend the short ascent trying to talk
Margaret out of her plan. If she was honest with
herself, she wasn't sure she wanted to. It would be
very nice indeed if they could find proof that
Yvonne was guilty of two murders. She remained
silent as she followed her aunt down the third-
floor hallway and watched her insert her master
key in the lock of Yvonne Quinlan's suite.

"I've been thinking about Nola ever since I left

your house earlier this evening," Margaret said when they were safely inside. "I owe it to her memory to clear her name and to see that she gets credit for the novels she wrote. That's the least I can do."

Liss studied her surroundings—a two-room suite with clothes scattered here and there and a complimentary fruit basket on the table. "What exactly are we searching for? It doesn't seem likely we'll find a diary with an entry reading *I did it. I pushed Jane off the cliff and then I did the same to Nola.*"

This was a bad idea, she thought. A really bad, really stupid idea. They were going to get caught. They needed to get out now.

But Margaret was already heading into the bedroom. "You search the drawers in the armoire that holds the television set," she suggested, "and the desk."

Unless she thunked her aunt on the head and dragged her bodily out of the suite, they weren't going anywhere until Margaret was satisfied she'd done her best to exonerate Nola. Resigned to helping, if only to speed things along, Liss joined, rather perfunctorily, in the search.

Free books from a conference goodie bag were neatly stacked on top of the desk, next to what looked like the script for a new television series. The desk drawer contained only hotel stationery and an HBO program guide. The rest of the living room yielded nothing more interesting than a bra discarded behind the couch. Liss couldn't help but notice that it was of the padded variety. She joined Margaret in the bedroom just as her aunt opened the door to the closet.

"Oh, Liss—good. Help me get this suitcase down."

Liss lifted it off the shelf. It wasn't locked, probably because it contained nothing but dirty laundry.

"I've been watching and listening to Yvonne Quinlan all evening," Margaret said, "and thinking about things I've heard her say in the course of the weekend. I think she may have managed to convince herself that she did write all those books. That means it will be a terrible blow to her ego if she's forced to admit that she didn't."

Halfheartedly, Liss checked the contents of the bathroom while her aunt continued to riffle through the actress's possessions. "So you think she might have killed two people to keep her secret?" Even though that had been her own theory in the beginning, Liss was starting to have doubts. Like Nola, Yvonne was much smaller than Jane. She'd have had a hard time tossing the bigger woman over the edge.

"Sometimes it doesn't take much to provoke murder." Aunt Margaret bent over to peer under the bed. Finding nothing, she turned to look at Liss. "And wouldn't a privileged, indulged actress be just the sort of person to think she was above the law? However, the more I consider the situation, the more I think someone else might have acted on her behalf."

"The faithful guard dog, Bill," Liss murmured. His career depended upon Yvonne's continued success, too.

But Sherri had made a good point earlier. Would book sales really have been damaged by Jane's revelation? Liss doubted it. Still, it didn't matter what she thought, or even what the truth was. It only mattered what Yvonne . . . or Bill . . . believed.

Just what was their relationship? Liss wandered over to the window and looked out, but she didn't see the view of lawn and trees. Her gaze was turned inward as she wondered if fear of potential loss of income could have been enough to motivate Bill Stotz to kill. If there was something personal between him and Yvonne, that would up the ante. But—Sherri's objection again, and Dan's, too—getting rid of Nola would be killing the goose that laid the golden eggs. The success of the mystery novels depended upon her talent.

Liss let the curtain fall into place once more and started back across the room. She stopped at the crinkle of paper beneath her foot and reached down to pick up what she'd stepped on. It was a green chewing gum wrapper. One of Bill's. Bill had been in Yvonne's bedroom since the last time the suite had been cleaned.

Margaret seized the wrapper. Her mouth curved into a grim but satisfied smile. "Well," she said. "This settles it. We have to search Bill's room next."

Chapter Thirteen

"We don't have time," Liss insisted as she followed her aunt back into the hallway. "We're pressing our luck as it is."

"Piffle. Yvonne's the star of the conference. Her fans will keep her busy for a while yet, and Bill Stotz sticks to her like glue. They're probably down in the lounge."

Liss gritted her teeth, marshaled a new argument, and stifled it when she saw that the elevator was about to stop at their floor. Margaret gave a guilty start when the doors opened to reveal Yvonne and Bill. Liss forced herself to remain calm. There was no reason for Yvonne to think they'd been in her suite, but she stepped back, giving the couple a wide berth.

Recognizing her, and no doubt remembering the scene in the bookstore, Bill frowned as he guided Yvonne out of the elevator with a hand on her elbow. The actress ignored Liss completely—or so Liss thought until she boarded the elevator and looked back the way she'd come.

Yvonne Quinlan had turned her head to glare, her eyes filled with loathing. She looked as if she wished she could make herself into the vampire she'd portrayed for so many years and take a large and fatal bite out of Liss's neck.

The elevator doors closed. Margaret mimed wiping sweat from her brow. "She looked seriously annoyed. You don't suppose she'll guess we searched her suite, do you?"

"She's still pissed off about what I said to her at Angie's Books. I think you may be right, that she's convinced herself she really did write all those novels. If that's the case, then I must have offended her very deeply."

The elevator stopped on the second floor.

"Oh, no," Liss objected. "We're not—"

Margaret stepped off and headed down the corridor.

"Margaret, this is insane."

"He'll stay with Yvonne for a while yet." She sounded confident. "Maybe even all night. When will we have a better opportunity to search his things?"

"I've got a bad feeling about this," Liss said, but she followed her aunt into Bill Stotz's hotel room.

They hadn't even begun to search when the door opened behind them and a man walked in. It wasn't Bill Stotz. It was worse. It was Dan.

Dan couldn't believe his eyes. Or rather, he could. He just didn't want to.

"Out," he ordered, his voice a low, threatening growl, "or I'll call the cops on you myself."

Margaret's cheeks turned a bright, embarrassed pink. Liss just looked exasperated.

"No, you won't," she said. "You don't want the bad publicity."

For a moment Dan saw red, but he quickly harnessed his temper. He was more frustrated than angry. And, as usual, Liss had scared the daylights out of him with her impulsive behavior. She was going to turn him gray before his time with her antics, and she'd never learn patience. He resigned himself to a lifetime filled with edge-of-the-seat moments like this one. His future wife simply wasn't the type who could sit back and let other people handle things, not even when those other people were duly authorized officers of the law.

"I have to admit that you two don't look like typical housebreakers," he admitted.

They were both dressed to the nines, or what passed for the nines in rural Maine. Dan couldn't remember when he'd last seen either of them in high heels or wearing so much makeup. Heck, he rarely saw anyone in Moosetookalook sporting anything but the most casual clothing. Most folks looked on a nice pair of slacks and a dress shirt or frilly blouse as putting on the dog. He didn't count the outfits Margaret had always worn when she was working at Moosetookalook Scottish Emporium. She'd just been modeling the merchandise, wearing a lot of long tartan skirts to showcase items she had for sale.

He caught a whiff of flowery perfume—something else Liss rarely wore—as she stepped past him into the hall. He was surprised she didn't realize—since she read so many crime novels—that she'd leave some of that fragrance behind, proof that an intruder had been in Stotz's hotel room during his absence.

Margaret dawdled, checking the drawer in the bedside table before she finally obeyed Dan's order to leave.

"I don't know why I put up with this nonsense," Dan muttered as he shepherded both women down the corridor in the direction of the stairs he'd used to reach the second floor. The elevators had been too slow for him, crowded with conference-goers on their way back to their rooms after the banquet. When he'd come out of the stairwell a few minutes earlier, he'd been just in time to see Margaret insert her passkey into the lock of a guest room door.

"You love me," Liss said in reply to his rhetorical question. "People in love put up with a lot from each other."

"You needn't sound so smug about it."

She stopped, turned, and threw her arms around him, hugging him tight. "I'm sorry, Dan. I know I promised to stay out of trouble, but—"

"It was all my fault," Margaret cut in. "I was determined to conduct a search, and Liss thought it would be safer if she came with me."

"So that both of you could get yourselves killed instead of just one?" Dan asked.

"So you *do* think we're onto something?"

Margaret sounded so elated that Dan hastily revised his analysis of the situation. Maybe it *was* Liss's aunt who'd been the instigator. This time.

"Did you find something?" he asked.

"Gum wrapper," Liss said succinctly, digging it

out of a tiny bag on a long thin chain. She'd slung it crossways to free her hands, an odd look with the slinky red dress and high heels. "Spearmint," she added, holding it up.

"Okay. So what? You already knew that Stotz is a gum chewer."

"I picked this up in Yvonne's room."

"So Bill shared a stick with her. Big deal."

"I think he shared a lot more than a stick of gum. I found this in her bedroom."

"The fact that they may or may not be having an affair doesn't make either of them a murderer." Even for someone with Liss's imagination, that seemed a leap.

"You're forgetting that another of these same gum wrappers was found at Lover's Leap."

"And you're forgetting that it could have been lying there for days. Jane and Nola and whoever was with them, if there even was anyone else with them, are hardly the only people who've ever been up there."

Dan could remember a few steamy evenings at the site himself, back when he'd been fifteen or so and leery of bringing a girl home. His mother had still been alive then. She'd had a strict rule about no girls in his bedroom.

"Time is getting short," Margaret said when they reached the foot of the stairs. "They're all leaving tomorrow. The conference attendees *and* the guest of honor."

"And I'm sure the police can track them down if they need to. It's time to go home, ladies, and leave sorting this out to the people who know what they're doing."

"Gordon still thinks it's a case of murder/suicide, that Nola killed Jane and then took her own life out of guilt and remorse," Liss reminded him. "What if thinking that way keeps him from looking at the other possibilities?"

"Tandy's good at his job," Dan said, albeit grudgingly. He had to give credit where credit was due. "Trust him to do it right. Now, not another word about it. Either of you. Go home, Margaret, and stay out of trouble. And you—" He was pretty sure that another kind of heat shone in his eyes when he glared at his fiancée. "What you need is a distraction."

Dan could tell she was receptive to that idea. He also knew there was a smart comeback on the tip of her tongue. Before she could utter a single word, her cell phone rang.

"I thought you had that thing turned off. Let it go to voice mail." Dan entertained a brief fantasy that involved sweeping Liss up into his arms, carrying her to his truck, and taking her away to someplace where they wouldn't even have to think about murder, let alone try to do anything about it. It occurred to him that they could catch a flight to Las Vegas tonight and be married by this time tomorrow.

"I did turn it off earlier." Unaware of his flight of fancy, Liss fished the small cell phone out of her tiny purse, giving him a brief glimpse of the rest of the contents—her house key, a lipstick, and a couple of tissues. "I turned it back on thinking I might need to call for help in a hurry if—"

She broke off when she looked at the caller ID. Dan shifted until he was close enough to see the readout over her shoulder. The incoming call was from the Carrabassett County Sheriff's Office.

"You don't have to answer."

"Yes, I do. It might be important."

Since cell phone reception was better outdoors, Liss shoved open the door that led to the floodlit parking lot behind the hotel, the one used by employees. Margaret had gone on ahead of them and was already backing out of her space. She and Liss exchanged waves and Margaret drove off. Only then did Liss answer her phone.

She paced while she listened to whoever was on the other end of the line and occasionally replied with a monosyllabic mumble. Mostly the conversation consisted of long silences on her part. The look on her face worried Dan. It combined disbelief with incredible sorrow. She'd gone pale, too. Whatever she was hearing, she was having a hard time accepting it.

At last she disconnected. "That was Stu Burroughs," she said. "He's in jail. He says he killed Nola."

Liss had never been to the Carrabassett County Sheriff's Office and Jail in Fallstown before, even though Sherri had once been a dispatcher there and Pete still worked for the county as a deputy sheriff. It was a long, low brick building with bars on the windows and a well-lit parking lot. Inside, a tiny lobby funneled visitors straight to a glassed-in area. On the other side was the dispatch center.

"I'm here because Stuart Burroughs phoned me," Liss informed the uniformed female who came to the window. She was a motherly-looking person, a bit on the plump side, but her expression was better suited to a junkyard dog.

"So, you were his one phone call, huh? Sit yourself down, then. Someone will be out to talk to you in a minute."

They settled into hard plastic chairs, the kind designed to discourage long stays. Five minutes passed, then ten. It was going on fifteen before Liss heard a loud click, the sound of a door being remotely unlocked, and Gordon Tandy stepped out of the secure area into the jail lobby.

Liss shot to her feet. "Did you talk to Stu? What did he say? Did he really push Nola off Lover's Leap?"

Gordon ignored her question and spoke to Dan. "I thought you were going to keep her out of this."

Dan's shrug spoke volumes. "I could hardly stop Stu from calling her."

To Liss's annoyance, they locked gazes for another full minute, as if they were silently exchanging ideas about how to control her actions. Finally, Gordon answered her question. "Stu Burroughs did not kill anyone, but only because he crashed his car into a tree instead of hitting another vehicle or a pedestrian. He was arrested for drunk driving. The bail commissioner isn't going to let him out until tomorrow, so you may as well go back home."

"But Stu said—"

"Yeah, I know what he said." Gordon ran his hand over his short-cropped hair and stared at the ceiling. "I interviewed him. What he *meant* was that he feels responsible for Nola's suicide. It seems they had a big fight yesterday at the hotel. He thinks she killed herself over some of the nasty things he said to her, and he's upset because he didn't really mean them. He was just trying to pay her back for abandoning him all those years ago."

"He's probably been carrying a torch for her since she left." Liss found that possibility both wonderfully romantic and heartbreakingly sad.

"Get a grip, Liss. Next you'll be saying that they quarreled because he asked her to marry him and she turned him down." Dan looked faintly disgusted by the idea.

"If that were the case, it would have been Stu who took the header off the cliff," Gordon said.

Liss glared at them both. "Whatever his reasons, Stu was terribly upset by Nola's death. He was drinking heavily all last night and into this morning." And after she'd left him all but passed out in his kitchen, he'd apparently slept off his first drunk and started on a second.

"You're partly right," Gordon grudgingly admitted. "He had a lot of unresolved feelings. It ticked Stu off that Nola accepted her ex-husband's offer to take her back to the hotel on Thursday night instead of going with him."

Gordon's stance was rigid, his face a mask, but Liss couldn't help but wonder if he was seeing parallels between Stu's disappointment in love and his own rejection when Liss decided to marry Dan. Of course, the situations were nothing alike, but she felt her cheeks grow warm all the same.

The three of them nearly filled the claustrophobically small lobby, but Gordon had not suggested they move into a meeting or interrogation room to continue their discussion. That meant he didn't intend to spend very long talking to them. Liss told herself she was relieved, but she still had questions.

"What happened when Stu and Nola met on Friday at the hotel?" she asked. "I know they quarreled and Nola was upset, but what did they say to each other?"

For a moment, she didn't think Gordon would answer her. She imagined he had to wage a brief but violent struggle with himself—not that she could see any evidence of such a thing in his stony countenance—before he relented.

"Stu taunted Nola with her lack of success. According to him, she had big plans and none of them materialized."

"He was wrong about that. Sort of."

"So I hear." Gordon sent a speculative look her way. "Been talking to Sherri, have you?"

Liss ignored the question. "After Nola's death, when Stu got good and drunk and maudlin, he must have decided that his taunts had driven her to kill herself. He didn't give her enough credit. She was stronger than that. And more successful, too."

"And maybe she was already distraught about something else," Gordon suggested.

"Guilt-ridden, according to your hypothesis, because she'd killed Jane Nedlinger? I don't think so."

"Let's just agree that Nola Ventress didn't kill herself because of Stu Burroughs. I've already informed him of that." Gordon's stiff formality eased for a moment when he added, "He wasn't as grateful as you'd think he'd be for that information. Then again, he's still pretty soused."

"Can we talk to him?" Liss asked.

"No."

"But I'm the one he called. If he'd used his one phone call for a lawyer, you'd let the lawyer in to see him."

"You're not a lawyer. However, if you want to be the one to pick him up tomorrow, I'll have dispatch call you just before he's released. His car's totaled, so he's going to need a ride."

Liss felt a headache coming on. She was already supposed to be in two places at the same time in the morning—the dealers' room and Lenny Peet's funeral. Splitting herself three ways just wasn't possible. "I'll find someone to come for him. Will you tell him that?"

"I'll see that he's informed." Gordon turned away, heading for the heavy, reinforced door that led back to the dispatch center.

"Will you also *inform* him of something else while you're at it?" Liss called after him. "Tell him I don't think Nola killed herself at all."

A spin on his heel and two quick strides brought them toe-to-toe and face-to-face. Liss took an involuntary step backward, bumping into one of the plastic chairs that were the only furnishings in the minuscule lobby. Gordon's face was no longer impassive. Temper sparked in his eyes and his mouth was set in a hard, thin line . . . until he opened it to yell at her.

"Damn it, Liss! I'm not going to go putting ideas into his head. The next thing you know, Stu will be trying to play detective. Bad enough that you are."

"I'm not—"

He silenced her with a look that promised retribution if she interrupted him again. "I'll be at The Spruces tomorrow. And, yes, I am pursuing other possibilities. I know damned well Sherri's just passing on ideas you've come up with. If something pans out, I'll be grateful. But if I even suspect that you're meddling in police business again, you'll be sitting in a jail cell, just like your pal Stu, waiting for someone to bail you out!" This time, when he turned away, he signaled for the dispatcher to unlatch the door the moment he reached it. It closed behind him with a solid thunk.

"There's no point in denying it, you know," Dan said as they walked back to his truck. "You can claim you only went along with Margaret to keep her out of trouble, but I know better and so do you."

"Is it so wrong that she doesn't want to see her friend blamed for something she didn't do? I can't help but sympathize with that." And nobody wanted a murderer to go free.

"I'm not going to argue with you about it," Dan said.

"Fine with me." She was too exhausted and discouraged to have much fight left in her.

They accomplished the drive back to Moosetookalook in contemplative silence. Dan parked in his own driveway and walked Liss back to her house, but when she would have said good night to him and gone inside alone, he slung an arm around her shoulders and went in with her.

"You're not going to be able to sleep," he predicted. "You're going to stay up, going over your lists, hoping you'll think of something the police haven't. Why don't you let me take a look at them with you? Maybe you can use me as a sounding board. Who knows? We might even come up with a solid lead."

"To tell Gordon? Do you really think he'd listen? He'll be too busy throwing me in the slammer. That'll really make his day."

Dan ignored her mini-rant and the long-suffering sigh that followed. He simply hung around until she did what he wanted. They settled down on the sofa, one cat on his lap and the other behind Liss's head, and Liss handed over her lists. He started with the page that listed all the people Jane Nedlinger had talked to and/or threatened at the opening reception.

"Bill Stotz," Dan read aloud. "Yvonne Quinlan. Me. Who's Eleanor Ogilvie?"

"She's the woman Jane talked to after she finished interrogating you," Liss reminded him. "Remember? You pointed her out to me the next day." At least, she thought it had been the next day. Events were beginning to run together in her mind. She shook off her lethargy and explained how Eleanor, the editor who was now an agent, was connected to both Nola and Yvonne.

"Okay," he said. "Then you've listed Nola. You left yourself off the list. Anyone else?"

"No one else that I know of talked to Jane Nedlinger that night. And that makes sense. The names on my list all fit into one of two stories Jane was writing. You and I represent one exposé. Bill, Yvonne, Eleanor, and Nola were connected to the other."

"But there *were* others," Dan mused. "Didn't Tandy tell you that he found some of Jane's notes in Nola's room?"

Liss nodded. "I've been assuming she deliberately left the ones about me behind, and she'd have destroyed anything relating to her, so if there were notes left for Gordon to find, they must have been about other people at the conference. There could be someone here we haven't even thought of who wanted Jane Nedlinger out of the way."

"Tandy has their names. He'll have checked them out."

"Yes. Good. That's good." She fought a yawn.

Frowning, Dan skimmed over the local names on her list—members of the Moosetookalook Small Business Association who'd attended the emergency meeting at Liss's house. "We can't discount anyone who knew Nola from before. Who knows what enemies she made when she lived in Moosetookalook? But with Jane's murder in the mix, I think we can narrow things down a bit."

"Wonderful choices there—your father, my aunt, Stu, and Doug."

"Too bad Lorelei Preston wasn't at the meeting. She strikes me as the jealous type. She wasn't happy to hear that her husband had spent time with his ex-wife."

"She didn't even know Nola was in town until we told her," Liss reminded him, "and that was after Nola was already dead. Besides, she'd have had no reason to kill Jane."

"I agree, but I'm trying to keep an open mind. Do you suppose there's any way we can include Dolores Mayfield among the suspects? She knew

Nola before, and she wanted very badly to talk to her on the day Nola died."

"About the class reunion," Liss recalled.

"So she said. What if Dolores wanted to see Nola for some other reason?"

"You think she had murder on her mind? Why?" Liss was just groggy enough from lack of sleep to give serious consideration to the suggestion. Hadn't Margaret mentioned something about Moose Mayfield having had a bad case of puppy love for Nola Ventress?

Dan shrugged. "Who knows? But Dolores had a link to Jane, too. She talked to her at the library on Thursday."

"Dolores doesn't kill people," Liss muttered. "She just talks them to death. Besides, knowing Dolores, she'd be the last person to want to get rid of Jane. She was probably hoping she'd be quoted in *The Nedlinger Report.* It would make more sense to suggest Davy Kline as a suspect."

"Davy Kline?" Dan needed a moment to place the name. "You mean the kid who found Jane's body?"

"If Gordon can suspect me just because I found Nola, then I can put Davy Kline on my list."

"He's what, twenty? He probably still has trouble telling the difference between the blood and gore in video games and real death."

"And you're *so* much older." But thinking about Davy, picturing him, sobered her. "He came to the conference with his invalid mother. Someone said she has a heart condition. Anyway, he sticks close to her, taking her wherever she wants to go, pushing her in a wheelchair."

"Altruistic?"

"He did climb down the goat track to try to help Jane. If he's accustomed to taking care of his mother, he probably has some training in first aid."

"My father said he recognized Jane. Do you know how?"

"He'd seen her at the reception."

"Seen her? Or talked to her?"

The realization that Dan was not only taking her seriously but also making suggestions—getting *involved*—gave Liss a second wind. Her brain began to function at full capacity again. "I don't know, but I think I should find out." She took back her lined tablet, turned to a fresh page, and scribbled a note to herself. There was one day left of the First Annual Maine-ly Cozy Con. Chances were good that Davy and his mother would pay another visit to the dealers' room. If not, she could waylay him at the tea, the last event of the day.

Flipping back to the list of people who might have wished to harm Nola, Liss made a few revisions. When she was done, she'd circled five names. Four were people who'd also had reason to dislike Jane.

"Bill and Yvonne, because of the ghostwriting thing," Dan said, studying the list. "Not Eleanor?"

"I don't think so. But add her if you like."

"Stu and Doug," he read. "But they didn't exactly hate Nola. It was more like she was the one who got away. The lost love."

"There's always the 'if I can't have her, nobody can' motive," Liss reminded him. "Plus love and hate sometimes get all mixed up. And both Stu and Doug have tempers."

"Okay. Leave them on the list. Who's Phoebe Lewis?" He pointed at the last name Liss had circled.

"She was Nola's second in command. I overheard them quarreling over conference business. My take is that Nola may have been charming to most people, but she treated Phoebe like dirt and Phoebe resented it. She did all the grunt work while Nola took all the credit."

"That's a pretty poor reason to push someone off a cliff."

"Is there any *good* reason?" Liss rubbed her forehead. Her headache was back, more fierce than it had been earlier. "The best scenario I can come up with involves Yvonne and Bill acting together, because the same argument I have against Nola killing Jane applies to Yvonne acting alone, as well. Jane was a big woman. Yvonne isn't as tiny as Nola was, but she's so slender she looks as if a good breeze could blow her away."

"I wonder," Dan said, "who was working the check-in desk Thursday night? Whoever it was might have seen Jane leave the hotel, and maybe who she was with, too."

Asking someone who'd know seemed so obvious Liss could have kicked herself for not thinking of it before. She supposed that Gordon had already thought to do so, but it wouldn't hurt for Dan—the boss's son—to make his own inquiries. She wrote herself a note about that, too. Then she turned to the page where she'd sketched out a time line.

"One big problem with figuring this out," she said, "is that just about anyone could have killed

Jane. As for Nola, anyone who was at the hotel that afternoon could have slipped away and followed her along the cliff path, just as I did."

"I don't like to think about that. The murderer could still have been in the vicinity when you found Nola's body."

"Then I'd have met him—or her, or them—on the path. Unless he, she, or they took the trail that comes out on Spruce Avenue and walked up the drive to get back to the hotel."

"Or into town," Dan added, playing devil's advocate.

"In any case, I didn't see anyone. Nola was probably already dead by the time I started looking for her. Yvonne or Bill weren't at the auction, but Doug was there and Stu—" She broke off, shaken by a memory.

"Stu what?"

"Stu came in late. He was out of breath. You don't suppose . . . ?"

"No, I don't. First of all, Stu is often late. That he was on time for the MSBA meeting on Friday was the exception to the rule. Second, if he'd killed her, he'd have confessed to it when he was arrested, instead of just rambling on about suicide. Who else did you see at the auction before you went to look for Nola?"

"Margaret. She was the one who asked me to find Nola. And—oh, you'll like this—Dolores and Moose."

He cracked the ghost of a smile.

"But I keep coming back to Yvonne and Bill, who weren't there. And when you add in the gum wrappers—"

"Which are pretty darned common. You can't build a case based on litter. Besides, if they were acting together, don't you think one of them would have been smart enough to make sure they didn't leave any evidence behind?"

Liss mulled over what he'd said, but she had a clear picture in her mind of the two of them ganging up on Jane and pushing her over. "She was a big woman," Liss mused. "It would have taken considerable strength to shove her hard enough so she'd fall and break her neck."

Dan hid a yawn behind his hand. "Pushing someone off a cliff seems like a pretty dumb way to commit murder. People can survive falls like that."

"That's what Gordon said, too. I suppose they hoped it would look like an accident. And it did, at first."

"Me, I think I would have broken her neck *before* she went over the side, just to make sure she died."

Liss stared at him, suddenly reminded of a scrap of conversation in the dealers' room, a careless comment that hadn't made any real impression on her at the time. "Oh my God," she whispered. "She wouldn't have needed help, after all."

"Who wouldn't?"

"Yvonne Quinlan. She was a stuntwoman before she was an actress. She all but came right out and told me that she knows exactly how to break someone's neck."

Chapter Fourteen

On Sunday morning, Liss awoke slowly. She was reluctant to get out of bed. She had so many things to do in the next few hours that she was tempted not to do any of them. She had not slept well. She didn't remember much about her dreams, but they'd definitely included an enraged Yvonne Quinlan, showing fang and gleefully snapping necks. Far-fetched? Only the vampire part.

She forced herself to sit up. The first order of business was to ask Dan to drive to Fallstown and bring Stu back to Moosetookalook. He could leave right after Lenny Peet's funeral, which was scheduled for nine that morning. It was an odd time for such a thing—right before Sunday church services—but that was apparently what Lenny had requested. Liss told herself she should be grateful. She'd only be an hour late getting to the dealers' room.

The smell of coffee drifting up from the kitchen told her that Dan had been up for a while and explained why the cats weren't still in bed with her.

She decided she could get used to having someone make coffee for her in the morning. Maybe
Dan would agree to do it every day after they were
married. On that cheerful thought, she dragged
herself out of bed and into the shower.

Brain and spirits both revived under the influence of hot water, soap, and shampoo, but that
meant Liss remembered more things she had to
do. There was the matter of Lenny Peet's dog, for
one. Skippy was still incarcerated at the animal
shelter. She had to find him a new home. She wondered if Stu could be persuaded to adopt a pet.

She needed to talk to Doug, too. Not about
Skippy. And not about Nola, either. There was no
point in dredging up what must be painful memories for him. But she'd promised herself that she
would take the funeral director to task over his
son's cavalier treatment of Lenny's remains. She
couldn't let that go undone much longer. Who
knew how many other bodies the boy, unchecked,
might treat with similar disrespect?

Once she got back to the hotel, she intended to
pursue yet another matter. Minutes after coming
to her stunning conclusion about Yvonne Quinlan
the previous night, she'd recognized the need for
a reality check. Yvonne's Caroline Sweet character,
the vampire, might be able to break necks with her
bare hands, but that might be just another example of the fallacies perpetuated by television and
movies—the sort of thing Nola had regularly
poked fun at in the books she'd written under
Yvonne's name.

Someone at the conference should know. A spe-
cific someone. According to the program, one of

the panels had featured a speaker who was an expert on martial arts. Liss hoped he'd be able to answer her question. And, with any luck, he'd drop by the dealers' room for the group signing after the morning panels or attend the closing tea so she could ask him.

By the time Liss had downed her second cup of coffee and eaten two slices of buttered toast, she'd completed a new list: Things To Do Today.

Dan read silently over her shoulder. He made no comment, but Liss suspected he planned to stick close to her until the conference was over. She was surprised to discover that she didn't mind a bit. Looking back, she realized that the change had come about shortly after their confrontation with Gordon Tandy the previous night. Dan was no longer acting like a bodyguard. He'd become her partner.

At a few minutes before nine, they left the house and crossed the square to the funeral home. Liss wore a simple dark blue pantsuit that was equally appropriate for a memorial service and a tea. Aunt Margaret showed up in one of her tartan skirts and a white blouse with a jabot.

"Lenny was always upbeat," she explained. "If he's looking down on us, I think this outfit will make him smile."

The service had a good turnout. It was simple but moving. The preacher spoke a few words and then invited Lenny's friends to share their memories. When Liss took her turn, she ended her remarks with a pitch for adopting Lenny's dog. "As most of you know, his name is Skippy," she told the crowd. "He's a two-year-old fox terrier, and it would make Lenny very happy to know that he had a good home."

Afterward, when the mourners were still milling about before leaving, she heard Dan's brother, Sam, talking to Pete's mother. "Dogs are great," he said. "My daughter would be lost without Papelbon."

"What kind of name is that for a dog?" Mrs. Campbell asked. "Papelbon is a baseball player, the closer for the Red Sox."

"And your point is? If I remember right, Lenny called the last dog he owned Tatupu." When she looked blank, he added, "Football player, for the Patriots, back when Lenny was younger. It's a fine old tradition to name pets after sports figures."

As Liss looked around for Doug, she wondered who Skippy had been named after.

"I was hoping to speak to your husband," Liss told Lorelei, who was resplendent in a black silk dress that clung just a little too tightly to her lush figure.

"If it's about adopting that dog, we're not interested."

"It's not." Liss debated mentioning Frank Preston's disrespectful attitude to his mother but decided it wouldn't do any good. Better to wait and talk to Doug. Lorelei indulged her only child. When he'd gotten in trouble the previous winter, she'd taken his side against her husband. Instead of being grounded for a month and losing his cell phone and MP3 player for that same length of time, as Doug had proposed, Frank had been deprived of those privileges for only a week.

"I wouldn't mind taking the dog," Betsy Twining

said. "Is Skippy in the animal shelter down to Falls-town?"

While Liss was distracted, Lorelei disappeared into Doug's office. She reappeared a few minutes later, looking disgruntled. Liss didn't bother talking to her again, but she stuck her own head into the office on her way out, expecting to find Doug there. As funeral director, he usually stuck around until all the mourners had left the building. To her surprise, the room was empty.

A glance at her watch warned Liss that she didn't have time to hunt for him. If he was down in the embalming room, she wasn't sure she wanted to find him anyway. Telling him his son was a lout would have to wait. She needed to get out to The Spruces.

Dan drove her to the hotel and escorted her to the dealer's room, then headed for Fallstown to pick up Stu. As promised, someone had phoned Liss before she left for the funeral to let her know that Stu had been able to post bail and was free to return home.

"It's been a dismal morning so far," Angie lamented when Liss slipped behind the Emporium's tables. "It looks to me as if everyone who wanted to buy a book has already done so. Or else they brought books with them to be autographed. Books they probably ordered online at a discount I can't afford to match."

"Cheer up," Liss said. "The group signing starts at eleven. People will come in then. While they're waiting in line, maybe they'll make a few impulse buys."

"Optimist!"

Dan returned while the last panel was still in session.

"How's Stu?" Liss asked.

"He's feeling very, very sorry for himself. And he's ticked off that he wrecked his car."

"He should be grateful he's out of jail."

"Oh, he is, and he seems to have gotten past the idea that he was responsible for Nola's death."

"Gordon probably told him *she's* the murderer," Liss muttered.

"If so, Stu didn't share. When I dropped him off, the only thing he was interested in was crawling into bed and sleeping for a week. He was still pretty hungover."

"Poor Stu." She shook her head. "And to think, for about a half hour last night, I actually believed he might have done it."

"And that's why we leave the detecting to the professionals," Dan said with a grin.

Liss made a face at him. "Did you find out who was working at the front desk on Thursday night?"

"I did. It was Tricia Lynd. I talked to her on the phone a few minutes ago. She worked Thursday night into early Friday morning."

"And?"

"She saw Nola return from the MSBA meeting."

"And?"

"Nola met Jane in the lobby."

"*Nola* did?"

Dan nodded. "Tricia said it looked like they were arguing over something, but she wasn't close enough to overhear what they said."

"Did they leave the hotel together?"

"Tricia says not. Nola took the elevator. Jane

stayed in the lobby a bit longer—she'd been sitting in one of the wing chairs, reading a magazine until Nola got back—then she left in the direction of the stairs. Tricia assumed Nola and Jane had gone up to their respective rooms. She didn't see either of them again."

"What was she wearing?" Liss asked. "Jane. Did Tricia say?"

"Is it important?"

"I don't know."

Dan pulled out his cell phone and hit redial. "Tricia. Sorry to bother you again, but Nancy Drew here has another question for you." He handed the phone to Liss.

Tricia, who was the hotel's only intern, a Jill-of-all-trades with an eye for detail, had exactly the information Liss wanted. She was smiling when she hung up. "Jane was wearing jogging clothes when she talked to Nola."

"So, she didn't change before she went out to the Leap. Maybe she never did go back to her room. But that doesn't really tell us anything we didn't know. In fact, the meeting in the lobby lends credence to Tandy's theory that Nola and Jane met at the Leap and Nola pushed Jane over."

"No. I don't buy it. There's still the problem of relative size. *Nola* never trained as a stuntwoman."

An influx of people signaled the end of the last panels and the start of the group signing. Additional tables had been brought in so that all the attending authors could be accommodated. The dealers' room was packed, but few bought books and no one showed any interest in the items Liss had for sale.

Liss did manage to spot her martial arts expert and lure him over to her table for a quick question. Unfortunately, he wasn't much help. Necks could apparently be broken more easily than she'd thought, but what she'd been thinking of as the "vampire snap" was, if not a Hollywood invention, then at least a skill usually reserved for Green Berets or Navy Seals or other muscular military types.

"But if someone were *trained*," Liss persisted. "Is brute strength a requirement?"

"Well, no," the expert allowed, "but you have to know what you're doing. Why are you so interested in this, anyway?"

Liss shrugged off the question. "Oh, you know— you see that sort of thing on television all the time. Take *Buffy the Vampire Slayer*, for example. The actress who plays Buffy isn't all that big or muscular."

The expert's expression brightened. "I love that show," he admitted. "But I'm pretty sure all the neck breaking is done by vampires. Angel. And sometimes The Master. Buffy pretty much sticks with her trusty wooden stake."

Liss was still mulling over this new information when she spotted Davy Kline and his mother in the line to have author Lea Wait sign books. She turned to Angie. "You want stock signed?" she asked.

"I was hoping the authors would stop by on their way out."

"Why don't I take the books to them?" She was already gathering up copies of Lea's children's books, all of which were set in Maine. When she started to add the volumes in her Shadows mystery series, about a woman who sold antique prints and therefore had reason to travel to antiques fairs and other potential venues for murder, Angie separated out the mass market paperbacks. "Hardbacks and trade paperbacks only."

In short order, Liss was standing behind Davy Kline. When he eased his mother's wheelchair up to the signing table and stepped back, she seized her chance. "You're the one who found the first accident victim, aren't you?"

He slanted her a wary look. "Yeah. But I don't really want to talk about that anymore."

"I understand how you feel. I was the one who found Nola Ventress's body. And what made it worse was that I knew her a little. Had you ever met the woman you found?"

Davy shook his head. "I just saw her around, y'know? I never talked to her."

"At the reception, I suppose?"

"Then, and again later that night."

Liss's interest quickened. She glanced toward Davy's mother and was relieved to see that she and Lea Wait were engrossed in a conversation about the books she'd brought to be signed. "Was this in the hotel?" she asked.

"Sort of."

"Meaning what?"

Davy looked uncomfortable. "When I saw her again, it was around midnight. I couldn't sleep, so I was standing at the window, looking out. They keep the floodlights on all night. Not real bright, but enough to see a little, and my room looks out across a roof. Over a porch, maybe. Anyway, she came out. I'm pretty sure it was her. She was kind of big and dumpy, you know? Easy to recognize.

And she was wearing this jogging suit, which just made her look bigger. Anyway, she walked straight across the grass and disappeared into the woods. I thought that was kind of strange, because it was so late and all."

"Was she alone?"

"Yeah. I didn't see anyone else out there, before or after, and I was there at the window for maybe fifteen minutes altogether. Pretty weird, huh?" He hesitated. "I've been wondering . . . well, you don't think I should have told someone, do you? I mean, an old lady wandering around at night like that— should I have worried that she'd have an accident?" He was looking at his mother as he spoke.

This was a very responsible young man, Liss decided, and one who did not need to be burdened with guilt. "You couldn't have known what would happen. And I can assure you that despite what happened to her, Jane Nedlinger knew what she was doing when she took that walk out to Lover's Leap."

She was willing to bet that Jane had arranged to meet someone there. That was still the only conclusion that made sense. Maybe it had been someone she'd been trying to blackmail, preposterous as that idea had seemed at first. The person she'd met might have been Nola, but Liss was more inclined to put her money on Yvonne Quinlan.

"You're sure you didn't see anyone else out there?" she asked Davy.

"I went back to bed maybe ten minutes after I saw the fat woman," Davy said in a low voice. His mother had started to back her wheelchair away from the signing table. "I didn't sleep well. I never do in a strange bed. That's why I was up early and decided to go jogging." He closed his eyes briefly. "Man, I really wish I'd just stayed in bed."

Liss stood for a moment looking after the young man as he and his mother left the dealer's room. Then she remembered the stack of books she was carrying. "These are for Angie's Books," she told Lea Wait, dumping the whole pile on the table.

"You'll just want my name, then," Lea said, and started signing.

Having once started, Liss felt obliged to continue taking Angie's hardcover stock to the other authors to be signed.

"Not Yvonne Quinlan," Angie said. "She already autographed all the extras while she was still at the store."

That was just as well, Liss decided. Yvonne's body language and facial expression, whenever she happened to look Liss's way, were decidedly hostile.

Following the group signing there was a break before the tea—actually a late luncheon. During that hour, having closed the dealers' room, Liss and Angie and the T-shirt dealer packed up all the items they'd offered for sale. Liss had her stock boxed and ready to load into the back of Dan's truck in record time. When she glanced at her watch, she saw that she still had a half hour to spare before the tea.

She turned to give Angie a hand and froze when she saw that the bookseller was ripping the front covers off one paperback after another and tossing the remains into a nearby trash bin that was already half full of similar discards.

"What are you doing? Those are books!"

"These are *returns*," Angie corrected her. "Titles I over-ordered. They didn't sell. Now they have to go back to the publisher. It's cheaper to send just the cover, and that's all the distributor requires."

Horrified, Liss struggled to make sense of such a system. How could the company that produced the books in the first place encourage their wanton destruction?

"At least I made money on Yvonne Quinlan's signing," Angie said. "Good thing, too. Hardcover books can't be stripped. I'd have had to foot the bill to ship them back to the warehouse."

"It was her popularity as an actress that brought out the fans. I'm surprised some of them *can* read." Making the snarky comment made Liss feel marginally better. Petty of her, she knew, but she'd take comfort where she could. "Stripped" books— what a loathsome concept!

"The woman certainly has had an interesting career," Angie remarked, "even if she did fake part of it."

"Overheard that, did you?"

"It would have been hard not to, since you were in my shop at the time. I've got to say, though, that she sure sounded sincere when she said she wrote her own novels."

"Aunt Margaret thinks she's convinced herself she did."

"Well, I don't suppose it would be the first time an actor got lost in a role," Angie said with a laugh.

Dan let himself into the dealers' room with a hotel passkey and was relieved to find that Liss was

still there. The only way he'd ever come up with to
keep her out of trouble was to stick close to her.
True, his attempt to protect her from herself last
January hadn't worked all that well. Liss had ended
up having to rescue him. But he didn't have any
better ideas, and this time around, she seemed inclined to accept his presence. Maybe being engaged to be married helped. In any case, in a few
more hours, when everyone at the First Annual
Maine-ly Cozy Con had left the hotel and gone
home, he'd be able to relax and worry about
something else—like how to talk the MacCrimmons out of formal Scottish dress as wedding attire.

"Ready to eat?" he asked after they'd loaded her
boxes and most of Angie's into the back of his
truck.

"Always."

"Tea, huh?" They walked back inside together
and headed up to the mezzanine.

"A substantial tea, with sandwiches and little
cakes. And a good crowd, I hope, since they sold
tickets to the general public."

In spite of that warning, Dan was surprised to
see so many Moosetookalook people in attendance. Margaret was there, of course, but so were
Dolores and Moose Mayfield, Doug and Lorelei
Preston, and his own brother, Sam, and his wife.

Dan began to relax as they ate. Liss filled him in
on her conversation with Davy Kline and the information the martial arts expert had given her. He
considered what she told him and came to the
conclusion that Tandy had been right, after all. He
didn't say so to Liss, but it made sense to him. Why

couldn't Nola have been the one to meet Jane at Lover's Leap? She'd been seen talking to Jane just beforehand. And if Nola had taken a self-defense course somewhere along the line, who was to say she might not have been able to counter an attack by a bigger, stronger opponent by using that opponent's own weight against her? He could see that—Nola flipping Jane right off the cliff. Of course he had no idea why Jane might have rushed at Nola, prompting her to defend herself, but he wasn't going to quibble over details. He liked his interpretation of the facts far too much.

If Nola had killed Jane and then committed suicide out of guilt, that meant Liss was safe. If the killer was already dead, there was no threat to his fiancée. She could ask all the questions she liked and no harm would come to her.

But he intended to stick close, just in case he was wrong about that.

When Margaret stopped by their table with the news that Tandy was in the hotel, Dan felt relief rather than irritation. That made a nice change.

"Gordon talked to Yvonne Quinlan this morning," Margaret reported, "and to Bill Stotz and Eleanor Ogilvie. I think he's finally decided to take Liss's theory seriously."

More likely he was just being thorough, Dan thought. Once again, he kept his opinion to himself.

When Margaret had moved on, returning to the table where she'd been sitting with several other local residents, Liss turned to Dan. "I need to talk to Gordon."

"Do you want to end up in jail?"

"He didn't mean that."

"I wouldn't be so sure. Anyway, what can you tell him that he doesn't already know?"

Liss smile looked forced. "He doesn't know I searched Yvonne's room."

"And since he's not likely to dust it for fingerprints, he never will. Leave well enough alone, Liss."

"I suppose he's already talked to Tricia and to Davy Kline."

"I know he questioned Tricia. She told me he did."

"But he came out here and talked to the people he knows I suspect. That means he's keeping an open mind. I wonder why he didn't arrest one of them?"

"Maybe because he was able to rule them out? I'm sure he has good reasons for theorizing that Nola killed Jane and then herself, probably more reasons than he's shared with you."

She leaned toward him across the table, her expression intent. "I agree, but I still don't buy that explanation. I have a viable alternative, one that doesn't involve Nola killing herself in the middle of the conference she spent most of a year planning. The Cozy Con meant too much to her, Dan. I know it did. No matter what—even if she did somehow manage to kill Jane—she'd have stuck it out until today. Until this tea and the closing ceremonies."

"And exactly how are you going to convince him you're right?"

"He doesn't know Yvonne was once a stunt-woman. That information might make a difference." She was already on her feet. "He's probably in the hotel library."

"If you're determined to do this, I'll come with—"

"No." She put a hand on his shoulder and left it there until he resumed his seat. "I need to do this alone. There's something else I want to say to Gordon, too. Something . . . personal. I've had the feeling, the last couple of days, that he and I need . . . closure."

Dan had no argument to offer against the pleading look in her eyes. She'd interpret any further objections on his part as jealousy. As far as he was concerned, the rivalry between himself and the state police detective for Liss's affections had ended the day she'd accepted his proposal of marriage, but if she felt she needed to make that clear to Tandy, so be it. Closure? Yeah, he was all for it if it meant she'd be finished, once and for all, with that chapter in her life.

"I'll be waiting right here when you get back," he promised.

Liss poked her head into the library and found it empty. "Damn," she muttered under her breath. She'd wanted to get this over with, finish it for Nola *and* for herself.

Here she was, all psyched up to set the record straight with Gordon, and he wasn't where he was supposed to be. She considered going straight back to the tea. The closing ceremonies were probably getting started about now. But maybe Gordon hadn't gone far. She tried to think where else he would be. Somewhere in the hotel seemed likely, maybe Nola's room, or Jane's. Or he could be re-interviewing staff members. The gift shop was on her way back to the lobby, so she stopped in to ask Fran Pertwee if she'd seen Gordon.

"Not a single living soul has come in here since well before noon," Fran told her. "I'm thinking of closing up and going home. There's not much sense in Joe paying me overtime to stand around and twiddle my thumbs."

Liss's next stop was the check-in desk. Joe Ruskin hadn't seen Gordon for at least an hour, but he did offer the information that the mobile crime-scene lab was still in the parking lot. "You could ask whoever's in there where Gordon's got to," he suggested.

The state trooper who'd been taking notes when Gordon had interviewed her was alone in the police trailer, but he knew where Gordon had gone. "He was headed out to the crime scene," the trooper said, "to take down the yellow tape."

"I wouldn't think that was Gordon's job," Liss said, surprised.

"Somebody's got to do it, and he wanted one last walk through the site."

Liss glanced at her watch. It would take at least ten minutes to hike out to Lover's Leap, but she'd certainly be able to talk to Gordon in private out there. He'd have to listen to her long enough for her to tell him that Yvonne Quinlan knew how to snap someone's neck with her bare hands. And, once she'd given him that information, she'd offer a long-overdue apology.

She'd taken the coward's way out and had Gordon's brother break the news of her engagement to him. She owed it to him to tell him straight out that she'd chosen Dan over him not only because she loved Dan, although that was the biggest part of it, but also because of the way she acted when she was around Gordon. He, or his profession, turned her into a daredevil. She took risks she shouldn't. It was as if he brought out her competitive nature, and in the worst possible way. She'd almost gotten both of them killed the previous winter, and the killer they'd been chasing *had* ended up dead.

No more Nancy Drew, she vowed as she started across the grass toward the woods. Or Jessica Fletcher. Or Buffy. She'd turn in her deerstalker cap and her magnifying glass, set the record straight between herself and Gordon, marry Dan, and stop meddling.

Closer to fifteen minutes elapsed before she came out of the woods at Lover's Leap. Gordon was nowhere to be seen. That the crime scene tape was gone told her he'd been there. She realized that she'd probably just missed him. Hands on her hips, a little out of breath from her trek through the trees, Liss fumed with frustration and disappointment as she crossed the clearing to the fence. She hadn't bumped into Gordon on the trail on her way in, so he'd no doubt left by way of the path that came out on Spruce Avenue. In all likelihood, he was already back at the hotel. And Dan, concerned that she'd been gone so long, would be worrying and wondering what had happened to her. Oh, this day just got better and better!

She turned when she heard footsteps on the

path behind her. Her first thought was that it was Gordon. He'd talked to his officer, heard she was looking for him out here, and come after her.

But it wasn't Gordon who emerged from the trees.

It was Yvonne Quinlan. She strode into the clearing, her fists clenched at her sides and her face an ugly, mottled red. "You've been spreading your terrible lies about me," she screeched. "I was questioned by the police this morning!"

Hands held out in front of her, palms out, Liss started to back away. After only a few steps, she came up against the fence. A quick glance over and down reminded her just how close to the edge she was.

"You'll be sorry you lied about me!" Yvonne hissed.

There was something feral in the actress's eyes as she came ever closer, stalking Liss like a leopard advancing on its prey.

"Nobody gets away with saying I didn't write my own books," Yvonne said with a snarl. "Not Jane Nedlinger. Not Nola Ventress. And not you!"

Chapter Fifteen

"Dan, have you seen Liss?" Margaret Boyd had a worried look on her face.

"She's off somewhere talking to Gordon Tandy." Dan glanced at his watch. It wasn't the first time he'd done so in the last half hour. She'd been gone longer than he'd expected, but he didn't want to rush her. He wanted her to be done with Tandy once and for all. *Let them hash it out,* he told himself again. *Then it will be over.*

"But Gordon's right there," Margaret said, pointing to the doorway.

The state police detective was obviously looking for someone. When he realized that Dan and Margaret were staring at him, he made his way across the room to them.

"Margaret. Dan. I expected Liss to be here with you."

"She didn't find you?" Dan asked, already halfway out of his chair.

"I didn't know she was looking for me. I walked out to the Leap and came back the long way 'round."

"I'm sure she wouldn't have gone out there after you," Margaret said.

Dan wasn't so certain. If Liss hadn't found Tandy, just where had she gotten to? It shouldn't have taken her more than five minutes to walk from the hotel library to the ballroom where the tea was being held, even if she'd dawdled.

"What did she want, anyway?" Tandy asked.

"Maybe the better question is why were you looking for her?"

Tandy shrugged. "I talked to several people this morning. I thought she might like to know that I cleared up that little matter of the gum wrappers."

"Really?" Margaret looked impressed.

"Some local kids were up at the Leap on Thursday evening around nine. Teenagers looking for privacy. Trust me when I say I've accounted for both the gum wrappers and at least one of the discarded condoms."

"Well, it's nice to know that our young people are practicing safe sex," Margaret said.

Dan and Gordon both stared at her.

"Well, it *is*," she insisted.

Gordon recovered his aplomb first. "Anyway," he said, "I also wanted to assure Liss that I interviewed Bill Stotz, Eleanor Ogilvie, and Yvonne Quinlan. The Quinlan woman wasn't pleased to be questioned about her connection to Nola."

"I don't suppose she admitted Nola was her ghostwriter?" Margaret asked.

"The very idea that she'd need one seemed to infuriate her. But, according to her agent, Liss was right on the money on that one. Nola did write the Toni Starling series."

"Are you telling me that Yvonne Quinlan *did* have a motive to kill those two women?" Dan scanned the crowd, looking for the actress who'd claimed to be a mystery writer. With a growing sense of dread, he realized that she was no longer in the ballroom. In fact, he couldn't remember seeing her since Liss left to hunt for Gordon Tandy.

Liss sidled along the fence, telling herself over and over again not to look down. Maybe fifty feet wasn't that far by some standards, but when seen from this close to the edge of a cliff, it was more than enough to have her stomach knotting and her head swimming. She was hoping to put more distance between herself and Yvonne Quinlan before she turned and made a run for it, but Yvonne kept pace with her.

"Stop!" Liss shouted.

To her surprise, Yvonne did.

"This is nuts," Liss said. "You may have gotten away with killing those two women, but if a third victim is found at the bottom of this cliff with a broken neck, Detective Tandy will figure out what happened."

Yvonne's jaw dropped. "I didn't kill anyone! And I don't want to kill you. I just want you to stop telling lies about me, *before* the press picks up the story."

A wave of relief washed through Liss. For a minute there, she'd really thought she was doomed. A little verbal abuse? That she could handle.

"Look, Yvonne, I've only told a few people about Nola writing your books. I didn't do so with any intent to hurt your career. It was only because that secret gave you a motive to kill both Jane and Nola."

"Who?" Yvonne demanded. "Who did you tell? How many?"

Liss had to think about it. She'd told Sherri and Margaret, Dan and Gordon. Had there been anyone else? She didn't think so. Angie had overheard her accusations when she made them in the bookstore, so she didn't really count. "The state police detective, a Moosetookalook police officer, my fiancé, and my aunt," she said aloud. "That's it, Yvonne. And none of them are likely to blab to the tabloids. We want to keep Moosetookalook and the hotel and ourselves out of the spotlight as much as you want to go on being known as a bestselling author."

The high color in Yvonne's face began to dim and the look in her eyes became more bemused than ferocious. "You thought I was a cold-blooded murderer?" she asked.

"It made sense."

Yvonne went up to the rail, leaned over to look at the drop, and gave a theatrical shudder. "And just how am I supposed to have managed to throw two women off this cliff?"

"You said you were a stuntwoman." Liss was starting to feel foolish.

"That was years ago. What am I—superwoman? I didn't even do my own stunts for *Vamped.*"

"Well, someone killed both of them." Liss still resisted accepting Gordon's murder/suicide solution. There had to be another explanation. "Jane may have arranged for someone to meet her out here in the middle of the night."

Yvonne's eyes widened. "Here? Why?"

"Maybe she just liked to jerk people around, make them jump through hoops. What did she want you to do, Yvonne? Did she ask for a payoff to keep the ugly rumor that you weren't the real creator of Toni Starling and her friend Simon out of her blog?"

"I did create those characters," Yvonne said through clenched teeth. "They were my idea."

And that wasn't quite the same, Liss thought, as writing novels that featured them. "Did Jane make such a threat or not?"

Yvonne affected indifference. "She may have been hinting around about *some*thing I wouldn't want my fans to know, but I ignored her insinuations."

"I thought you said your conversation with her at the opening reception was all about her review of the new Toni Starling novel. Or was that just the story you made up rather than admit that she'd just tried to blackmail you?"

"You just don't quit, do you? Do I have to pay you off, too?"

Stunned, Liss stared at her. "Too? You mean I'm right? You *paid* her?"

Yvonne drummed her fingers on the top rail of the fence and stared out at the view. It was another clear, balmy, sunny day. The vista should have inspired a sense of calm. Instead, Liss tensed and

tried to readjust her thinking yet again. Was
Yvonne a threat to her or not? She couldn't decide, but she thought it might be wise to stop bait-
ing her.

"I don't want anything from you," Liss said after
a moment, "except the truth."

"Fine," Yvonne snapped. "Nola Ventress *assisted*
me in writing the books in the Toni Starling series.
I'm a terrible speller."

And I have a bridge in Brooklyn I'd like to sell you,
Liss thought. She waited for Yvonne to continue.
The silence stretched between them for a long
moment before she did so.

"Jane Nedlinger was a nasty piece of work. She
was intimidating, both physically and in the power
she wielded in her blog, and she knew it. She liked
making people dance to her tune. You're probably
right that she arranged for someone to meet her
out here. But it wasn't me. I had Bill write her a
check. What's the point of having a manager if he
can't handle petty annoyances for me?"

"Maybe Bill did more than write a check. Or
maybe he decided to take steps to avoid writing
one."

Yvonne's lips quirked into a smile. Then she
laughed out loud. "*Bill?*"

"Nice way to talk about your lover."

Yvonne shrugged. "Haven't you ever heard of a
business associate with benefits? The point is, I
know him very well. He's a dynamo in bed and a
barracuda in contract negotiations, but turns into
a wimp when he's up against a force of nature like
Jane Nedlinger."

"Well, *someone* killed her," Liss said.

"Not me." Yvonne leaned against the railing, apparently relaxed.

"Not you," Liss agreed, finally believing it. "And probably not Bill. Or the two of you together. But not Nola, either. Nola just wouldn't have had the strength to toss a woman of Jane's size off this cliff."

"Maybe she had help," Yvonne said. "That's the logical scenario, isn't it? Nola didn't do it alone, and then her partner in crime turned on her and killed her to hide his part in Jane's death."

"Oh, no," Liss murmured. "That couldn't be."

But even as she voiced the denial, she knew Yvonne was right.

Liss had overlooked the most obvious explanation of all, the one that answered every question, but produced one new one—who else had been out here at Lover's Leap that night with Nola and Jane?

There were only two possibilities that Liss could see. One was Stu, but she'd already ruled him out because of his drunken confession. She didn't believe he'd faked his grief or his misplaced guilt.

That left one other.

"Doug," she said aloud. "It had to have been Nola's ex-husband who helped her kill Jane Nedlinger."

"I didn't know she'd ever been married."

Yvonne had been admiring the view and now turned her head to look at Liss as she spoke. A moment later, her gaze shifted and an annoyed expression crossed her face.

"If that's a reporter," she hissed, her narrow-eyed gaze on something behind Liss, "we need to give him the slip."

Liss glanced over her shoulder toward the cliff path. A shadow moved among the trees. Someone was there. Someone who'd been watching them; listening to them. She squinted, trying to get a better look at the dark, sinister-looking figure. There was something familiar about that silhouette.

"That's not a reporter." She knew him now—both his identity and the reason he was skulking about in the woods, spying on them. She grabbed Yvonne's arm. "We need to get out of here. Now."

Before they'd taken two steps toward the section of the trail that would bring them out on Spruce Avenue, a cold, hard voice stopped them in their tracks. "Stay right where you are," it ordered, "or I'll shoot."

Slowly, Liss turned to confront the man who had killed both Jane and Nola. "Why, Doug?" she asked. "Why did you do it?"

Yvonne's willowy body was stiff and her wide, dark brown eyes narrowed once more as she took in the man and the gun in his hand. Then her gaze slid sideways to Liss. "Why is he pointing a gun at us?" she asked.

Liss had to hand it to the actress. She didn't scare easily. Even as a double murderer advanced on them, armed and dangerous, Yvonne used both hands to smooth back her short cap of blue-black hair with its purple highlights and then slid easily into the role she'd played for so many years on television—the haughty, self-confident, *immortal* Caroline Sweet of *Vamped*.

"This is Nola's ex-husband," Liss said. "His name is Doug."

"Know him well, do you?"

"I thought I did." Boy, had she been wrong! "I guess you didn't just drop Nola off at the hotel on Thursday night, did you, Doug?"

His thin-lipped smile was devoid of humor. "In fact, I did. But she called me on my cell phone less than fifteen minutes later, begging me to come back."

Yvonne edged slowly closer to the fence. Liss thought that was the wrong direction to go, but she said nothing. The more distance between targets, the less likely it would be that Doug could shoot both of them. She hoped he wouldn't fire his gun at all, but she wouldn't bet her life on it. His desperation showed clearly in his eyes and she could smell the acrid scent of his sweat. He was no longer the polished, overly formal gentleman who ran the funeral home and served as a town selectman. He'd already killed two women and was terrified enough of being found out that he was prepared to kill two more to keep his earlier crimes secret.

"There's no need for violence," Liss said in the most soothing voice she could manage. It didn't sound all that calm, especially when it broke on the last word.

"Don't you mean *more* violence?"

His grim expression and the tight grip he had on the gun made Liss's palms sweat. Her knees felt wobbly, but she held her ground and kept talking. If she could only buy enough time, maybe she could figure out a way to escape. Or she'd be missed, and Dan would come looking for her.

That possibility sent a new wave of panic through her. Bad enough that she and Yvonne were in danger. She would not have the man she loved putting his life at risk. She'd nearly lost him once. She wasn't going to go through that agony again.

"Yvonne and I won't say anything," she promised. "Right, Yvonne? There's nothing to tell, anyway. We weren't here. We don't have proof of anything. And Gordon Tandy thinks Nola killed Jane and then took her own life out of remorse. No one suspects you of anything."

Doug's gaze darted back and forth between Liss and Yvonne, but his gun hand remained steady.

"I never thought of you as the type to own a gun," Liss blurted out. *Let alone use one,* she silently added. But he carried the weapon with the ease of someone accustomed to being armed. "Do you need protection from all the dead bodies you deal with?" Now she was babbling, but she couldn't seem to stop.

"Maybe he secretly believes vampires are real." Yvonne hissed the words, giving them an eerie sound that went well with the maniacal look on her face.

Taken aback, Doug stared at her.

Liss had to tamp down a hysterical bubble of laughter. Obviously, he'd never watched *Vamped.*

And, in that moment of distraction, she saw her chance.

Liss's years as a professional dancer had left her with strength and agility. Once she'd recovered from a career-ending knee injury, she'd taken pains to get back in shape and stay that way. Two running steps brought her close enough to Doug to take a flying kick at his gun arm.

Her foot struck his wrist, hard, and the hand

jerked upward. His finger squeezed the trigger and the gun fired, but the bullet went wild.

Yvonne rushed at him from the other side. When she threw herself bodily into the air, she kicked him in the chest with both feet. Apparently, her training as a stuntwoman hadn't been so very far in the past, after all.

Doug fell backward. Yvonne went with him, but the gun flew toward Liss. She scrambled to pick it up. She had no idea how to fire it, or even how to keep it from going off in her hands by accident. She'd be as likely to shoot Yvonne as Doug if she tried to use it. Slipping around them, she tossed it over the edge of the cliff.

By the time she turned back to the pair on the ground, Yvonne was using her fists to beat the crap out of the man who'd threatened to kill her. Doug tried ineffectually to fend off the blows, batting at Yvonne with open hands. A shaky laugh bubbled up and escaped before Liss could quell it. Doug fought like a girl. And Yvonne did not.

Her head jerked around at a shout from the cliff path. Gordon and Dan emerged from the trees at a dead run and skidded to a stop when they got their first good look at the scene in the clearing.

"Well, damn," Dan said. "You were right."

He was speaking to Gordon. Liss goggled at them. Gordon had *known* Doug was involved? It would have been nice if he'd said something! She'd have given him a piece of her mind about that if he hadn't been fully occupied wading in to separate the combatants. It took considerable strength for

him to haul Yvonne off Doug. The moment her
blows stopped raining down on him, he curled himself into a ball, sobbing.

Liss didn't feel a bit sorry for him. In fact, if
Gordon hadn't moved so quickly to get him to his
feet and slap handcuffs on him, she'd have gone
over there and given him a kick herself, while he
was still writhing and whining on the ground.

Yvonne retreated to the fence, leaning against it
not because she needed to catch her breath—she
wasn't even breathing hard—but to get control of
her temper. Still keeping her eyes on Doug, she
reached up to fluff her short hair.

"Try to kill me, will you," she muttered.

Engulfed in Dan's tight embrace, Liss rested her
head against his chest. She could hear how rapidly
his heart was beating.

"You scared the life out of me," he whispered.

"I didn't mean to." She hugged him back, but
after a moment, she pulled free and walked over
to Yvonne. "That was amazing," she said.

"You didn't do so badly yourself. What can I say?
Kick-ass women rule."

They shared a grin and a high five. Right at that
moment, Liss didn't care who had really written
the Toni Starling series, not when she owed Yvonne
Quinlan her life.

Behind her, she heard Gordon read Doug his
rights and ask him if he understood them. A mumble indicated that he did. "Let's go," Gordon said,
his voice gruff.

"You can't arrest me," Doug whined. "I haven't
done anything."

"You've got some nerve claiming to be innocent," Liss said, marching right up to Doug and getting in his face. "You threatened us with a gun and you killed Jane Nedlinger and Nola Ventress."

"What were doing with a gun, Doug?" Dan asked. "Most people who use the jogging path don't need protection from the chipmunks."

"Back off, Ruskin," Gordon warned. "This is police business."

Dan ignored him. "Tandy already had it figured out, you know. All you did today was drive the last nail into your own coffin."

There was little trace now of the suave, dignified, almost staid gentleman Liss had always imagined Doug to be. "I had no choice," he whined. "That Nedlinger woman brought it on herself. And then Nola was going to confess. I had to stop her, didn't I? She ruined my life once. I couldn't let her do it again."

"You already told us that you came up here with Nola that night, after she phoned you and asked you for your help," Liss reminded him. "You said that meeting here was Jane's idea. But why here?" That still baffled her.

"Can't you guess? She wanted Nola good and scared and she knew her weakness—her little phobia about the great outdoors, especially at night. It wasn't hard to discover. Nola never could shut up about herself."

"She never told anyone about her ghostwriting," Liss said.

"Her what?" Doug looked blank, which just confirmed Liss's statement.

"This is not the time or place for an interrogation," Gordon cut in.

"It is if Doug wants to talk about what happened that night. Isn't it, Doug? You do want to tell your side of the story, don't you?"

Doug looked confused. Liss wondered if Yvonne had given him a concussion. She didn't much care. To her mind, he owed them an explanation for trying to kill them.

"Perhaps you can clarify the situation," she suggested. "Convince us you've done nothing wrong."

"I need to sit down," Doug said.

Reluctantly, Gordon allowed his prisoner to collapse atop a convenient boulder. Then he pulled out a miniature audio recorder, turned it on, and recited the date, time, location, and names of all those present. "You've been read your rights," he said. "Do you want a lawyer?"

"No," Doug said.

Liss repressed a smile. Good. Any confession he made now would be admissible in court.

"You were telling us about Jane Nedlinger, and how she wanted Nola to be frightened when they met up here," she prompted him.

Doug nodded, then winced and rubbed the back of his head. "Nola told me that the Nedlinger woman had been waiting for her in the lobby when I dropped her off at the hotel. She insisted Nola meet her at the Leap, precisely because it would scare Nola half to death to walk all the way up here alone through the woods in the dark. She was a cruel woman. She wanted Nola to suffer."

"So you came to her rescue," Liss prompted him.

"Yes and no." A sly expression came into Doug's eyes. "A part of me wanted her to suffer, too. She had a lot of nerve asking me to bring her up here when she knew that just the mention of this place would bring it all back—what she did to me."

It took a moment for Liss to realize what he was talking about. Then she remembered. It was here that Nola and Stu had been caught—how had Aunt Margaret put it?—"buck naked and going at it like rabbits." The discovery of Nola's extra-marital affair had led directly to Doug and Nola's divorce, and to Doug's public humiliation. No wonder he'd jumped at the chance for a little pay-back.

"So, you agreed to accompany Nola," she said aloud. "Did she tell you why she'd agreed to Jane's demands?"

"She just kept saying she didn't have a choice, that she had to save her career. She told me to pull into the employee parking lot, so no one would see her leaving the hotel, and she slipped out the back door and into my car. Then we drove down to the Spruce Avenue end of the path and came up that way."

Doug was calm now, and telling his story in such a matter-of-fact tone of voice that he might have been relating an everyday anecdote to a group of friends. Liss wondered if he'd lost his grip on reality. He didn't seem aware of Gordon's audio recorder, and he had a faraway look in his eyes.

"The Nedlinger woman was some startled when I showed up with Nola, but she already knew who I was. She knew all about Nola's past. That story was

going to go into her blog, too, she said, unless
Nola was willing to pay what she called a 'kill fee.'
She said she was building up her retirement fund
and she laughed—a real nasty laugh. Nola was
ready to pay her off, even if it took all of her savings to do it. I told her not to be a fool. A woman
like that doesn't stop with one payment. And I figured she'd be after me next, demanding money
not to repeat all the old scandal. Maybe even suggesting that as a town selectman I could dip into
the municipal coffers to keep the good name of
the town of Moosetookalook from being smeared
in her damned blog."

Liss found the possibility that Doug might claim
to have killed Jane as an act of public service a little hard to take.

"I was so disgusted by her tactless and offensive
demands that I started to leave, taking my flashlight with me. There were no lights along the path.
All we had to see by were the Nedlinger woman's
flashlight and mine, and it was a miserable, overcast, drizzly night. When Nola realized I was going,
she went into a panic."

His humorless smile combined with his thin
face and general boniness put Liss in mind of a
grinning skull, an image that made her shudder
even before he told the rest of his story.

"The Nedlinger woman grabbed hold of Nola to
stop her from leaving and gave her a shake for
good measure. I may have wanted to make my ex-
wife suffer for her sins, but that doesn't mean I'd
let someone else hurt her. I shoved the bitch.
Hard. And she fell. She cracked her head on a
rock. She was dead as a doornail. No pulse. Nola

really freaked out then, saying I'd *murdered* the Nedlinger woman. Well, obviously, I hadn't. It was an accident. But Nola was unreasonable about it, going on and on about how all her secrets were going to come out if we told anyone what happened. To shut her up, I helped her toss the body over the cliff."

So that it would *look* more like an accident, Liss presumed. Clearly neither Nola nor Doug had been entirely rational at the time.

"What happened to the rock Jane Nedlinger hit her head on?" Gordon asked in a quiet, nonthreatening voice.

"Oh, I tossed that over, too."

"Weren't you concerned about fingerprints?" Liss asked.

"Of course not. You know I always wear driving gloves when I go out at night. I feel the cold in my hands something terrible."

"So, you'd have gotten away with it," Liss said softly. "I don't understand why Nola had to die."

His derisive snort spoke volumes. "Nola *promised* to say nothing about what happened up here, but when I saw her the next day, she was in a terrible state. She was fussing about how guilty she felt, how she had never meant for me to hurt anyone. I knew then that I had to take steps to protect myself or she'd ruin my life, right along with her own, by confessing to the police. I suggested she salve her conscience by creating a memorial to the Nedlinger woman. I told her to buy some flowers and meet me at Lover's Leap. She was reluctant, even though it was still daylight, but I convinced her that I had a way for her to make amends."

"You walked up the other way, as you had the previous night." It was not a question.

Doug nodded. "Who would believe it was a suicide if I'd been seen?"

"But she didn't kill herself, did she? You may have suggested it, but Nola had priorities you knew nothing about."

Doug shrugged again. His voice was devoid of emotion. "She may have had a little help, but it was what she wanted to do. She was the one with the guilty conscience." He frowned. "That should have been the end of it. I know dead bodies. No one would be able to say exactly when Nola died. I made certain I was seen at the auction less than twenty minutes later. It was an excellent alibi. I even bid on a few items. I won a hand-crocheted pillow with a cat on it." He made a moue of distaste.

Silence descended on the little group gathered around the boulder. Doug's seeming indifference made the tale seem even more hideous.

Gordon cleared his throat. "I think that's enough. Come on, Doug. Let's get you back to civilization."

"Hold on a minute," Liss said. "I have more questions."

She waited until Doug looked up, wanting him to meet her eyes. She was momentarily disconcerted by the blankness of his gaze. He seemed to look right through her. She had to swallow hard, but she asked her questions anyway.

"Why did you bring a gun to the tea? Why did you follow me out here? Did you think I knew you were guilty of murder?"

"Don't play dumb with me, Liss MacCrimmon. My wife told me you were looking for me after Lenny's funeral this morning. What else could you have wanted except to ask nosy questions? And if you were asking, then you were getting close to the truth. Everyone in town knows that when you stick your nose in where it doesn't belong, people end up in jail."

"I only wanted to talk to you about your son," Liss whispered.

He didn't seem to hear her. She didn't suppose young Frank's attitude mattered now. His life would be shattered when he found out that his father was a murderer. She doubted the funeral home would stay in business after the news broke. That was not the way she'd expected to correct the boy's lack of respect for the dead, but it would certainly solve the problem.

"If you knew," Doug volunteered, "then I had to eliminate the threat. I had it all worked out in my mind. I meant to force you into my car at gunpoint and drive you somewhere remote, somewhere I could shoot you and no one would hear. Then I'd hide your body." He chuckled. "That part would have been easy. I have plenty of caskets. No one would think twice about it if I buried one more, and no one would ever know what happened to you."

Liss shivered convulsively, although the sun was high in the sky and the day was pleasantly warm. Doug's voice sounded so ordinary, his tone almost conversational.

He'd followed her when she left the hotel looking for Gordon. He'd overheard part of what she

said to Yvonne—overheard his own name. How
ironic that, until that very moment, she hadn't
had the slightest suspicion that he was involved.

This time, when Gordon hauled Doug to his
feet and led him away, she did not object. As soon
as they disappeared around a curve in the trail,
she turned to Dan, standing patiently beside her,
and walked straight into his waiting arms.

Epilogue

A full day later, Liss was still haunted by Doug's confession. Filling Sherri in on the details helped. Repetition dulled the sharp edges and reinforced the most important facts: She was safe; Yvonne was safe; and Jane and Nola's killer would get what was coming to him.

After Sherri left, Liss sat in the rocker in her bow window, waiting. She'd left a message on Gordon Tandy's voice mail, asking him to stop by. She'd not yet had the chance to clear the air between them on a personal level. She could not move on until they talked.

Gordon arrived just before five that afternoon. Liss invited him in, settled him on her sofa with coffee and coffee cake, and resumed her seat in the Canadian rocker with her hands primly folded in her lap. Out of the corner of her eye, she saw Dan crossing the town square. She knew the moment he spotted the state plates on the unmarked vehicle parked in front of her house. He stopped dead, right in the middle of the street, then turned back the way he'd come.

He wasn't angry, or jealous, either, only considerate. He would keep watch from his own front window and when Gordon left, he'd return.

The thought comforted her and gave her the courage to say what needed to be said to the only other man she'd ever considered as a potential husband.

"I should have told you myself when I accepted Dan's marriage proposal," she said. "You shouldn't have had to hear about it from your brother."

She'd succeeded in surprising him. He set his cup aside and left the coffee cake untouched. "*That's* what you wanted to talk to me about?"

"Yes, it is."

"Liss, I wasn't around for you to tell. I was out of state at the time."

"Right before you left, I wasn't sure you wanted to be around me. I caused you a great deal of trouble. You broke the rules because of me. And I almost got both of us killed."

"You have a way of convincing me to let you in on things you shouldn't know anything about," he admitted, with a rueful smile. "That doesn't seem to have changed since you got engaged to Ruskin. What the hell was I thinking yesterday, letting a civilian conduct an interview with a suspect?"

"Will Doug's confession hold up in court?"

"It should, especially since he broke down and repeated it a couple of hours later—with his lawyer present." He reached for the coffee and sipped.

"Are you in trouble because of my meddling?"

"I doubt it. It got results." He started on the coffee cake.

Liss sighed. "You wouldn't tell me anyway, would you?"

"As to that, it's on a need-to-know basis and you don't need to know."

"Well, at least your sense of humor is improving." Liss bent forward, inclining her body a little closer to him in an attempt to gauge his reaction. "I need you to know this, Gordon. It wouldn't have worked—you and me."

"I know." He polished off the coffee cake. "If I'd ever gotten around to proposing, and if you'd been foolish enough to accept, we'd probably have been divorced within a year." His eyes locked on hers. "Still, it would have been one hell of a year."

"Be serious!"

"What makes you think I'm not?"

"I've never been able to read you," she complained, exasperated. "I'm trying to apologize here, Gordon. I should have phoned you, or at least written to you."

"Because a 'Dear John' letter would have made things so much easier on me?" The glint of amusement in his dark eyes was unmistakable.

"You're not going to make this easy on me, are you?"

"In fact, I am. I'd already done a lot of thinking about us before my brother sent me the news of your engagement. I'd decided it wouldn't be smart to continue to see you after I returned home. I was planning to keep my distance. We aren't good for each other, Liss. I don't know how to explain it any better than that, but that's the honest truth."

"I can't explain it either," Liss admitted as she sat beside him on the sofa, "but I know exactly what you mean. You tell me things about your cases that you shouldn't, even when I don't ask. And I . . . take risks. I still get the shakes every time I think about what happened just before Christmas. I should never have—"

He touched a finger to her lips to stop her words. "It's over. Done with. And so is this case. You're going to marry a good man and try harder to avoid getting tangled up in unsolved murders."

"Yes, I am. And you?"

He chuckled. "I've been seeing someone for the last couple of months. It's getting serious."

"That's wonderful, Gordon. I'm happy for you. Is she anyone I know?"

He rose and she walked him to the door. "You met her once," he said, "back when you first got back to Carrabassett County." He stepped out onto her front porch, turned, and grinned at her again. "Her name is Penny Lassiter."

Liss was frowning as she watched him get into his car and drive away. The only Lassiter she knew was—

"Good grief," she whispered.

"Good grief, what?" Dan asked, overhearing. As she'd expected, he'd lost no time trotting across the square to her house once he saw Gordon leaving.

"Gordon is dating Penny Lassiter."

"Who?"

"Penny Lassiter—the sheriff of Carrabassett County." Liss could see them together, and the image made her very happy.

"So, loose ends all tied up?" Dan asked as they went inside. "Air cleared?"

She slipped her hand into his, savoring the warmth and firmness of his grip. "Now all I have to worry about are my lists of things to do before our wedding."

"Uh, Liss—about the wedding?"

"You're *not* backing out," she said, giving him a poke in the arm with her free hand, "and we're not eloping." A laugh caught in her throat when she looked up and saw the serious expression on his face.

"I got a phone call a little bit ago," Dan said, turning her so that they were standing face-to-face in the center of her living room. "From your parents. You remember how they were going to leave ahead of schedule and drive straight here because Dolores Mayfield told them what was going on?"

"Please tell me they decided against it. I love them dearly, but there was no reason for them to change their original plan. They'll still be here in plenty of time for the wedding."

"They certainly will." He glanced at his watch. "They decided to fly instead of drive. Their plane landed at the Jetport in Portland about an hour ago and they rented a car. In, say, another forty-five minutes, they'll be on your doorstep."

Liss felt her jaw drop.

"Before they show up, there's something I need to tell you."

Watching Dan swallow hard and hesitate made Liss's heart stutter. *Was* Dan going to call off the wedding? Had her reckless meddling finally pushed him too far?

"When Tandy came back into your life, I had to wonder if you were really certain you picked the right man to marry."

"I'm sure. I—"

"Let me finish. Please. I figured out pretty quick that I had nothing to worry about. I know you love me. And I love you. And because I love you, seeing you with Tandy this morning made me realize that I want to do more than *tell* you I love you."

"You show me how you feel every day," Liss assured him.

"Yeah? Well, good. But I wanted you to have *proof* of that love. I'm not going to change my mind about this. I'm resigned to making the ultimate sacrifice."

She blinked at him in confusion for a moment before she saw the twinkle in his molasses-brown eyes. She started to smile. "You mean—?"

"Yes, Liss," Dan said. "When we get married, at the Western Maine Highland Games, I will be wearing a kilt."

A Note from the Author

Some of the mystery writers attending my fictional First Annual Maine-ly Cozy Con, or mentioned by fictional fans at this conference, are real. They all write their own books. The others, along with all editors, agents, book doctors, managers, and conference organizers who appear in these pages, are figments of my imagination and bear no resemblance to any real person, living or dead. The same is true of the residents and business-people of Moosetookalook, Maine, a made-up town in a fictitious county.

I've taken a liberty with television news coverage here in Maine. Although there is local news at 5:00, 5:30, and 6:00 every weeknight, on weekends there is only one broadcast, at six, and half the time that one is bumped because of sporting events that run long. In my fictional Maine, however, Liss and her friends have three chances to hear the local news, even on a Saturday.

To learn more about Moosetookalook and its inhabitants and to see photos of "Lumpkin" and "Glenora," you can visit www.KaitlynDunnett.com.

Moosetookalook, Maine, has never seen so many bare legs walking its streets. It could only mean one thing: the Western Maine Highland Games are in town for the weekend. But instead of wondering who'll win the hammer throw, everyone's asking who got kilt . . .

Even if Liss MacCrimmon, soon to be Mrs. Dan Ruskin, spends her days running the Moosetookalook Scottish Emporium, all she wants is a simple white wedding as she walks down the aisle accompanied by her father. When it comes to weddings, however, her mother, Vi, has another idea about tradition. Instead of white, Vi sees tartan, and more tartan.

What bonnie luck then that Liss and Dan's wedding is scheduled on the same weekend as the Western Maine Highland Games. What could make a nuptial weekend more memorable than a hammer throw or medieval reenactment group to go along with the tossing of the bouquet? How about a charming college professor found slashed to death by his own reproduction of a broadsword?

But who'd go medieval on a professor, no matter how nutty? Turns out the deceased had plenty of enemies, including a line of female conquests stretching back to the dark ages, a band of picketers protesting his historically questionable theories, and a strapping collegiate with a howdy-doody smile. And topping the suspect list is Liss's own father, Donald "Mac" MacCrimmon!

As much as Liss tries to keep her fingers out of the sleuthing cake, she finds herself again dead center of a Moosetookalook murder mystery. If Liss doesn't solve this one, and quick, she might never say "I do," let alone "'til death do us part."

Please turn the page for an exciting sneak peek of the next Liss MacCrimmon Scottish Mystery BAGPIPES, BRIDES AND HOMICIDES coming next month!

Chapter One

Liss MacCrimmon's mother's idea of "helping out in the shop" consisted of rearranging every bit of merchandise sold at Moosetookalook Scottish Emporium. True, Violet MacCrimmon dusted as she went, but the overall result was chaos. By the end of the first week of her parents' visit, Liss no longer knew where anything was. If an entire rack of ready-made kilts could disappear—she'd finally located it tucked away behind a large display case—Liss feared that the search for any of the hundreds of smaller Scottish-themed gift items she kept in stock might last hours, even days.

"Mother, please!" Liss exclaimed, fighting the urge to pull at her hair in the best cartoon-character tradition. "I know you're trying to be helpful, but I like that section of the shop the way it is."

"Nonsense," Vi said. "Nothing is ever so perfect that it can't be improved."

She disappeared behind one of the bookcases that gave the illusion of privacy to the shop's "cozy corner," an area furnished with two overstuffed chairs and a coffee table. There customers could make themselves comfortable while they examined Liss's offering of novels set in Scotland or featuring characters of Scottish descent and volumes of nonfiction with a Scottish theme. There were a few histories and biographies, but for the most part Liss stocked cookbooks, instruction manuals, and coffee table books full of pictures. The how-to books covered everything from dancing the highland fling to preparing your own haggis.

The lemony scent of furniture polish wafted across the showroom, making Liss's nose twitch even as her hackles rose. Vi MacCrimmon was accustomed to getting her own way. She'd only recently retired after teaching world history to junior high school students for thirty-five years. Nothing fazed her, least of all objections from her only child. There was no stopping her, short of seizing her bodily and shoving her out the door.

For a brief moment, Liss toyed with the idea of doing just that. Vi was five inches shorter than she was and proportionately petite. But Liss reassessed the idea as one of those comfortable, overstuffed, *heavy* chairs shot out from behind a bookcase and traveled a good two feet beyond. Vi kept her figure with ruthless workouts at a local gym. For a woman of fifty-eight, she was in great shape.

And you *are almost thirty years old,* Liss reminded herself, *not thirteen.* It was absurd to revert to the behavior of her childhood simply because her mother hadn't changed one iota in all the years they'd lived apart. Besides, there was something more important at stake here than the arrangement of displays in her place of business. Liss's parents had returned to Moosetookalook because she was about to get married. Unchecked, Vi's meddling wouldn't stop with the Emporium. She'd already talked her daughter into making major changes in the wedding plans. Liss had no doubt but that Vi had other "improvements" in mind.

Grimly determined to reclaim control of the situation, Liss marched across the shop and flattened her palms against the soft fabric of the easy chair. Putting her back into it, she shoved. A loud scraping sound made her wince and fear for the state of her hardwood floor, but she didn't stop until she'd returned the cumbersome piece of furniture to its original location.

Vi turned from one of the bookcases, a dust cloth in one hand and a spray bottle of furniture polish in the other. Her frown was a formidable weapon and she knew how to use it. Liss had to squash the impulse to back away, apologizing with every step. She held her ground, but it was a near thing.

Her mother's eyes were pale blue behind stylish glasses and her hair was still the same dark brown as Liss's. At first glance, Vi looked a good ten years younger than she was. Liss reminded herself that Vi's hair needed help to stay that color. Then she looked closer, homing in on the lines inscribed in her mother's face. They were deeper than she remembered.

Liss faltered. Both her parents were getting older. One day, perhaps sooner than she expected, given

that all four of her grandparents had all died before they reached the age of seventy, she wouldn't
have her mother to complain about anymore.

Vi frowned. "Is something wrong, honey?"

"Sit down, Mom." Liss sank into the chair she'd
just manhandled and pointed to the other. Giving
direct orders rarely worked on either mothers or
cats, but that had never stopped Liss from trying.
This time, she lucked out.

Vi hesitated for a moment, then shrugged and
sat. She placed the polish and the dust rag on the
coffee table with exaggerated care before she
folded her hands in her lap. The pose put Liss in
mind of the deceptively prim heroines of Regency
romances. In collusion with those dauntless fe-
males, Vi attempted to appear demure but the expression in her eyes shattered the illusion.

Fixed on Liss, Vi's steely stare sent her daughter
straight back into adolescence. It might be irrational, but Liss felt exactly as she had the time
she'd been caught sneaking back into the house at
three in the morning. She'd been fifteen and determined to attend the midnight showing of a
movie her girlfriends had been raving about. All
these years later, she couldn't remember the title
of the film, but she'd never forget how devastated
she'd been by her mother's disappointment in
her.

She cleared her throat. "The shop looks lovely,
Mom. It hasn't been this clean in months. But I
don't want to change the cozy corner. It's always
been kept just this way."

If there was one thing Vi MacCrimmon understood, it was tradition. Throughout Liss's child-hood, Vi had been the one who'd drummed her Scottish heritage into her head, all the while encouraging her to take up traditional Scottish crafts and skills. Because of Vi, Liss had won prizes for dancing at Scottish festivals all over New England during her youth and had gone on, after two years of college, to pursue a career as a professional Scottish dancer.

The curious thing was that Vi didn't have a single drop of Scottish blood in her veins. When she'd become Mrs. Donald MacCrimmon, however, she'd wholeheartedly adopted her new husband's family background. She'd become more Scottish than any native-born Scot. That was hardly surprising, Liss supposed. At the time of their marriage, he'd owned and operated Moosetookalook Scottish Emporium in partnership with his sister. The store had been opened thirty years before that by Liss's grandparents.

"I was just trying to help." Vi sound more reproachful than apologetic.

Liss read the subtext with the effortlessness of long practice. It was: *Do you kick puppies, too?* She squirmed in her chair. What was it with mothers and guilt? She felt like the worst kind of bully when all she'd done was ask Vi to cease and desist.

Stop rearranging my shop, she thought. *Stop trying to take over my life!*

Aloud, she said none of that. She kept her voice as soothing and conciliatory as she could manage. "I know you mean well, Mom. And I appreciate all you've done here. But you didn't come back to

Maine to clean the cobwebs out of my shop. Look outside. It's a beautiful day. You and Dad should go for a drive. Maybe visit old friends."

"Well, I suppose there are one or two people I'd like to see," Vi mused, "and there are some wedding details that need attention."

Alarm bells sounded in Liss's head. Loud ones. "Everything is right on schedule, Mom. I've checked off nearly every item on all my to-do lists." Liss was a champion list maker.

"But you haven't taken care of the most important item. Here it is the end of May, with your wedding scheduled for the twenty-fifth of July, and you still haven't found a wedding dress." Vi leaned forward, her expression earnest and concerned. She took Liss's right hand in hers.

"I'm thinking about it." Put on the defensive, Liss felt her muscles tense. She willed herself to relax. This was *her* wedding. She had to stick to her guns.

"You said you liked my suggestion of a Renaissance-style gown." Vi gave Liss's hand a squeeze, then released it.

"I did. I do." Liss had the feeling that she was digging herself deeper into a pit with every word. Agreeing with her mother was always risky. "I just haven't decided which one I like best. I've narrowed it down to two choices, both pictured in that magazine you sent me." It had arrived in the mail shortly before Vi herself had turned up on Liss's doorstep.

"Well, then, I have the perfect solution. I know a wonderful seamstress who can *make* your dress. She can incorporate whatever elements you want."

There had to be a catch, Liss thought, but she couldn't find one. "That's a wonderful idea, Mom, but are you sure she'll be able to take on a commission like that on short notice?" Liss regularly dealt with kilt makers and they always needed eight to ten weeks to deliver the finished product. Her wedding was exactly eight weeks and one day away. That was cutting it very close.

"Oh, yes." Vi's face wore a smug smile. "I've already talked to Melly about it on the phone. That's her name: Melly Baynard. If you really like the idea, I'll drive down to Three Cities this afternoon and discuss the dress with her face to face."

Three Cities, actually only one city, wasn't very far away, perhaps an hour and a half by car, but Vi sounded much too willing to take on the chore. "Maybe I should be the one to go talk to her," Liss suggested.

"Oh, I don't mind. It's been years since I've seen Melly. We went to college together. Back in the dark ages," Vi added with a self-deprecating chuckle. "I've been dying to spend some time with her and catch up on what she's been doing. The only things I know for certain are that she's currently the wardrobe mistress and costume designer for the theater department at our old alma mater, and that, since it's summer semester now, she isn't as busy as she would be during the school year."

Translated, that meant Liss's mother had *already* made arrangements for Melly Baynard to make the wedding gown. Liss's first instinct was to balk at the idea. Then she remembered that old adage about not cutting off your nose to spite your face. She didn't have a better idea, and in her mind's eye she could envision the perfect dress. Her mother was right. It needed to be custom made.

Decision reached, she stood. "Okay, Mom. Go talk to her. I'll give you the pictures from the magazine and write notes right on the pages to make sure there's no confusion about what I like and don't like."

That, she reasoned, would keep her mother's contributions to the design at a minimum. It was too much to hope that she'd entirely keep her fingers out of the dress pie.

Beaming, Vi bounded up from her chair and leaned across the coffee table to give Liss a quick hug. For a moment, Liss was engulfed in the scent of violets, Vi's signature perfume. A peck on the cheek followed.

"This is all that's wonderful, darling. I promise that you won't be sorry."

As she watched Vi waltz out of the Emporium, humming cheerfully to herself, Liss wasn't so sure about that.

Ten days later, Liss had almost all of the contents of Moosetookalook Scottish Emporium back where they belonged. The pieces of her life were another matter.

She got up early on that Tuesday morning, slipped into workout clothes, and trotted three doors down the street to a newly opened business called Dance Central. Before she got started on the exercise program that had once been a daily part of her routine, she executed a spin and a few moves from a Scottish step-dance in front of the floor-to-ceiling mirrors.

The reflective surface extended the length of one wall and gave her a clear view of every flaw in her out-of-practice performance. The body in the skintight, long-sleeved black leotard was still good—five-feet nine-inches tall, lithe, and slender, if a few pounds heavier than it had been during her pro career—but the knees would never be the same. The long scar across one showed plainly in the glass.

Liss shifted her focus upward, meeting blue green eyes framed by pale skin and shoulder-length dark brown hair. She made a face at her reflection and turned her back on it. The rosin she'd stepped in with her dance shoes, to prevent sliding on the wooden floor, made a faint whooshing noise as she walked.

Sandy and Zara Kalishnakof, old and dear friends from the days when she'd made her living as part of a Scottish dance troupe, had moved to Liss's hometown, Moosetookalook, Maine, after the company disbanded. They'd bought a building on the town square, settled into the upstairs apartment for living quarters, and turned the storefront into a dance studio. The first classes had begun just a bit more than a week earlier, on the first day of June,

Sandy and Zara gave lessons to both children and adults in a variety of disciplines, everything from ballet to competitive ballroom to break dancing. All the offerings had attracted a satisfying number of pupils. It had helped that there were no other dance teachers nearby. And that dance

competitions had recently become so popular
on TV.

Even before Dance Central officially opened,
Zara had been urging Liss to join her private workouts, both for the exercise and for the companion-
ship. Liss hoped to make it a habit, but so far she'd
been lucky to manage three days out of seven.

"So how are the wedding plans coming?" Zara
asked.

"The idea of eloping is starting to sound better
and better," Liss said as she headed for the barre
set into the wall opposite the mirrors.

"Wedding jitters?" Zara was a slender, green-
eyed redhead of the carrot-top variety. She sat on
the floor, bent double over long legs encased in
hot pink tights. They were stretched out straight in
front of her. Since her forehead was now resting
on her knees, her voice was muffled. "I had them
right before Sandy and I tied the knot. But I'm
glad we went through with our small family wedding. It wouldn't have been the same without his
folks there."

"I could handle a small family wedding." Liss extended one of her own legs along the barre and
bent at the waist, reaching for her toes.

It had been just over two years since her knee
had given out on her during a performance, ending her career as a professional dancer at the age
of twenty-seven. She'd regained her mobility but
she'd never again be quite as agile as she'd once
been. Her left leg would always be a little weaker
than the right. If she tried to go back to dancing to
earn a living, she'd have been like a football player

who insisted on playing after he'd had a knee or ankle replaced.

Athletes who kept going too long paid a terrible price when they finally retired—more surgery and lots of pain. Liss hadn't seen the point in either when both could be avoided. She'd come back home, joined her Aunt Margaret in the family business, and settled down to start a new life.

She hadn't expected it to include love and marriage, although she had no complaints about that aspect of things. Her fiancé, Dan Ruskin, was just about perfect. What flaws he had, she could live with. Her only complaint was that actually *getting* married seemed to be so darned complicated!

At times, eloping *did* seem very appealing. Back in February, on Valentine's Day, their good friends Sherri Willett and Pete Campbell had done just that. Rather than cope with her divorced parents and his controlling mother, they'd taken Liss and Dan along for witnesses and gone to a local justice of the peace. The only other person invited to the ceremony had been Sherri's seven-year-old son, Adam.

"Why does planning a wedding have to be such a hassle?" Liss mumbled into her knee.

"Now, Liss—surely the worst hurdles are past. You're all set on the venue, right?"

Liss gave a short bark of laughter, switched legs, and resumed stretching. "Some venue! We're getting married at the Western Maine Highland Games instead of in a church because my mother decided it was fate that the date Dan and I picked and the weekend of the Scottish festival were the same."

"You *agreed*," Zara reminded her.

"I had no idea what I was getting into. I was a little distracted at the time. And ever since my folks got here—*weeks* ahead of time—my mother has been slowly but surely taking over *every*thing. First it was the dress, then the cake. Now she's gotten it into her head that Dan and I should jump the broom!"

"It is a fine old Scottish tradition," Zara teased her.

Liss groaned. "I should never have let her talk me into a historical theme for the wedding in the first place. When she first suggested it, it sounded romantic, like something out of a fairy tale. I was always a sucker for Disney's *Cinderella* when I was a kid." She sighed. "Even after I realized that Mom had something more medieval in mind, I thought I'd be fine with it. The modern versions of the gowns are gorgeous, and I liked the idea of a circlet of flowers instead of a veil. But now—Mom doesn't just want the broom in the ceremony, she wants the sword *and* the anvil. It's too much."

Changing position, Liss began a series of pliés.

"What Mom has in mind is a complete revamping of the wedding ceremony to include the medieval Scottish tradition of handfasting. Along with anvil, sword, and broom, it involves—literally!—tying the hands of the bride and groom together with silken cords or ribbons."

"I get the anvil," Zara said, "because in the old days a blacksmith could perform the wedding ceremony. And I know the bride and groom jumping over a broom is supposed to bring good luck to the marriage. But what's with the sword?"

"According to some sample ceremony Mom found online, the groom is supposed to drop to his knees and offer the wedding ring to the bride on the tip of his sword."

Zara giggled.

"Get your mind out of the gutter! The sword is supposed to symbolize his promise to protect her."

"A real sword?"

"A real sword. I'd be lucky not to cut off a fingertip trying to get the ring off the blade."

A bemused look on her face, Zara paused in her routine. "Then what? Do you put the ring on your finger yourself?"

"Oh, no. There's far more to it than that." Liss's pliés began to more closely resemble deep knee bends than a graceful ballet exercise. Just thinking about the details Vi had dropped on her ratcheted up her tension level. "The bride just holds on to the ring while she takes the sword. Then she makes like the queen of England conferring a knighthood. You know—touch the blade to the left shoulder, then the right shoulder, then the top of the head."

"I don't think the queen does the top of the head."

"Whatever!" Liss scowled as she realized she'd lost count of how many pliés she'd done. "Anyway, then the bride returns the sword to the groom and gives the ring back to him, too, so he can put it on her finger."

"Still on his knees?"

"Probably. Mom didn't say."

"How about his ring?"

"The bride presents it to him inside a chalice.

The groom takes the ring out and hangs on to it while he pours wine into the chalice, which the bride is holding for him. Then he drinks a toast to her before he hands the chalice back to her. Then he returns the ring so she can put it on his finger."

"While balancing the chalice?"

"Apparently."

"Just a tad chauvinistic, don't you think?"

"That's the least of the reasons why I'm not doing it. Tradition is all well and good, and I'm sure some couples would find all the trappings of a medieval wedding romantic, but my Cinderella fantasy stopped at the dress. Besides—kneeling in front of me with a sword? There's no way Dan would ever agree to that! I had trouble enough convincing him to wear a kilt."

Zara stifled another giggle. "Chill," she advised. "You'll work it out. Compromise with your mother. And don't worry about Dan. He's crazy in love with you. He'll go along with whatever you decide *you* want to do."

"On some things, sure. Like agreeing not to wear earplugs when the bagpiper plays." Dan was not a fan of Scottish music. "And he did manage to convince his brother to get with the program. Sam didn't think the best man should have to wear a kilt just because the groom was going to."

"What was Sam's problem?" Zara asked between stretches. "Bowlegged?"

Liss had to smile at that as she left the barre. "Trust me, *all* the Ruskin men have excellent legs."

She settled herself on the floor and began another series of bends from a sitting position. Zara was right, she admitted to herself after the first set. Dan had been more agreeable than she'd expected. She knew he'd have felt far more comfortable wearing a tux. She might have been persuaded to let him if he'd made an issue of it, but it was too late to change their minds now.

The kilts would arrive at the shop sometime this week. She hoped Dan would wear his a bit around the house, so he'd get used to the feel of it. It would help that the Black Watch tartan was very dignified. It had a nicely macho military connection, too, since the Black Watch was an infantry battalion in the British Army, a part of the Royal Regiment of Scotland.

Zara scooted closer and curled her legs beneath her, tailor-fashion. Liss envied her ease of motion. Once upon a time, she'd been able to move just as smoothly. Now her knee made an annoying crackling sound when she bent it at too much of an angle, and it started to ache if she stayed in one position for very long.

"You fuss too much, Liss. Everything is going to be just fine. And after the wedding, you and Dan will be married. Trust me when I say that makes it all worthwhile."

"Yeah, but I have to survive till then. I just hope Mom doesn't come up with any more inspired ideas."

For the rest of the exercise session, Liss made a concerted effort to shake off her gloomy mood and stop grumbling. By the time she returned home, in spite of the steady drizzle of rain that greeted her the minute she stepped outside Dance

Central, she felt much more cheerful. A quick shower, another cup of coffee, and a few minutes of playing with her two cats, Lumpkin and Glenora, completed the cure. She was about to slip out the back way, cross the narrow strip of lawn and the driveway that separated her house from Moose-tookalook Scottish Emporium, and enter the shop through the stockroom door when her mother burst into the kitchen.

"Everything is ruined!" Vi MacCrimmon wailed.

Liss stared at her in bewilderment. It wasn't like Vi to lose her composure. "What happened?" she asked, catching her mother by the arm and steering her toward the kitchen table.

Once there, Vi sat, propped her elbows on the placemat, and buried her head in her hands. "Disaster," she moaned.

"Mom!" Concern had Liss speaking more sharply than she'd intended. "Snap out of it. Tell me what's wrong."

Vi reared up, eyes flashing. "Those idiots at the fairgrounds have cancelled their contract with the highland games!"

Liss blinked at her in surprise. "Can they do that?"

"They *say* there's a conflict—some other group with a prior claim to that weekend. Oh, what does it matter how or why? If there are no Western Maine Highland Games, then there is no Medieval Scottish Conclave, and if there is no Medieval Scottish Conclave, then your beautiful wedding will be *ruined.*" Once again her voice rose to a wail.

"Oh."

"'Oh'? Is that all you have to say?"

"It's not a disaster, Mom. Dan and I can always be married in the church." For her mother's sake, Liss tried to sound disappointed, but inside her head she started doing a happy dance.

"Absolutely not! I won't see all my plans ruined!" Vi got to her feet and starting pacing.

"Now, Mom, be reasonable. If the games are cancelled, what choice do we have?"

It was the wrong question to ask. Liss knew it the moment the words left her mouth.

A determined expression came into her mother's eyes. Her jaw hardened. She stiffened her backbone and squared her shoulders. Then she glanced at her watch. "You'd better be off to work, Liss. You don't want to be late opening the shop."

"There's no rush." That was the advantage of being her own boss. "What are you up to, Mom?"

"Nothing, dear. I just have some phone calls to make." Vi continued to pace, wearing a path in the floor from the table to the stove and back again. "I need to talk to Joe Ruskin. We'll have to make some changes in your wedding plans. What a pity you already mailed the invitations. We'll have to let everyone who's coming know there's a new location."

"I suppose so."

Liss wasn't particularly concerned about that aspect of things. The wedding was still weeks away and almost everyone who was coming could be reached by e-mail. What did trouble her was the determined look in her mother's eyes. She felt uneasy about leaving Vi to her own devices, but what choice did she have? She knew from past experience that nothing she said or did right now would slow down the force of nature that was her mother. She'd have to wait until Hurricane Vi blew herself out and then try to repair whatever damage she might have done.